DEATH ON A WINTER STROLL

The Merry Folger Nantucket Mystery Series

Death in the Off-Season
Death in Rough Water
Death in a Mood Indigo
Death in a Cold Hard Light
Death on Nantucket
Death on Tuckernuck
Death on a Winter Stroll

WRITTEN UNDER THE NAME
STEPHANIE BARRON

Being a Jane Austen Mystery Series

Jane and the Unpleasantness at Scargrave Manor
Jane and the Man of the Cloth
Jane and the Wandering Eye
Jane and the Genius of the Place
Jane and the Stillroom Maid
Jane and the Prisoner of Wool House
Jane and the Ghosts of Netley
Jane and His Lordship's Legacy
Jane and the Barque of Frailty
Jane and the Madness of Lord Byron
Jane and the Canterbury Tale
Jane and the Twelve Days of Christmas
Jane and the Waterloo Map
Jane and the Year Without a Summer

DEATH ON A WINTER STROLL

FRANCINE MATHEWS

SOHO
CRIME

Published by
Soho Press, Inc.
227 W 17th Street
New York, NY 10011

Library of Congress Cataloging-in-Publication Data

Names: Mathews, Francine, author.
Title: Death on a winter stroll / Francine Mathews.
Description: New York, NY : Soho Crime, [2022]
Series: The merry folger nantucket mysteries ; 7
Identifiers: LCCN 2022011536

ISBN 978-1-64129-274-0
eISBN 978-1-64129-275-7

Subjects: LCGFT: Novels.
Classification: LCC PS3563.A8357 D439 2022 | DDC 813/.54—dc23
LC record available at https://lccn.loc.gov/2022011536

Printed in the United States of America

10 9 8 7 6 5 4 3 2 1

For all those who survived the pandemic,
and in memory of those who did not.
Have yourself a merry little Christmas.

DEATH ON A
WINTER
STROLL

PROLOGUE: The Plague Winter

IT WAS SLEETING and nearly dark when the woman reached the overgrown turnoff to the house. There was no one else on the Polpis road to glimpse her battered green van hesitate an instant before wheeling into the rutted drive. She was unidentifiable in any case: a shapeless figure in a gray parka, hood bunched around her ears, and a blue paper surgical mask over her mouth. Her van's wipers struggled against the intermittent gusts of rain. A single grackle lifted from the scrub oak as she passed and winged indifferently toward the sea.

It had been raining for days, as March came in like a lion and contagion spread throughout the world. The wrong season for crowds on Nantucket; in fact, she had counted on that—on slipping undetected beneath the invisible cordon that separated her from her past. The freight boat out of Hyannis was half full; people were scared of getting sick. Most were avoiding travel. Those who were forced to cross the Sound, she noticed, did not make eye contact. They hunched over their phones and hugged themselves against the heavy winter chop. The passenger cabins were too warm, laced with a sickening fug of diesel fuel, wet raincoats, and burnt coffee. She chose to spend the crossing outside on the bow deck, her hands shoved for warmth in her pockets and her gaze fixed on the low charcoal smudge of home coming up on the horizon.

The raw air was laced with the fresh tang of the sea and

despite being buffeted and chilled, she felt her soul begin to sing. *Returning. At last.*

THE WESTFALIA SHE'D bought in Oregon and driven across the country, sleeping fitfully in the back at night, was the sixth vehicle off the MV *Woods Hole*'s freight deck. It had 155,763 miles on its odometer and a minifridge beneath its tidy window curtains.

Now, she sat motionless for a moment behind the wheel, engine running, and studied the house she'd found at the end of the drive. It looked worse than she'd hoped, but not as terrible as she'd expected. A typical old New England place, with rooms and extensions added or subtracted over the years as generations swelled or not. The front windows looked blank and sightless, covered with sheets of plywood. The gray shingles, black with damp, ought to have been replaced years ago. A rime of lichen etched them in phosphorescent green. She noted the sag in the roof near the chimney joist, the way the roof itself undulated across the unseen attic rafters. Wisps of plant life were growing there and she knew without question it leaked. The utilities had been shut off long ago.

Her gaze drifted to the front door, which had once been painted deep rose and was now the color of a healed scar. The quarter-board above read *Stella Maris*. The name her great-grandfather had given his farmhouse, which *his* Quaker great-grandfather had built in the middle of the eighteenth century. It would be cold inside, and smell of mold, and she had not yet bought wood pellets for the ancient iron stove or dug the winter blankets out of the attic chest. She'd have to bring in water and flush the toilet manually. And what about baths? Until she shut off the engine, there was still the possibility of retreat, of actions considered but not taken.

She debated thirteen seconds longer. Then she silenced the

van and stepped out into the small noises of late winter and dusk. She drank deeply of the forgotten air. *Salt spray, damp sod, marsh.* He would have changed the locks, of course. But there could be no alarm system; that required electricity.

She kept a tool box in the back of the van as insurance against catastrophe. A pandemic seemed to qualify. She rummaged among her things until she found a flathead screwdriver and a hammer. Then, with a briskness that surprised even herself, she walked around the side of the house and smashed the window of her own back door.

1 | Twenty Months Later

THE FIRST WEEKEND of December had been Meredith Folger's favorite time of year for as long as she could remember. People often say that about holiday traditions, of course, but Merry was convinced that nowhere on earth was the winter solstice heralded with such enthusiastic conviction as during the three days of Nantucket's Christmas Stroll.

Anticipation started to rise all over the island in late November. The day after Thanksgiving, crowds gathered at the head of Main Street for the ceremonial lighting of the massive evergreen tree that shed its glow throughout the darkest hours of the year; the following weekend, Santa would arrive at the end of Straight Wharf by Coast Guard cutter. Waving from the back of an antique fire truck, he'd follow the Town Crier and a drum section of grade-school kids who'd been practicing with Ms. Benton the music teacher for weeks, parading up from the harbor and winding through town. Everybody standing on the curb—islanders, tourists, daytrippers—would fall in behind and follow the truck with guttural cheers. Eventually Santa would be enthroned next to the lighted town tree and take requests from a long line of children. This was what gave Christmas Stroll its name. It had been going on for half a century now, and although imitated by towns all over New England, Nantucket's weekend remained unrivaled. People who loved the island arrived each year by land and sea, from all over the country and the world, to celebrate.

Over time the holiday had morphed into three full days of permission to wander amiably around town with steaming cups of cheer and weird hats, bells jangling from the ankles of elf booties. Over ten thousand tourists crowded the sidewalks of downtown. The shops and restaurants were full. People laughed freely and called jokes to friends across the brick sidewalks and paused in the middle of the morning to sit on available benches. They bought things they didn't need, simply because they wanted them, then gifted them to others without a thought.

Costumed carolers sang on street corners. Tourists took selfies in front of window boxes and beneath mistletoe balls. A few of them found someone to kiss. They jostled each other goodnaturedly, butting armfuls of colorful bags, as they trailed down the streets in their red and green Stroll scarves.

In lucky years, it snowed.

In less fortunate ones, it rained.

This year, the forecast was for Windy and Gorgeous.

Uniformed members of Merry's police force would be up early and out on Main Street Saturday morning with sawhorses, barricading the heart of town against vehicular traffic. They'd stand in the crosswalks and near the sundial planter that sat right in the middle of the cobblestoned street. The Garden Association decorated the urn each year with fresh greens and red bows and tiny white lights. The police were there to maintain order and most of the Strollers were orderly, except for the occasional drunken jerk who vomited without warning on the uneven brick sidewalk. Merry had observed the rhythms of Stroll her entire life, she reflected, and usually it never got old.

But this year, she was clenching her teeth and grinding her way through the holiday. This year, she was struggling to find the Joy of the Season. This year, she barely had time to care.

This year, she wasn't merely another happy reveler hiding mysterious boxes on the top shelf of the spare bedroom's closet, the scent of vanilla and cloves in her hair. She wasn't pausing to rub pine or spruce branches on her early morning walks, so that the resinous oil lingered on her fingertips, or losing track of time while she snapped pictures of festive window boxes. This year, she was the Nantucket Police Department's chief of police. And Christmas Stroll, to be completely honest, was shaping up to be a royal pain in the ass.

She'd been police chief the previous year as well—her first in that elevated position—but Stroll was canceled that December due to the pandemic. She and her husband, Peter, had spent the holidays cozily enough in their farmhouse on the moors, spelling their quarantine cabin fever with long tramps through the cranberry bog or chasing their dog, Ney, down the trails that riddled Nantucket's conservation land. Because Merry was an essential worker, on the front line of the island's pandemic and obliged to interact with a heterogenous public, Peter was one of the few people she exposed to her germ-laden self for nearly a year. She was fortunate that he didn't mind the relative isolation; an introvert who preferred workouts and reading to loud gatherings, Peter had always lived something of a Socially Distanced life.

But *this* December, two days out from the Stroll kickoff, Merry was already exhausted. Because the man who was now president of the United States—as he had done every year for four decades except during the pandemic—had once again descended on Nantucket to celebrate Thanksgiving. He had brought three generations of family with him, naturally. A familiar sight in his aviator shades and bomber jacket, a dog lead in one hand and a cup of joe in the other, he'd been known in the past to pose for selfies, show up at book signings with a stack of hardbacks, and do a bit of Christmas shopping among the island merchants. But until this year, he hadn't been president—someone who a nutjob might actually want to kill. This year, weeks of planning and Readiness Exercises had preceded the family holiday. Airspace

was restricted around Ackerman Field, private jets were hang-
ered until further notice, C-17A Globemasters lumbered like
awkward water buffalo down the simple island runways and
disgorged armored vehicles and raincoat-clad advance teams.
As protection against a car bomb careening across the tarmac straight for Air Force One, every available piece of heavy
equipment on Nantucket—front loaders, dump trucks, mass
excavators and graders—was lined up with their noses flush
against the airport's perimeter fence in an intimidating picket of
steel. The Coast Guard forbade boating traffic off Abrams Point,
where the president was due to spend the holiday, and a fleet of
State Police motorcycles (for motorcade escort) was offloaded
from the freight boat and parked in readiness at the old Water
Street station.

Thankfully, it was the State Police who coordinated with the
Secret Service and White House staff, and the fire department
that was responsible for airport safety. But as chief of police,
Meredith was in the loop for every local planning meeting and
Readiness Exercise required to game out possible crises. Her turf
was the island community, forced to put up with road closures
and traffic snarls due to the president's security. It was her Public Information Officer who issued the press releases she signed,
informing Nantucketers that the heart of town would be inac-
cessible from noon until six the day after Thanksgiving while
the Secret Service posted snipers on various roofs, because the
president and his family were attending the annual tree-lighting
ceremony at the top of Main Street. It was Merry and her people
who received emails and phone calls from pissed-off islanders
outraged that their traditions had been hijacked, that motor-
cades bisected their shopping routes, and that the president
disappeared before they'd captured his face on their cell phones.
How was she to control the crowds trolling Abrams Point? What
if demonstrators with bullhorns broke the president's peace? Or

mobs halted foot traffic in town when he stopped for ice cream? Never mind the fear of foreign assassins in scuba gear circling in the waves off the presidential house, with silenced air guns and scopes trained on that famous silver head. Merry already had too much to worry about.

"Washington is why we can't have nice things," Peter reminded her three nights before Thanksgiving. Normally, he'd be spending the holiday with his sister, Georgiana, in Connecticut, but this year he'd elected to sit tight with Merry. Never mind that she was working the entire holiday. Peter was a better cook than she was; the cranberry sauce would certainly be excellent, and she'd have it on a turkey sandwich at midnight if she was forced to miss the actual bird. But for an instant, she gave way to wistfulness.

"Why didn't the Pres just go to Martha's Vineyard this year?" she moaned. "It was good enough for the Clintons and Obamas."

"He's not a Vineyard guy," Peter said simply. Which was, of course, unanswerable. It was accepted fact that you were either a Vineyard person or a Nantucket one. The loyalties were fierce, utterly distinct, cultivated over generations, and immune to criticism. No one could be both.

Which made it a little easier to put up with the security craziness, Merry reflected. It was kind of cool to know that the president cherished exactly the same place she did.

THIS CHEERFUL THOUGHT carried her through Thanksgiving week. It buoyed her as Air Force One taxied heavily down the runway at Ackerman Field to waving fans that Sunday, bound once more for Washington, and allowed her to breathe a sigh of relief when the final C17 left with the last of the White House staffers. She spent Monday writing reports, debriefing her key counterparts on snafus and successes, and commending the uniformed patrol people who'd killed themselves to keep everyone happy. By dinnertime Merry was kicked back in her fleece bed-room slippers in front of a roaring fire, with a glass of Peter's favorite red in her hands.

She allowed herself to take Tuesday off—or rather, on call. She spent Wednesday on call, too. It was a midweek breather, her chance to snag some extra sleep before the Stroll crowds slapped her on the head Friday like a cold curler off Surfside. This was her chance to follow Ney on a morning walk through Peter's cranberry bog, and finally have that leftover turkey sand-wich, with mayo and a slather of stuffing.

It was a good hiatus, and it turned out that she was wise to take it. She returned to the station, refreshed and humming "Have Yourself a Merry Little Christmas," Ralph's favorite old carol. Growing up, he'd told her it was written especially for her, the Little Merry in the Folger household. She couldn't actually sing the words this year without her voice breaking.

Only a few hours later, the first body was found.

2 | Thursday Morning

"WE'RE ABOUT TO land, babe."

Janet glanced up from the briefing book spread open in her lap. Ron was leaning near the cabin bulkhead, still in his shirtsleeves; he'd been hanging with the pilots again, watching the clouds sweep past the windscreen as the jet flew north from Washington.

"You might want to wake Ansel," she said.

Ron glanced at his son, who was sprawled with his legs akimbo and his head thrown back, mouth open and earbuds dangling, on the opposite side of the plane. Although it was nearly noon, the kid looked like he'd never rolled out of bed—his hair, dyed half red and half green, was standing on end. His cheeks were puffy. Was he hungover? Janet wondered. Coming down with something? Please God, don't let it be Covid—Ron had assured her Ance was fully vaccinated. But there were breakthrough infections, and his demographic was full of idiots who thought they were immortal . . .

She could *not* afford to get sick.

Janet slapped her binder closed and handed it without a word to her chief aide, Micheline, who raised a significant brow in her stepson's direction. The photographers would love it when he rolled bleary-eyed off the plane in his gray Champion hoodie.

Involuntarily, Janet frowned. Sensing her tension, Ron moved immediately to shake Ansel's shoulder, his voice low but his hands urgent and nervy. He was as alive as any of them to the possibility of blowback, this first family vacation of the new administration. Nobody wanted the headlines dripping with innuendo as soon as the secretary of state's plane touched down on Nantucket. And for too many reasons, Janet mused, Ansel was a press magnet. People loved reading about failure, particularly when it lived in the homes of the powerful; the media obliged, serving up every lurid detail of Ansel's colorful history and doubtful future. Gossip was far more compelling than the status of Taiwan or the threat of war in Ukraine or the delicate balance between carrot and stick. Janet got it. Her every act and word demanded something difficult—that people think. Whereas Ansel inspired schadenfreude, the simplest emotion on earth.

Ron exhaled in exasperation as his son blinked and yawned. "Dude," he ordered. "Hit the john. Splash some cold water on your face. And do something about that hair." His tone was clipped and tight; Ansel's vagaries drove him insane, further evidence, he told Janet in private, of the shitty gifts that genes kept on giving. Ansel was his mother all over again, a destiny Ron had dreaded since the boy's birth; but at twenty-three, Ansel was proof, Janet thought, that nature was infinitely more powerful than nurture.

She tried not to get involved. Most of the time Ron's son was his problem, one he'd brought into their decade-old marriage, and she had no dog in that fight. Janet had always been childless herself; kids were a ridiculous burden for anyone with a real career.

"You good?" Ron shrugged into his blue blazer as Ansel stumbled past him.

She nodded, and pulled a lipstick from her bag.

Ron looked perfect as usual, she thought: tall and rangy, with the leanness of a runner, although he rarely hit the gym. Janet was curvy herself, and the constant sitting required by her job didn't help; she'd put on fifteen pounds in the past year. She felt a flicker of gratitude for Ron's *message discipline*—his dark hair was neatly cut and swept back, with just a touch of gray at the temples; his brown oxfords were hip enough to telegraph that he was on trend, without going rogue. She wished Ansel had half his father's savvy.

Her stepson eased through the plane's folding bathroom door, his eyes drifting to meet hers. He gave a tentative little wave. She attempted to smile in return, but her anxiety must have been visible; Ance's gaze dropped and he slouched back into his seat, fastening his belt for the descent. There were water stains now on the front of the hoodie, and a fluorescent orange smear from the pizza they'd had three days ago. She'd known Ance since the age of twelve, and the arc of the kid's universe had always bent toward chaos.

"Do we know when he bathed last?" Micheline murmured.

"He was relatively clean on Thanksgiving. If you ignored the paint. I think he showered in it."

Ansel described himself as an artist. He'd picked up painting in rehab—abstracts in acrylics, mostly, that had the color sensibility of a circus clown on acid. He liked to inform people that art had saved his life. Ron routinely called bullshit, of course—Ance was wasting time in the name of *therapy*, and doing it on his dad's dime. Ron planned to tell him this weekend that they were cutting him off financially unless he agreed to finish college. She hoped Ron waited until Sunday to drop that bomb.

For an instant, Janet wished Ansel hadn't come along to ruin Christmas Stroll—but the next few days on Nantucket were supposed to be Family Time, on a direct order from the president. It was hard to trumpet *Family* without at least a token stepchild. And she needed to reassure her boss that she was handling the stress of the job just fine. That she could hit any curve ball the world threw. That the president could have complete confidence in Janet Brimhold McKay . . .

"You're no good to me if you collapse from exhaustion," he'd said on the call the day after Thanksgiving. "You've been run off your feet. I know how bad the jet lag can be. And hell, a relaxed American posture might reassure the world right now. Not every day has to be hair-trigger."

Is that the vibe she telegraphed? A woman who was *hair-trigger*? Unstable? Liable to lose it completely and thrust the US into World War III? Janet drew a deep breath. Sure, it had been a definite leap from the Senate Foreign Relations Committee to secretary of state. The media had done their best to fan doubts about her. She'd inherited a State Department in disarray after the travesties of the previous administration—all hiring on hold, entire cadres of seasoned professionals sidelined or fired, the politicization of hallowed aid programs and fear of retribution rampant among the ranks. Her people needed confidence building and healing, support and leadership, yet she'd been traveling ten days out of twelve since her confirmation and was still down too many deputies and key ambassadors due to the snail's pace of the confirmation process. She was trying to learn on the job, but sometimes the lessons came from failure, and self-doubt gnawed at her. It was alien and unsettling for a woman who'd sailed through the world with complete certainty since kindergarten.

Ron figured she could leverage this post straight into the White House if she played her cards right. *If she was good. If people liked her.* Maybe; but was that what she wanted? The White House? And did people like her? Was she any good?

The president passed over a lot of men to hand her this plum cabinet post. Her enemies called her a token, appointed for gender balance and as a sop to the party's moderate wing. They brayed that she'd flame out in a few months' time. Worse, that she'd take down the Administration when she fucked up. If an international crisis hit while she relaxed over Stroll Weekend, Janet thought with a stab of anxiety, the headlines would be shrill: *Administration Blindsided While SecState Parties on Exclusive Island.* She was kicking back and killing time for somebody else's *relaxed American posture.*

So many things could go wrong over the next few days. With work, sure, but right here on Nantucket, as she twiddled her thumbs in the old house on Hulbert Ave. she'd inherited from Nana Brimhold, while Micheline fed her prep papers for next week's Ukraine trip and Ron tried to pull her away for a *family bike ride* or a *photo op.* If Ansel pulled one of his stunts—

She felt the landing gear judder into place, glimpsed the flaps on the wings extending. She slipped her stilettos back on her feet, wincing slightly—her toes had swelled in the fifty minutes of flight—and positioned her sunglasses over her eyes.

"Your mask, ma'am," Micheline said, handing her a navy blue scrap of fabric embroidered with State's seal. Mick had been with her for years, through stump speeches, election nights, and the insurrection at the Capitol. Janet had brought her over to State without hesitation; she trusted Micheline completely. Like Ron, Mick understood optics and was perfectly on message: as whip-smart as her Vietnamese neurologist father, as chic as her French film agent mother, in black wool trousers and a white shirtwaist, her jet-black bob grazing her chin.

Janet tucked the mask's straps over her ears. The jet bumped heavily onto the island runway. A few days of cheer. Of family and relaxation. She would have to survive them somehow.

3 | Ingrid's Gift

"Wow, look at this place!"

Chris Candler dropped his carry-on and surveyed the guest cottage's main room. It screamed both elegance and comfort—a balance that could be hard to strike. At one end was a grouping of chairs and a sofa in front of a gas fireplace, flat-screen TV above; at the other was an open kitchen, all white marble and pale gray cabinetry that echoed Nantucket's aesthetic. The floors were reclaimed wide-plank teak, he guessed, with sheepskin rugs scattered over them. He immediately shed his boat shoes; per usual, he wasn't wearing socks. He sank his toes into the nearest fleece and sighed.

His daughter drifted into the cottage behind him. Her eyes were on her cell phone, a faint pucker between her brows. Had she even heard him? Had she noticed where they were? Or was her head still back in LA, tripping among the impossibly gorgeous holiday posts of her frenemies?

"Hey. Look up."

Winter's gaze lifted, and Chris swam for a second in her blue eyes. *Blue* didn't begin to capture it, really; Winter's eyes were large and oval, framed with thick dark lashes, brilliant and faceted as sapphires. Encountered by chance, they demanded a second look, and then a second guess—were they somehow fake? He'd known people to stop, mesmerized, when Winter was just a baby, then sink down to stroller level and stare. He'd been ridiculously proud when she was young—as though her otherworldly beauty was a credit to his taste, when in fact it was entirely by chance. Maybe he'd enjoyed the fact that for once, people weren't staring at *him*—Chris Candler, Hollywood hottie and action-movie hero. When Winter was around he didn't need to hide behind a four-days' growth of beard and a wool cap pulled low on his forehead. When Winter was around, he was irrelevant. She had her own adoring public. Maybe that was why at thirteen, every talent agent he knew was trying to sign her, and why in high school everyone hated her.

Why at nineteen, she was lucky to be alive.

"Isn't this great?" he prompted.

She shrugged, and wrapped her arms around her ribcage. "It's so dreary and cold."

Because you're too thin, Chris thought. But she was right; they'd landed in rain this Thursday evening, and dark had already fallen by the time their driver reached the compound off Polpis Road. No sign out here in the coastal moors of Christmas lights or holiday cheer. Maybe Town would be more festive?

"Your mom loved Nantucket."

"My mom also killed herself," Winter replied.

He repressed a sigh of frustration and moved to switch on the gas fireplace. Flames whipped across a base of fractured glass chips the color of obsidian. "It'll warm up soon. You should probably add a layer. The cold feels worse when you're near the sea."

"Not in Malibu," she murmured, and flopped down on the sofa, her eyes back on her screen.

Winter hadn't wanted to come on this shoot. Chris had basically forced her onto the plane. He'd thought a bit of traditional New England Christmas might help them both. Not for the first time, he wondered if he'd done the right thing.

He picked up their bags and went in search of the bedrooms. Maybe there'd be sun in the morning.

"LIGHTS JUST WENT up in the guest cottage," Vic Sonnenfeld announced.

He stood at one of the large front windows, peering out
into the dark. The rolling lawns of the twelve-acre compound,
known as Ingrid's Gift, were hidden now and had been difficult
to see for most of the day—fog had rolled in off the harbor along
with scattered bouts of rain. It was an impressive property, if a
bit sodden; the main house, where he and Carly had the primary
suite, was about ten thousand square feet and came with a live-in
housekeeper and cook. The guest house was apparently for over-
flow, and there was an additional apartment above the boathouse
where the owner of Ingrid's Gift—a guy named Mike Struna—
was living this week while they were all using his property. He'd
claimed it was no trouble to move into what was essentially a
garage on his thirty-million-dollar estate; from the bedroom he
had a prime view of the harbor and his private dock, a rarity on
Nantucket.

Vic had met Mike for the first time last night, when the
tech genius showed them over the main house and introduced
them to Brittany, the housekeeper/cook. "She trained with
Tess Starbuck at the Greengage," he'd confided *sotto voce*, as
though Vic should be impressed. Carly had made up for his
apparent indifference, oohing and ahhing over every detail of
the arrangements and thanking Mike profusely. She could be
charming as hell, Carly—when it served her interests. He wondered briefly whether her interests included Mike himself. The
man was smooth and attractive enough, not to mention thirty
years younger than Vic and an old college friend of Carly's;
probably good the man had removed himself to the water's
edge. Part of the deal when Mike offered Carly the compound
was that he would stay out of the way.

Vic would have to keep an eye on things.

His wife finished pouring a glass of scotch and handed it to him; he chinked it automatically against her red wine. "Cheers."

"Cheers." She took a sip then grimaced as her cell phone pinged. She thumbed the keypad with her free hand. "Marni LeGuin and Theo just landed. I hope the cook knows we'll be six at dinner."

Marni. A tingle of excitement stirred at the base of Vic's spine. She was one of the most talented young actors he'd ever signed to CMI—the Hollywood talent agency he'd founded, Creative Management International. She was a blonde perfectly suited to rom-coms, but in recent years she'd grown into meatier roles, a deepening of her work that stemmed naturally from greater experience and the wisdom that sometimes comes with age. This project of Carly's was a perfect platform for Marni: paired with Chris Candler, who was also attempting to pivot from action roles to ones with gravitas. Carly had cast them in her streaming television series, *The Hopeless,* for strategic reasons: she knew they'd jump at the chance to work in her brooding, atmospheric police procedural, and their box office power would persuade millions of viewers to watch.

Now, Vic thought, *if we can only encourage them to have an on-set affair and promote the crap out of it in the tabloids, The Hopeless is a slam dunk. What would be a good paparazzi nickname? Marnichris? Chrismarn? CanGuin?*

"Apparently the kid is a vegan," Carly muttered.

"What kid?"

"Chris Candler's. Her name is Winter." She set down her phone. "Glad I'm not cooking for this crew. Theo is probably only eating pink food this week, or something equally bizarre."

"I'm sure the cook will cope." Vic tossed back his entire scotch. "She trained with Somebody, Somewhere, remember?"

"WE'RE APPARENTLY IN the main house," Theo Patel told Marni LeGuin as the car the production people had sent pulled away from the airport's tiny terminal. Rain was sheeting down; they'd run across the open tarmac from the jet, but were damp anyway. "I've just had a text."

"Shit," Marni said. She had spent the flight counting to a thousand and then back down again to zero, her personal form of meditation. She hated small planes and had almost balked at boarding. "I don't want to be in the main house."

"You've never seen it, darling."

"That doesn't matter. I never sleep down the hall from my director. Distance is critical."

"Hush, child." Theo's slender brown fingers were busily swiping his keys. "Carly says your room is palatial and there's an en suite bath. Also a cook. She wants to know if you're vegan. Do I break it gently that I'm only eating raw fish? Or do I wait until she's air-kissed my cheek?"

"I was promised a guest cottage," Marni attempted.

"Not in your contract. Candler has the cottage. And there's top production crew in what's known as the Barn." Theo shuddered. "I'm sure those poor sods are *sharing* baths. Try to remember, Sweetness, that life can always be worse."

"That's what I'm afraid of."

At last, his dark eyes flicked up to meet hers. He set down his phone and folded his hands in his lap. This was Theo's invitation to tell him everything, to vent while she could, in the safety of their intimate bubble. They had been sharing it for six years, now.

He was a beautiful man, Theo; Anglo-Indian by birth, meticulously groomed and tailored by habit. She called him her personal assistant but he preferred the old theatre term of *Dresser*, and introduced himself as such around Hollywood. Theo's husband was a master gardener who tended their country house in Sussex and amused himself during Theo's frequent absences by singing bass in a local opera company.

"Dish," Theo ordered. "Why the willies? You're not usually *such* a princess. I've known you to sleep on the ground in a leaking tent for the right production."

For a second she almost told him. She caught herself in time.

"Princess?" she repeated, with one of her most enchanting smiles. "This week I plan to be a *queen*. This is my Emmy vehicle, remember?"

"That's my girl." Theo reached once more for his phone. "And not to fret. If Vic tries anything on in the night, I'll kill him, shall I?"

Marni's stomach swooped to her knees. *What did Theo know?*

But the time to ask him had passed. His slim fingers were pressing keys again.

She leaned her head against the chill car window and began to count backwards from one thousand.

4 | Stella Maris

SHE AWOKE TO rain that Thursday morning: a half-hearted and fitful shower that pummeled the rafters of the old house before easing off with an audible sigh. In the dripping silence that followed, crows called from the trees that fringed the property and a mourning dove muttered in the shelter of the attic dormer. She lay listening to it, half-dozing, in search of the shreds of a dream that fluttered just beyond reach, like a forgotten bit of laundry left hanging in the dark. She had been wearing an evening dress. Washing her hair in a basin, as she did here. A man in bare feet was laughing at her, pouring champagne, but she could not make out his face—

The unheated house was cold enough that she could see her breath; it would get colder in January and February. There would eventually be snow. She had lived through one winter already at Stella Maris and had adapted to the gradual loss of warmth and color in sea and sky. She would never grow used to the winter winds, which for periods of time could howl senselessly about the house, battering her. But this, too, she knew now to expect.

Once she accepted that her dream was irretrievable—*whose face?*—she emerged from the cocoon of blankets beneath her grandmother's pieced quilt and set her socked feet on the floor, which was as canted as the deck of a ship under full sail and as worn as the spine of a well-loved book. Buildings of Stella Maris's vintage were raised on poor foundations, subsided through centuries, strained the seams of their joints, buckled under the weight of vanished footsteps. Nothing in the house was level. She had acquired her sea legs after a few days of tipping up and down the stairs and lurching through doorways. Now, twenty months on, she found the stability of other properties disorienting. The aisles of the grocery store rose up to trip her as she shopped.

She relieved herself in the one toilet she used for that purpose, and flushed it with a bucket of cold seawater left tidily nearby. Then she set bottled water to boil on the kitchen's cast-iron stove for simple filtered coffee. Later, when the flames died down a bit, she would stab an English muffin with a fondue fork and toast it close to the coals.

She made bacon this way, too, and at dinner time set potatoes to roast in the embers.

She contemplated the landscape beyond the kitchen's picture window while she drank her black coffee. This year, fine weather had lingered on Nantucket, and the flushed colors of the moor scrub—low bush blueberry, drifts of corema, reindeer moss, and false heather still flared here and there beneath her eye, though subdued and blanched under the leaden sky. The harbor's water was mercury colored, a barely discernible line on the horizon. There would eventually be fog. She would not take her camera and tripod to the UMass Field Station today, as she had planned; she would wait for better weather, when the mergansers she hoped to sight and capture on film would be visible.

But there remained the more familiar wings of her home ground, the tufted titmice and common wrens and the occasional wonder of the eastern blue jay, flashing like a scimitar across the overgrown patch of what had once been lawn just beyond this kitchen window. They would be hungry. Hungrier than usual, perhaps, because of the chill rain. She drained her

cup, thrust her arms into her winter jacket, and padded out the
back door in her bedroom slippers.

The pockets of her coat were filled with sunflower seeds.
Shelled raw peanuts. Small lumps of suet. As she trudged across
the frowsy lawn, which glinted silver with the remnants of frost,
she scooped some of this into her palm. Her first pandemic July, she
had been surprised to glimpse the pale blue heads of hydran-
geas among the wild Queen Anne's lace at the old garden's edge.
Planted by her mother once, and overtaken by the moors. She
had not attempted to restore order in the backyard; chaos was far
more beautiful. The birds preferred it, and to her, the birds were
always the point.

The hydrangea heads were bleached of color now, their florets
transparent as rice paper, nodding on desiccated stems. As she
crossed the tousled back lawn, a deer—startled from its brows-
ing among the shrubs—leapt into the air and bounded away.
A juvenile whitetail buck, she noted, its antlers not yet shed.
She slowed to a halt just where memory merged with wildness, and
held out her right hand. A wealth of feed gleamed on her extended
palm. She willed her breath to slow, inaudible to her own ears.
Felt her heart rate steady. The early rain had faded to cold mist
that napped her face in velvet; her skin was dewy as a teenager's.
Her mind stilled.

A whirr of wings, a sudden breeze—some of the sunflower
seeds spilled to the ground—and a living flutter lit on her palm.
Three toes clutched forward and one to the rear: the term for
this is *anisodactyl*. The bird perched on her fingertips, tail tipped
down and inward for balance. It had been many years since she
had flinched at the nip of claws, thin and tensile as steel wire.
She did not shake herself free. A female northern cardinal,
browner and rosier than the male, cocked its head rapidly, first
left, then right. A brilliant eye assessed her. Then the head bent
to the feed. The open beak grasped a suet lump, turned to stare

liquidly at the sky, where another bird was incoming. The wings lifted. The cardinal flicked to the tip of a scrub oak, throat working, as a black-capped chickadee grasped the side of her index finger and stabbed at a peanut.

She stood like this, almost motionless, while the wings of countless birds swooped and lifted in turn. She had coaxed them to this level of intimacy over the past five-hundred-odd days in patient stages: First, setting out a conventional feeder to inform the birds that she was home; then, removing it and placing feed in the palm of a stray glove set out at feeder height on the railing of the kitchen steps; then donning the glove, filling it with feed, and offering it to the skies; and at last, removing the glove to extend her bare, food-filled palm. It was a technique she had learned from other bird photographers—and from other birders who cared nothing about capturing wings on camera—and she had perfected it during her years of exile in Oregon. She was quietly pleased to have replicated the results on Nantucket.

A grackle, familiar from past feedings. A common wren. Two tufted titmice, tufts lifted aggressively at each other. Damp seeped through her slippers and her locked knees began to ache. The tips of her fingers chilled to a bloodless gray.

Only when the feed was nearly gone, seeds slipping between the seams of her fingers, did she dust her hands together and turn back to the house. That was the extent of her work for the morning. She would wait out the damp by the fire and drink another cup of hot coffee. Then she would change into her work clothes and drive yesterday's roll of film to be developed in town.

She was smiling with contentment and peace, as free as the birds she'd fed, when she walked back into the derelict house.

5 | Friday Morning

Ms. Thompson's 4th Grade Class, Ansel read from the tag on the fir tree. Like the others that stood up and down Main Street, it was decorated and strung with lights, in this case by a group of nine-year-olds from the island's elementary school. They'd cut disks and diamonds from colored construction paper and glued photographs to them, of kids sitting in study groups, or volunteering at local charities, on field trips, and with special members of their families. The pictures were uniformly cheerful, filled with goofy and gap-toothed faces clowning for the lens. He wondered, as he studied them, what even one child really felt or thought as the shutter clicked. In his experience, no one's inner world was as relentlessly upbeat as the images people curated for public approval and judgment.

He moved to the next tree, a few yards farther up Main. He found it less interesting—it had been decorated by the local hardware store with tools. But it stood directly in front of a place called Lemon Press, and Ance stopped short to study the glass storefront windows, which had been exuberantly and lovingly painted for Stroll Weekend with a townscape of Nantucket. Each building, even the Congregational Church spire, was depicted as gingerbread.

He preferred abstract to representational art, particularly the schtick that proliferated around the holidays, but the mural was pretty cool, he decided. It was perfectly festive for the day—which was sunlit after the rain, but chill enough for a proper Winter Stroll. His gaze drifted over the exuberant paint swirls, over the evergreens and branches that filled the window boxes below, and came to rest on a brilliant and bottomless pair of blue eyes that stared out at him from Lemon Press's interior.

Everything in Ansel went still, except his pulse. That accelerated.

The girl—she had long dark hair and a pale, elfin face— smiled at him tentatively. She was studying his hair, he realized, and he reached up to smooth it. Remembering, only then, that he'd dyed it Christmas red and green for Stroll. What had he been thinking?

He was an idiot. He should walk on, quickly, and stop embarrassing himself.

He glanced up at the Lemon Press sign, and realized it was a café. Or bakery. He could go inside and order coffee. The pot had been empty this morning when he came down to the kitchen and he'd debated making more, but it was clear he was the last one to get up and his dad was already on a conference call, Janet was closeted in her office with her aide, Micheline, and it seemed like a perfect time to slip outside without anyone noticing him.

From habit he'd left by a side door and walked straight down Hulbert Ave. toward the Coast Guard Station on Brant Point, his hands in his jeans pockets and his hoodie pulled up around his ears. It was his ritual each time he came to the island, a way of checking in on past Ansels and the distance the present one had traveled. He'd stood for a few minutes near the old lighthouse, watching a cocker spaniel chase a ball in the shallows and the high-speed ferry pass through the channel. One or two people on deck waved; Ansel waved back. Then he walked slowly down Easton Street toward the heart of town. Tourists just off the boat were making their way up Main toward the Jared Coffin House, suitcases bumping across the uneven brick sidewalks behind them.

It was excellent to be free, Ansel thought—of his dad, who was constantly exasperated with him these days; of his step-mother's staff, who rarely spoke to him but watched him like an unpredictable vagrant; and naturally of Janet, who looked too harassed to deal with the complications of an extraneous sub-relative. He took his time ambling up Main Street, studying each of the trees, and resolved to come back that night, when all the strings of lights would be on. If past experience was any guide, the sidewalks would be deserted until Saturday evening of Stroll.

Which is how he came to be ambushed unexpectedly by this pair of remarkable and arresting eyes. Ansel stepped back and considered running straight to Hulbert Avenue, but the truth was, he was hungry, and he wanted a cup of coffee, and he was old enough to own his hair and the choices he'd made about it for the holiday weekend. So he opened Lemon Press's door instead, and walked inside.

The girl's gaze followed him. He tried to look unconscious of that while he studied the menu. There were other people in the place and she'd lose interest in a matter of seconds. *Falafel, vegan harissa aioli, muhammara, avocado,* he read. What was muhammara? Were eyes that color even real? He strayed from the menu and caught the girl still looking at him. Ansel walked stiffly to the counter and asked for a cup of coffee and a breakfast sand-wich. Then he pulled out his phone, and made a pretense of studying it.

"I like your hair." She had actually gotten up and come over to him, although to be clear, she was also dumping trash in the nearby garbage can. "Strangely festive."

"Thanks." He glanced up and fell immediately into that mes-merizing blue. "You, too, can have it for the price of spray dye. Although I can't vouch for how it'll turn out on your color hair."

She frowned. "What's yours when it's . . . normal?"

"Pretty blond. Although *normal*'s eluded me for at least two decades. You here for Stroll?"

She nodded. "My dad dragged me. You?"

"Same."

"But it's okay, I guess. Now that the rain's over. I don't do rain."

"You mean, there's a choice?" He shoved his phone back in his pocket as the woman behind the Lemon Press counter set down a wrapped sandwich.

"For Ansel!" she called.

"Ansel," the girl behind him repeated. "As in, Ansel *Adams?*"

"Sure." Not many people got the reference; icons of print photography were obsolete in the TikTok age.

"I love his pictures of Yosemite," she enthused. "Half Dome. El Capitan. But you can't be from California without being an Ansel groupie, right?"

"You came all the way from California for Stroll?"

"Sort of. My dad has to work this week. Here, on the island. It's just an accident that we showed up for the holiday—but I guess he thought it'd be fun." She looked worried for an instant, as though *fun* was a form of pressure. "At least he's not keeping me on a leash."

"Well—" Ansel glanced at the door, his sandwich warm in his hand. "If you like art, you should check out the gallery on Water Street. The Artists' Association of Nantucket. They've got a show mounted for the holidays. There should be some photographs."

"Where's Water Street?"

He jerked his head to the left. "Bottom of Main. Turn right just past Ralph Lauren. You'll find it."

"Thanks," she said. "Maybe I will."

They stood awkwardly for a second while Ansel wondered if

he should offer to show her the gallery himself, but that seemed overly familiar for a casual chat near a trashcan, so he said instead, "Nice talking to you. Have a good Stroll."

"You, too!" She reached into her pocket for a face mask. "What'd you get to eat? The muhammara was totally great, by the way."

"What is that, even?"

"Muhammara?" She was surprised. "It's like a . . . dip, or a spread. Made from walnuts and red peppers. Pomegranate molasses?" she added, as he still looked bewildered. "I take it you're not into Middle Eastern food. Or . . . vegan?"

He shook his head.

"This is, like, the only vegan-friendly restaurant on Nantucket." She laughed, and it transformed her; the waif was gone. "At least, as far as I could tell from my super-swift search this morning. What are you actually eating?"

"An egg, cheese, and sausage sandwich."

She wrinkled her nose and shrugged into her jacket. It was fleece, which relieved Ansel because it was cold outside and this girl had no body fat. Her knit top was severely cropped and exposed an expanse of tanned midriff oddly at variance with her pale face. She wrapped a wool scarf several times around her neck—one of the special red and green Stroll ones sold at the Boat Basin every year.

"I'm Winter, by the way. Winter Candler."

"Ansel McKay. Most people call me Ance."

"Nice to meet you, Ance."

Those amazing eyes had a glint of friendliness in them as she pushed open the door. He did a minor salute with his wrapped sandwich, but stayed where he was, because he didn't want to look stalky by following her out into the street. She headed right, toward the head of Main, her chin tucked into the collar of her jacket and her black hair bouncing as she walked.

Fifteen seconds later, a tall woman in yoga pants and an emerald-green half zip rose from her seat, gave Ansel a hard stare, and followed Winter Candler out of Lemon Press.

Ansel felt a prick of shock. The woman was wearing an earpiece! Not the usual earbuds anybody might use to receive phone calls or music, but the kind with a tightly spiraled transparent cord that disappeared into the neck of her pullover. It would be connected to a radio and pager. She'd successfully hidden most of the device with her long brown hair, but Ansel knew what he was looking at; his stepmother's Diplomatic Security Service bodyguards wore the same thing.

He sprinted to the front windows. Winter's fleece and dark hair were about to turn into Nantucket Looms—and a few paces behind her, attempting to look like any other holiday reveler, was the girl's female bodyguard.

What the *hell*? Who were these people?

Nobody from the Administration, he thought. The name didn't ring a bell. And she'd said her dad was here on business.

He pulled out his phone and did a quick internet search on her name. It was distinctive enough that he wouldn't have to scroll through too many social media accounts to find her.

He had no sooner finished typing *Winter Candler* before the girl's face appeared on his screen. Ansel's mouth opened, and he sank onto a chair provided for Lemon Press's takeout customers.

She was walking down a sidewalk in sunglasses, but it was the same hair, the same slender frame, the same elfin chin. She had extended her right hand in the universal sign for *stop*, and her lips were set in a grim line. *Winter Candler Reality Show?* the blurb queried. Ansel saw the dateline; Los Angeles, about six months ago. So she was somebody famous?

The next shot was a close-up of her face, and the words beneath it said: *Are Winter Candler's Blue Eyes Fake?* He scrolled to another image—Winter on a beach in a bikini, taken from the rear. Her ribs and shoulder blades were frighteningly sharp beneath the skin. *Winter Wasting Away*, this one was captioned. *Chris Candler's Daughter No Better After Anorexia Treatment.*

Chris Candler!

Ansel expelled a gusty sigh. He'd probably seen every Chris Candler action movie ever made, at least once; the buddy gambling films, too, and even the Star Trek reboots. There'd been that medieval Crusader epic he hadn't loved, but no fault of Candler's. And she was his *daughter*? No wonder she had security. Snatch Winter and stuff her in the back of a white van, and you could ask her dad for twenty million dollars.

He returned to the link about anorexia. Pulled it up and read through it quickly. It was a few years old—she'd been sixteen when she was shipped off to a treatment facility in the Adirondacks for half a year of therapy.

Rehab. They had that in common, at least.

She would be about . . . he checked a few dates, did some math . . . nineteen now. She hadn't looked anorexic this morning, and she'd eaten breakfast, even if it was vegan. That had to be good, right?

Why was he worrying about someone he didn't even know?

Ansel shook himself slightly and put his phone away. *Coffee*, he thought. He'd order a cup to go, then walk up Old North Wharf while he ate his sandwich. He'd look for Killen's Dory, the boat with the lighted Christmas tree on it that the Killen family anchored in the Basin each year. It was another one of his rituals, and it was on his way home. It was also the very last place he'd expect to run into a celebrity and her bodyguard.

6 | Ingrid's Gift, Friday

"I T L O O K S L I K E he's been dead for a few days," Marni LeGuin said tersely. "Probably went into the water farther north and washed down with the current."

"Think he drowned?" Chris Candler asked.

"Maybe—but look at these needle tracks. He may not have been conscious when he entered the water. We'll have to wait for the autopsy."

"With the coroner's backlog, it'll be weeks before we know what happened to him."

"Oh, we *know* what happened to him." Marni lifted her head to meet Candler's eyes. "Trick is, how do we prove it?"

"Let's stop there," Carly Simpson-Sonnenfeld broke in.

She stood up from the long, square dining table that bridged the main house's open kitchen and the comfortable great room. She'd chosen to sit in the neutral middle of the table rather than at the ball-busting head, placing Vic there instead. He had no formal role in the read-through, but he was at loose ends this week while she shot the initial outdoor scenes of *The Hopeless* on Nantucket—the two main characters, female cop Quincy Reynolds and her male subordinate Nate Trask, finding a drug addict's body on an isolated stretch of winter beach. Vic would be less restless if she included him, and she needed him to behave. Once they returned to the set in Toronto for interior scenes, he'd head back to LA and find his own sources of amusement; but this week, he was her problem. As if she didn't have enough to do, directing her first serial project for a major streaming service! Managing a seventy-three-year-old man, she sometimes thought, was as challenging as entertaining a tired toddler. If she'd known how difficult he'd be when she'd married him six years ago . . .

She'd have done it anyway. Vic had networks, financing, influence. A stable of talent he could tap for any size package. Vic had power. And Carly needed it.

She smiled at Chris Candler, who was stretching his arms over his head and cracking his spine. The walnut Windsor chairs grouped around the live-edge dining table were antiques sourced on Nantucket. Mike, who owned the house, was proud of how many things his designer had managed to buy locally—but the spindly wooden chairs were uncomfortable. Chris had lots of reasons to feel stiff anyway—he'd taken a beating in all those action films. Rumor had it he'd done his own stunts in his early hungry days. He was wise to pivot to deeper narratives in his mid-forties. There was only so much a body could take, even one as beautifully toned and maintained as Chris Candler's.

Mid-forties. Carly was roughly in the same ballpark, twenty-eight years younger than her husband, Vic. She knew for a fact that she was five months younger than the beautiful Marni LeGuin, who could pass for early thirties and made a rule never to disclose her actual age. Vic was fawning over Marni—he had her right hand captured in both of his, now, and was patting it avuncularly. As though she were a prized niece or granddaughter. He'd never treat Chris that way in a million years, out of terror of being mistaken for a homosexual. Once again, Carly felt a stab of disgruntlement at Hollywood's persistent gender disparities. Too many old white men had Vic's death grip on power.

"Tea?" Chris called from the gleaming kitchen.

"Love some," she replied. "Chamomile, if there's any."

That was another rumor about Chris—that he'd quit drinking

after he found his wife dangling from a halter in his daughter's horse barn. When was that, three, four years ago? He didn't look like he was grieving any longer, but then again, what did Carly expect? That he'd wear his loss on his sleeve while he was working? Carly drifted toward him, seeing the fine dark hair on his forearms, the immaculate, crisp white shirtsleeves rolled to the elbow, the long-fingered hands deftly filling the pot. It was true that certain people in the industry had star quality—a palpable magnetism that flared like an aura around them as they moved. Even in something as mundane as making tea. Chris had it. She'd been lucky as hell to catch him between projects. The air in the room shimmered when he walked through the door.

"There's a boiling water tap near the sink," she offered.

"Blasphemy," he said. "And always disappointing."

He gave her a crooked grin—one of his famous ones, but no less real for that—and Carly wondered suddenly if Chris thought of her as a peer, as a woman around his own age, or if in his mind a director was firmly off-limits.

"I'm glad we're doing this table reading," he volunteered. "Any thoughts about character yet?"

"I like the deference you're showing Marni." She opened a cabinet door in search of a tea mug, and found one with the Whaling Museum's logo on it. "Too many police procedurals stick a woman in the lead role and then let her male colleagues treat her like shit. You've got respect. A careful distance. That's critical at this stage in the script, but it's entirely in the nuances of the reading."

"Until I fall into bed with her in the final third?"

The kettle whistled. Chris's head swiveled as he reached for it. His dark hair was as crisp and immaculate as his tailored shirt, his jawline close-shaved. Carly closed her eyes for a second and took a deep breath.

"Only if the chemistry is there."

"Really?" A line of surprise now on his brow.

"That's a principle of mine. Let's see where the dialogue and the characters take us. If you and Marni feel it's right, then go with the pulse. If there is no pulse, we'll write romance out of the script."

"And keep the viewers guessing?" He poured the boiling water into her cup, wincing slightly as it splashed his hand. "That's an excellent strategy if you're angling for a Season Two."

"Who isn't?" The back of her fingers grazed his as she reached for the tea, and Carly swore she felt an electric shock.

"It's early days yet." Chris's eyes were on something beyond Carly's shoulder. She turned to follow his gaze.

Vic's right hand was extended in supplication, and Marni LeGuin was striding out of the room. Every line of the woman's retreating back screamed fury. Theo Patel, her personal assistant, let her go—but said a few words in an undertone to Vic.

Her husband's hand dropped. Carly watched his thumb rub his forefingers pensively. She muttered under her breath, "What the fuck?"

"Bathroom break," Chris said. "I'm sure we could all use one."

He set down his tea and left her.

MARNI MEANT TO go upstairs—slam the door of her suite, which was, as Theo had assured her, perfectly beautiful and in keeping with the spirit of her contract. An entire wall of windows overlooked the rear of Ingrid's Gift, the sweep of faded winter lawn running down to the rough path through the moors, the blue water just beyond. She'd had coffee in bed, her tablet propped up on her knees while she read the headlines, lifting her gaze every so often to absorb the untrammeled peace of the view. The linens were exquisite, the quiet of the house was deep, she'd slept well and shaken off the anxiety that had shadowed her on the flight.

Dinner the previous night had been entirely cordial and professional, each of the principals determined to position themselves well, and it had ended blissfully early. She'd kissed Theo's cheek—his room was right next to hers—lingered in a hot bath, and chewed some melatonin gummies to help with the time change. She had barely moved until Theo tapped on her door eight hours later. She opened it to find the breakfast tray: warm, homemade cranberry muffins and oatmeal.

Clearly, the kitchen staff hadn't flagged the no-carb rule in her contract. She left the food out on the tray and carried the coffee service inside.

Now, however, as she hesitated furiously before the stairs in the wide center hall, the prospect of the bedroom was prisonlike. In fact, it made her gorge rise with ancient trauma. She would *not* be forced into retreat barely half a day into the shoot! This role she'd won—Quincy Reynolds, rising detective star—was too important. It might renew for multiple seasons, become a national obsession, catapult her into the awards. She would *not* let the stupidities of the past force her into a position of weakness. She had fought too hard to compromise now. She would—

She would burst into tears if she stood here another minute.

Marni glanced to her right: the front door, leading out to the long driveway and the Barn, where principal members of the production crew were staying, by the electronic gate. Too symbolic of flight, and ultimately leading nowhere. If she trudged down to the main road now, it would be tough to trudge back; humiliating, in fact. She glanced to her left: the French doors leading out to the back lawn. There was that path she'd seen, winding toward the water. A contemplative choice. She could say she'd merely needed a bit of fresh air.

She hurried to the doors and pulled one open. A light breeze, brisk with salt and the scent of old hay and something else— marsh?—drifted over her skin. She stepped out onto the deck and breathed deeply. Last night's rain was gone, and everything around her looked fresh, clean, unspoiled. Thank God something was!

She was wearing only jeans and a cabled cashmere sweater. It didn't matter. She wanted her skin to prickle with gooseflesh, she wanted to feel cold. She glanced at her watch and set off across the lawn. She'd give herself fifteen minutes before she went back into the table read. Breaks were written into her contract, for fuck's sake.

HE GLIMPSED HER from the boathouse's upstairs windows, which overlooked the long wooden dock snaking out into Polpis Harbor. She was standing at the landward end, as if debating whether to walk all the way out. She was equally interested in the boathouse, however, he could tell. Deliberately painted to look like the Coast Guard Station on Brant Point, fresh white clapboards with black trim and a red door, it had an irresistible appeal to people who knew nothing about the water. *What did it look like inside?*

Sure enough, in another instant the figure below him disappeared, and he heard the ground floor's barn door slide back.

He set his laptop on the coffee table and walked deliberately downstairs, making enough noise so that he wouldn't startle the woman when he appeared.

She was looking right at him when he came into sight on the steps, her expression inquiring.

"I'm sorry, I hope I didn't disturb you . . ." she managed. "I've just never seen inside one of these before."

"No worries," he said, and offered his hand. "Mike Struna. I own Ingrid's Gift."

"So these are your boats!" she exclaimed, gazing around.

He almost laughed. His real boats were moored or docked in town. What Marni LeGuin was staring at—yes, he knew who she was, her face was immediately recognizable—was the small fry. A couple of sea kayaks and a rowing scull on racks, and in the water a meticulously restored Chris-Craft Deluxe Runabout Barrelback. He had to admit that was a bit of eye candy; twenty-three feet of polished red mahogany, triple cockpits, a bird's-eye maple dashboard. He'd paid a quarter of a million dollars for it. The boat's name was *Miss Janey*, after the original owner's wife, but he'd renamed her *Equity*. He used her to run guests over to Topper's at the Wauwinet for dinner.

"And my boathouse," he agreed. "I'm bunking upstairs at the moment to give Carly some room."

"That's really lovely of you."

He shrugged. "We're old college friends. Lived in the same dorm as NYU freshmen. I was a computer geek and she knew everything about film. It's good to see her get a chance to direct. I was happy to help anyway I could."

"You make *The Hopeless* sound like a present," Marni said. "Something she's been given."

"—Instead of something she worked for?" He found himself smiling at that. "I know how hard Carly works, believe me. But Vic put together her financing. I'm probably just too aware of what that takes."

"I see." Her voice was carefully neutral, her expression less open now. He wondered if she *did* see, if she could possibly see, how essential money was to the world she took for granted—an actress walking into a shoot, a role, a project. Or did she say her lines, accept her salary, and move on to the next set with the assumption that there would always be one waiting for her?

Did Marni LeGuin know what life, and its choices, really cost?

He knew. So did Carly. She'd told him as much when she'd called him six years ago to explain why she was marrying a man old enough to be her father . . .

He hadn't made his fortune in Silicon Valley then, hadn't taken his startup public or been bought out for half a billion dollars. He had nothing to counter Vic Sonnenfeld's influence and power except hopes and promises. Belief in himself. A certain depth of hunger . . .

"That's like something out of a movie," she said, motioning at the Chris-Craft. "All it needs is an American flag hanging off the back."

"She waves one all summer. Usually I pull her from the water by this time of year—it's not good for her bottom to be continuously exposed to the sea like this—but since moving up here full time I've gotten lazy. And too used to having her around."

"You don't normally live here?" Marni asked.

He shook his head. "I'm a New Yorker, have a place on Central Park West. And a vineyard in northern California. But when the pandemic started, I decided an island was the best possible place to be. Ingrid's Gift is all about isolation. So I quarantined here. Turns out I was right—Nantucket had the lowest number of Covid cases of any county in Massachusetts. And by the time summer rolled around, it was way too gorgeous to leave. I can work from anywhere."

"That's fortunate," she said evenly. "Actors can't isolate, I'm afraid. We need sets, productions. The pandemic was one long cancellation of my life. I'm so glad Carly decided to go ahead this winter."

"One person's cancellation is another's opportunity."

"Maybe."

Again, she was carefully neutral. He was usually able to read people quickly, but Marni LeGuin was proving difficult to gauge.

"Did the boat come with the house?" she asked.

A calculated change of subject, safely impersonal. "Not even remotely. I bought her at auction in Minneapolis. She spent the past seventy years on a lake."

Marni reached out and stroked the satin-smooth wood of the barrel back. "That's a long time. Does it still run?"

"Like a Lamborghini. There were only thirty-one of these built—by hand. About twenty are still on the water. The motor is *not* original 1941, but it's refitted, and close."

She smiled. "I like the fact that you care about details."

"Something else Carly and I have in common. Are you looking forward to the shoot tomorrow?"

She glanced at him then, and he was intrigued to glimpse a shadow in her eyes. But she said, "Of course. Speaking of which, I should probably be getting back. We're reading through the script. I just ducked out to stretch my legs, get a sniff of the air. It's such a beautiful day—and beautiful spot. You have a lovely home, Mr. Struna."

"Mike," he said.

"Call me Marni."

He nodded. "Let me know if you'd like to take a spin in the boat while you're here, Marni. She's at your disposal."

7 | Stronghold, Friday

RON MCKAY CLICKED out of his conference call and set down his phone. He'd been sitting with his feet propped on the William IV writing desk Janet's grandmother had placed in the library's bay window. The leather surface had once been bottle green, and was scarred with the impressions of nearly two centuries of pen nibs and hard leather heels carelessly dug into its surface. Like everything in the weathered shingled house on Hulbert Ave., it reeked of old money. Stronghold, as the Brimhold place was called, had not been winterized until the 1970s, and even now the landscaping was limited to the traditional rose trellises and privet hedge—none of those carefully manicured set-piece gardens for *us*, thank you very much. Those screamed New York, and the Brimholds had been Massachusetts for nine generations.

The bay window in front of him overlooked beachfront running down to the harbor. He'd watched the freight boat round the point twice during his conference call and measured the expense of his time according to the blasts of the ferry's deep horn. A few people had strolled by with dogs—who were forbidden on the beach in summer—and a gull or two dipped and wove through the air currents. But this Friday morning of the Christmas kickoff weekend, most people were elsewhere, wandering the festive streets of town.

Ron noted with satisfaction that one of the Diplomatic

Security Service officers who protected his wife was positioned on the sand twenty yards in front of his view, partially obscuring it. Frank was securing the house against beach gawkers in search of the secstate's place. He looked nondescript and warm enough in his insulated windbreaker and baseball cap, but Ron didn't envy him. December on the water, even under weak sunshine, could be raw.

"You're done with your call, Mr. McKay?"

Ron swung his legs off the desk and looked toward the door. Micheline, standing with an iPad in her hands. The electronic intel briefing had ended, then.

"I am. Is the secretary available?"

"She has forty-five minutes before her next teleconference."

Micheline turned away. She was ruthlessly efficient around Ron and entirely impersonal. Although he had heard her laugh once, when she had no idea he was lingering in a corridor out-side Janet's office. The mirth had sounded genuine, and it was in response to something his wife had said. Ron frowned slightly; Janet was many things, but funny wasn't one of them.

When he left the library, he found Janet already descending the stairs. Her female body person, Sasha, was two steps behind her. Both wore coats and the red and green Stroll scarves Micheline's Advance Team had bought for them.

"Town?" he asked.

Janet nodded. "Where's Ansel?"

"I haven't seen him this morning."

"It's noon, Ron." A spasm of irritation crossed her face.

"Ance!" he shouted up the stairs. "An-SEL!"

Silence.

"Don't tell me he's still asleep." Janet pulled on her fleece-lined gloves in angry jerks. "He's not a teenager anymore."

"I believe your son left the house earlier, sir." This from Janet's bodyguard.

"Left the house!" Janet looked appalled. Ance at large; a loose cannon. God knows what might damage he might have done.

"Ian, my colleague on the front gate, reported him walking eastward on Hulbert. Around . . . ten-thirty-seven A.M."

"You should have told us." Ron's annoyance flared. "I'd have gone after him."

"What good is a family holiday if the family is AWOL?" Janet muttered.

Ron glanced at Sasha. "You're now an honorary stepdaughter. For as long as it takes to get some shots at Mitchell's. I'll buy you a book."

"We're going to Bookworks," Sasha said firmly. "Better sightlines, less claustrophobic. Plus, stuffed bears. In Christmas sweaters."

"Okay." Ron held out his hands for the SUV's keys. Normally, they would have walked into town—but that was dangerous now. Too difficult to defend. The car, too, had been brought in a few days ago by the Advance People. "I'll drive."

It would look sweet, he thought—the Sec's husband taking her into town, instead of her DSS driver. But Janet would have to sit in the back, safely shrouded in dark glass. Sasha would fill the passenger seat.

She wore an insulated jacket that matched the one Frank sported out on the beach—navy blue with the Department of State's seal on the left breast. She probably had an armored vest beneath. Ron loved the quiet discretion, the gravitas, the sheer luxury of it all. He had spent twenty-six years in political consulting and understood the slightest nuances of power. Janet, however, was the closest he'd come to possessing it himself.

No marriage was perfect—he knew that better than anyone, for chrissake—but he'd made the right decisions all those years ago.

Maybe someday even Ansel would realize that.

WHILE HIS DAD waited for Ian, the DSS guy, to open the
manual driveway gate—it was white-painted wood, to match
the shingle house's trim, and would never thwart a hostile
breach from a weaponized vehicle—Ansel decided on a photo
op of his own.

He had sauntered up Old North Wharf, chewing his breakfast
sandwich contentedly, his head turned toward Steamboat Wharf
and the calm waters of the Boat Basin. Almost the only vessel
anchored there was Killen's Dory—the family usually launched it
over Thanksgiving—with its stout little Christmas tree secured
amidships. Another reason to escape the house tonight; it blazed
in the profound darkness of the island winter like a flaming torch,
casting red and green ripples across the basin's water. Ance was
surprised how nostalgic he was feeling this morning—a rush of
memories flooding his mind, all of them achingly warm. It was a
good sign, he thought. Another marker in his long recovery. He
hated that word; it smacked of therapy groupthink, of optimistic
euphemisms for restoring a broken life. But in his more solitary
and reflective moments he recognized the justice of the term. He
was recovering. He had been seriously unwell two years before.
His emotional response to this familiar landscape was a salutary
thing.

He stopped short in front of the Wharf Rats club. It seemed
like a weird sort of thing to join, a group of old Nantucketers
swapping stories. Janet's grandfather—a federal judge—had been
a member most of his life. Ance had never known him. He had
no memory of grandparents on either side of his family, and only
fleeting mental pictures, like dust motes caught in sunlight, of
the mother who'd abandoned him when he was three.

The freight boat was docking across the water, easing slowly
into its berth like a floating building, and Ance waited for the

horn to sound. He felt a deep satisfaction as the ferry's bellow echoed across the basin. It was as regular and comforting as fog horns at night, guiding ships home as he fell off to sleep. His childhood room at Stronghold had been secure and deeply slumberous, vivid with cinematic dreams, laced with the odors of salt and wind-borne roses through the screened windows left open to the summer darkness. But it was sharp, clear, winter now, and he was no longer a boy. He did not want to go back to the house on Hulbert Avenue at the moment. He might not escape so easily for the rest of the weekend. He would risk another hour of stolen freedom.

He crumpled the waxed paper from his breakfast and shoved it into his pocket. Then he set off back the way he'd come, toward the foot of Main Street and the free shuttle bus that would carry him away from Stroll and out into the rest of the island, half-empty and wild in the isolation of its third pandemic winter. He was ready for whatever awaited him in a house off the Polpis road.

8 | Stella Maris, Friday Afternoon

SHE WAS OBLIVIOUS when the young man trudged down
her rutted gravel drive. She was on the wrong side of the house,
for one thing—making lunch in the kitchen: liverwurst from
Stop & Shop, with mayo and lettuce on Portuguese bread. She
ate the same sandwich almost every day, with two cups of scalding Assam.

Both the food and the tea were welcome, because she'd
risen before dawn and driven out to Great Point, stopping near
the Wauwinet hotel (which was closed in winter) to deflate the
ancient green van's tires. The gatehouse to the Coskata-Coatue
Wildlife Refuge was deserted; and her spirits rose in the hope
that she would find herself completely alone.

She drove over the sand at a snail's pace for nearly forty minutes, sipping black coffee from an insulated bottle, windows
cracked to welcome the crash of the Atlantic waves. At 6:49
A.M. by her watch, the sun rose out of the sea like a burning god-
dess, and it almost seemed possible that she was the only person
on earth alive to witness it.

Great Point is Nantucket's outflung upper arm, a narrow pen-
insula of sand that trails northward for miles. At its tip, the calmer
seas of the Sound run headlong into the open water of the
Atlantic Ocean, creating dangerous shoals and rip tides and cross
currents. Bluefish and bonito, false albacore and striped bass lurk
in the rills where the two waters meet, and the fish draw birds.

Which, in turn, drew the green van filled with photographer's equipment, lurching along a beach still wet and compacted from yesterday's rain.

She parked not far from the lonely white tower of Great Point's lighthouse and carried her tripod to the lee of its empty keeper's quarters. It was odd, she thought, that the presence of the buildings did nothing to humanize the spot. If anything, their desertion intensified the solitude. She was surrounded on three sides by ocean and buffeted by wind. Later in the day, gray seals would haul out of the Atlantic to sun themselves. In this first hour of daylight, little stirred except the fitful branches of beach plum and bayberry. But the air was filled with wings.

She sighted sanderlings, running back and forth in the wash, as she set up her equipment, and a few dunlins as well—common to the Arctic Circle in summer months but hugging a different latitude now that it was December. Gulls of all kinds stalked the waterline, crying harshly. She did not waste her film on them. She waited, her coffee thermos drained and the cold beginning to seep into her toes, for the northern gannets.

She had come out this morning hoping for the heavy white predators of winter seas, with their bright blue eyes and black flight feathers. Gannets had dagger-sharp bills and dove straight from the air into the waves with a terrific splash, stabbing their prey at depths of up to seventy feet. Remarkably, they used their six-foot wingspan to swim underwater. Gannets were the Olympians of the Atlantic, and the ways they manipulated wind and sea fascinated her.

She had brought two camera bodies, both Nikon F2 35mm, that she'd bought as a baby in the 1980s. They were loaded with two different speeds and types of film—the first, with Fujichrome Provia 100f slide film that offered the speed and saturated color she sought for both birds and landscape; the second, with Ilford

HP5, a 400 speed ISO black and white film that was brilliant for capturing movement without blur. She also had four different lenses with her, interchangeable on both bodies: the standard 50mm, useful for close-up and still shots; a 24mm wide-angle lens she rarely needed but packed as part of her kit; a 105mm and a 180mm for zeroing in on objects far away.

She had attached an MD-4 motor drive to one camera body to advance her film swiftly as she pointed and shot, and she had brought along a handheld light meter to supplement the one in the camera viewfinder. It was light that influenced how widely she set the f-stops on her various lenses; the viewfinder's, which operated with a 3V lithium battery, showed only light reflected from the subject, not the depth of her field. For that, she needed the handheld one.

Yes, her work verged on art; but it began with science.

She tested the light now as she moved around the sand, focusing out on the roiling waters of Great Point Rip. It was stronger at twenty past seven, with the persistent heaviness of early December. Moving to the tripod, she attached a camera body and 105 mm lens for closer focus and snapped a roll's worth of snow buntings, quietly enjoying the plump little birds' alert briskness in the higher dunes. Then she reached for her second camera and attached the 180mm lens, scanning the horizon. Set her f-stop to 5.6, the aperture quite open to capture swift birds in flight. The gannets were out there; she had only to wait.

THEY APPEARED AT 8:37, a great cloud winging in from the east with the sunlight gilding their feathers. The air was filled with high-pitched cries as they circled a hundred yards above Great Point Rip, a, searching the seas all around her for schools of fish. She pivoted to follow the birds' flight with her camera's eye, resetting her f-stops and snapping the powerful wing thrusts, until the first gannet glimpsed prey and, folding its wings back along its body, torpedoed into the water.

It was like watching a fighter jet plummet in a death spiral. The gannets' speed was suicidally fast. They knifed into the waves at sixty miles an hour, as though punching through concrete. The fish they devoured underwater, at point of impact, then bobbed up to the surface to cry out their satis-faction. She knew enough about them to realize that one or two might not survive the morning's feeding—the slightest miscalculation of angle as head hit sea, and the bird's neck would snap.

The cacophony was immense. When she paused to reload her film her hands were shaking with the excitement and pleasure she witnessed. She forgot the cold entirely. Her heart raced and she could not stop smiling.

She had no idea how long they remained, only that after a time the wild calls faded again into the distance, the gleaming white and black bodies were pinpoints on the horizon, and once again, she was alone with the rearing stone tower and its empti-ness. Exhausted.

SHE WAS POURING the water over her tea when the knock came at the door.

The kettle jerked in her hand, a gout of hot water hitting the cast-iron surface of the hot stove with a hiss. She drew breath and steadied herself for an instant, then set the kettle back down on the burner.

No one, not even a stray tourist in July, had knocked on her door in twenty months.

Perhaps if she did nothing the intruder would go away.

She held her breath, teacup suspended in her left hand, steaming furiously.

The second volley of knocks was closer, at the back kitchen

door, loud and inescapable. She started so violently she burned her hand, head swiveling to the kitchen window.

He was large, unfamiliar, his eyes roaming the back façade of the house, taking in all the details. His hair was a riot of color. But when his gaze dropped at last and he met her eyes through the glass pane, he smiled.

And in that instant, she knew exactly who he was.

Ansel.

She set down her tea and ran to open the door.

9 | Ingrid's Gift, Friday Evening

BRITTANY NOVAK PLATED the pink slices of duck breast on a decorative smear of sweet potato puree, then spooned the succulent quince sauce over them. The scent of Chinese five-spice powder drifted to her nostrils, and she smiled with satisfaction. She'd gauged the duck's grilling to a nicety, and the presentation was spectacular. The Boss would be pleased. Wild rice with dried cranberries and arugula salad rounded out the entrée, the berries sourced from Peter Mason's nearby bog.

The Boss had chosen a Bouchaine Merlot from his extensive cellar that had undernotes of clove and anise, echoing the five-spice powder. Brittany handed the first two plates to her sister Cara, one of the hired servers tonight, and watched as she carried them through the swinging kitchen door to the main dining area in the Barn.

This was a spectacular semi-modernist structure that greeted visitors to Ingrid's Gift. The Barn sat at the entrance to the long drive off Polpis Road, its outflung arm forming the property's entrance arch. It was the sole building Mike Struna added to the compound's structures, intending it to house caretakers when he was absent from the island for months at a time. But when he was in residence, the Barn doubled as a party venue. There was a theatre screen and stadium seating at one end, a kitchen at the other, and a flex area in between that tonight was set up with tables for Carly Simpson-Sonnenfeld's entire production crew.

Forty-eight camera operators and technicians, props people and continuity people and makeup artists, the most valued of them staying in the bedrooms upstairs, held down six tables scattered near the fireplace, which was roaring with flames against the December cold. The actors, along with Mike and the Sonnen-felds, were grouped in the center.

Brittany had overseen the placement of fresh pine boughs and cedar, swagged with exuberant red and green taffeta bows, and waist-high silver planters filled with lighted winterberry and willow twigs. A special ventilation system wafted the scents of balsam, orange, and moss through the air. The Boss had ordered soft Christmas jazz in the background.

This was the one massive event Mike Struna was hosting as fairy godfather of *The Hopeless*, and Brittany knew she'd done them both proud. Everything Tess Starbuck had taught her in five years of catering for The Greengage had paid off. She brushed back a stray wisp of curly brown hair, escaped from her neat bun, and reached with tongs for another perfectly sliced fan of breast meat.

She'd hated leaving Tess—who was a friend more than a mentor at this point—but the pandemic hit The Greengage hard, and Brittany's survival was at stake. Tess had cut her tables and staff to a quarter of the restaurant's capacity, and shifted her kitchen's focus to takeout. Tourism was negligible that year—no one was traveling—and the offseason was an absolute dining des-ert. Nantucket turned inward under quarantine. Tess applied for federal aid while Brittany volunteered with a food truck—a joint venture among the island's restaurateurs that brought free break-fasts and lunches to Nantucket's kids during the worst months of remote learning. It was a quiet fact that 42 percent of the island's children relied on free meal programs in the elementary and high schools—the flip side of an exclusive resort commu-nity—and when the state shut down all in-person learning, a lot of them went hungry. Local cooks tried to fill the gap. Brittany had felt good about the effort, and it had kept her involved with other foodies during a time when she needed emotional support, but handing out sandwiches hadn't exactly spurred her creativity. She was worried and restless even as she joked with the kids whose parents pulled up in the parking lot line.

Tess shut down The Greengage completely and turned to curbside service. She was wary of the possibilities of contagion. She and Rafe da Silva had a toddler now, their adorable daughter Kate, and they were afraid the virus might strike close to home.

Then one morning in March, Tess called Brittany out of the blue.

"Mike Struna wants a full-time personal chef," she said.

Mike was the founder of GoldenEye, a software company based in Palo Alto. Rumor said he was worth about a billion dollars. He was a regular at The Greengage, sitting alone at the bar for dinner when he didn't bring a party of twenty into the private room upstairs. That was in the pre-pandemic days, of course, but even now he'd remained loyal, and Tess made sure his takeout orders were delivered to his door free of charge.

"I told him you were the best I'd ever worked with," Tess continued. "But he wants a general housekeeper, too—just say no if that's not your jam."

Brittany had driven out to Ingrid's Gift immediately and walked all over the property with Mike. She had tried hard to look cool and unemotional during the interview, but her adrenaline was up; the estate was gorgeous and she was dying to work a real job again. Nobody was hiring during the pandemic. Frankly, she'd been at her wits' end.

"I'm moving here to work remotely for the duration of this Covid thing," Mike told her. "Could be as long as a few months, some people are saying. I don't want to have to think about the logistics of toilet paper or hand sanitizer. You'll order everything, make sure the main house and guest quarters are properly cleaned, cook all the meals, and manage the service contractors. My cleaning staff comes in twice a week, more often when people are staying here, and in spring the landscape crew shows up." He mentioned some names. Brittany had gone to high school with the landscaper and the cleaner was a distant cousin.

"I can manage that," she'd said bravely.

She was twenty-five years old and had learned most of what she knew from Tess. She did not have a "real" credential (culinary school, a degree in hospitality management) to her name. She was prepared to fail spectacularly. But she figured quarantine would give her time and space to rise to the job and test some recipes.

She was right. Twenty months later, Mike Struna still raved about her meals and wondered how he'd ever coped without her. He'd never moved back to his condo in New York. But on seven different occasions this past year he'd flown her on his private jet to cook for friends in Manhattan and Sonoma. It was the first time Brittany had left the state of Massachusetts. She was hoping Europe would be next. As the pandemic wound to a close, Mike was talking about renting a place in Umbria for the spring.

Now, as she turned away from the final raft of plated duck and her four hired staffers swung through the Barn's kitchen door, Brittany knew from the happy buzz of voices beyond that dinner was already a success.

"Check the level in the wine glasses," she told Cara.

It was time to assemble dessert.

CHRIS CANDLER WAS drinking Fever Tree tonic with a slice of lemon and enjoying the way the flavors played off the quince. There were times when he missed red wine, but not as profoundly as he missed his wife, Sonya. In the ghastly hours after finding her body, he'd offered up prayers and vows to a force in the universe he no longer believed in. Death was chaos, a rift in his soul's fabric, and he'd craved rules to contain his terror. One of them was vigilance. He was Winter's only parent now. He had to be awake to danger, constantly alert, to keep her safe. That meant a refusal to dull his senses or chemically escape.

His daughter was toying with her food in the comfortable armchair across the table, although her meal was vegan, exactly as she requested—a roasted gnocchi and brussels sprout dish that smelled appetizing enough. Chris felt a spasm of worry. Under her delicate makeup, Winter's expression was subdued, her eyes fixed on her plate. Slender fingers twirled her fork in a pantomime of feeding. Her coffin-shaped nails were painted Christmas green and had a sparkle of snowflakes etched on them. They flickered in the candlelight.

Seated beside her, their host, Mike, said something to Winter that Chris couldn't catch, and for an instant her lips quirked in response. But the smile was automatic, pro forma, there was no real feeling behind it. Was she getting sick? Worried about something? Just *bored*? Chris hadn't seen her for most of the day. A car had taken her into town to shop and catch the holiday sights. Laura, the bodyguard who'd escorted her, confirmed she'd eaten breakfast. But what if she'd slipped away to vomit in a bathroom? He couldn't bear for that whole nightmare to start again—

"I like your daughter," Marni said.

He dragged his eyes from Winter's face and focused on the woman to his right. "You're kind to say so."

"We talked during cocktails. It's refreshing to run into somebody raised in the film world who wants absolutely nothing to do with it. If I'd had the chance to run away to Normandy at her age, I'd have gone like a shot!"

Chris smiled at Marni. He had no idea what she was talking about. Maybe she'd had too much merlot. She'd held onto a glass all night, but her duck looked barely touched. That, he felt, was a crime. The food was so good, he was ready for seconds.

"Winter's my whole life," he told her. "People in the industry might not believe that, but . . ."

"Oh, I believe it." She sipped her wine, her eyes on his daughter. "I mean, seriously, none of us lives to act."

"Marni!" He filled his voice with mock dismay. "That kind of talk ends careers. Don't let Vic Sonnenfeld hear you."

"Fortunately, he's ignoring me tonight."

Chris glanced at the man across the table; he was seated on Winter's other side, and appeared to be engrossed in conversation with Theo Patel. Something about racehorses; British versus Arab stock; it meant little to Chris. Winter was the one who loved horses. Sonya had placed her on a pony at the age of two, and from the age of seven she'd been schooling high jumpers. Not during therapy, of course, and if he was honest, not for a few months before that. She'd been too weak, too lost in the miasma of her own sickness to do more than binge and purge, binge and purge, until he'd frantically broken the cycle and flown with her and a private nurse to the facility in the Adirondacks—

He quelled a flare of anxiety. Winter was *fine*. She was healthy and starting to train again. But he was surprised she wasn't right in Vic's face, talking about Ardennes, her beloved Selle Francais, and trading barbs with Theo, whom Chris knew she liked. Her self-absorption tonight was painfully obvious.

"I thought most of us wanted more attention from our agents, not less," he said.

Marni set down her empty glass. "Vic is *not* my agent. He handed me off to Bella Griswold years ago, and to be honest, she's all that keeps me at CMI—which is no small sacrifice."

Chris was surprised. Vic had persuaded him to meet with Carly in the initial stages of the project and the agent's backing was a big part of why he'd signed on to *The Hopeless*. He'd assumed Marni had done the same. From the edge in her voice, however, it was clear she felt no love for CMI's chief. The wine must have made her reckless. She was eating with the man, and talking too much.

Time to do her a favor and change the subject.

She had no kids to talk about, and relationships were off limits.

"Where are you living in LA these days?" Chris asked.

And as she enthused about her 1930s Tudor in La Cañada, he felt his uneasiness pass. He was keyed up, over-sensitive about his daughter, and too prone to suspect crisis in everything. He needed to chill. It was the night before a big project started, sure, but it was also the holidays on Nantucket—nostalgic and peaceful as a lost dream from childhood. The island was full of memories. Sonya had loved it here. He'd reached the point in grieving her where he could remember the good more often than the bad, one reason he'd been able to return to the island. In a few days, he might even be ready to wander around town, in sunglasses and a camouflaging hat, and revisit places Sonya loved—the old mill, the Tiffany glass windows at St. Paul's, or the house called Greater Light. But tonight, the beauty of Ingrid's Gift was enough. He'd walk back to the guest house with Winter under the stars, and persuade her to make hot chocolate. Maybe she'd even watch *Home Alone* with him in front of the fire.

TWENTY MINUTES AFTER Chris Candler politely declined a glass of vin santo with his white chocolate and pistachio biscotti, Theo Patel took his leave. Marni was engrossed in conversation with the head of costuming, and while he had decided opinions on his girl's preferred color palette, he wanted desperately to talk to his husband, Algernon. It was nearly two o'clock in the morning, but Algie was a night owl. He'd just be turning in, after a performance with the local opera company.

Theo walked briskly up the long, crushed-shell drive, his face lifted to a sweep of Milky Way dazzling overhead. It was startling how little he thought of stars when he was in LA, how clouded they were by light pollution, but the pricks in the firmament tonight were mesmerizing. He was flooded suddenly with images he hadn't thought of in years: himself, shivering and wet from a midnight drenching at school—a bout of hazing in his first year—and his silent, hateful sobbing as he huddled in a ball on the slates of the school roof, blessedly alone but wretched. The vast scrawl of the stars overhead, and the sound that had drifted to his ears, then, of a soprano singing Tosca; someone was playing it from an open window in the middle of the night, in violation of all the rules. He had been stabbed with a brittle realization: beauty existed regardless of pain, it could pierce even the heaviest shame and self-hatred; and for some reason, that truth had given him resilience.

He smiled to himself in the darkness. He had never been someone who broke easily.

"Theo."

The deep voice was calm and authoritative. Instantly recognizable. Theo stopped short. "Vic."

"I enjoyed our conversation this evening." The older man fell into step beside him. His expression was impossible to read in the darkness. But Theo knew what Vic meant; he'd relished their back-and-forth about horse breeding. It was a relief to talk about something other than Hollywood for once.

"So did I," he said warmly.

"Unfortunate, then, that it was our last."

"I'm sorry?"

"Our last conversation." Sonnenfeld sounded amused. "You're leaving tomorrow."

"Actually, Vic, I'm planning to be here until—"

"You're leaving tomorrow." The agent's footsteps slowed,

delaying the return to the main house. "You see, Theo, you threatened me this morning. That will never happen again. You will leave on the first plane out."

Theo laughed, a startled noise full of nerves. He *had* warned Vic to watch himself, but he thought the older man had taken it in stride. "I think you're forgetting, Vic. I don't work for you."

"You don't work for Marni anymore, either."

"*What?*" This time, Theo's voice cracked.

"Carly's telling her right now. About the news that's going to break in all the trade papers tomorrow."

"What news?"

He could feel Vic smiling.

"About you, and that thirteen-year-old boy you destroyed a few years ago. He committed suicide, remember? Jumped off the fifth floor of a parking garage in Anaheim, after a special day out at Disneyland?"

"What boy?" Theo drew a ragged breath. "I've never—"

"Tell it to your lawyer," Vic suggested distantly. "If you can find one to represent you after tomorrow. And Theo—"

Vic Sonnenfeld strolled by him, his expression benign. As though Theo were already irrelevant, already dead. "Safe travels."

IT HELPED THAT her room came with a private bath, and that it was on the opposite side of the cottage from her father's bedroom, and the third one that his assistant Carlos was snoring in. Because Winter felt sicker that night than she had in months, the Brussels sprouts and gnocchi and butternut squash swelling in her stomach like grotesque sponges, until she finally threw back the duvet and catapulted out of bed and fell at the foot of the toilet and retched until she was aching and weak.

A nerveless peace washed over her as she lay on the marble tiles, which were chilly at thirteen minutes past one o'clock in the morning. Her cheeks and forehead were hot and the tiles blessedly cooled them.

Peace never lasted more than a few seconds, though. Once it ran off, giggling in the dark, she felt emptied out, soulless, a husk that needed filling. She pushed herself off the floor with both hands, rinsed her mouth at the sink, and stared at herself in the mirror. It was beginning again. She hated it, hated it, she hated herself and what the therapists insisted on calling her *choices*—

She crept down the hall carefully toward the cottage's kitchen. What was in the fridge? Milk. Cheese. Wine and fruit and crackers. Her stomach turned over, too empty. She needed to eat the world until she was full and then empty herself of all the bad feelings inside.

A bar of bittersweet chocolate—artisanal—with nuts and fruit, a confection for the holidays, sat near a bottle of champagne her father hadn't opened. She tore the gold foil with shaking fingers and stuffed pieces in her mouth, choking horribly on the smear of sugar at the back of her throat. There were gingerbread cookies, too, wrapped in a plastic sleeve tied with a red ribbon, and she didn't bother to undo the bow, just split the bag with her fingernails and swallowed great pieces of the scented ginger girl and ginger man. She washed down the cashews with champagne and then moved to the fridge—an entire salami and a log of goat cheese studded with bourbon-soaked apricots and a wedge of soft Gorgonzola. A package of Parmesan crisps. Smoked oysters, oily and curry colored. They smelled like rot and tasted like semen and she was violently sick in the kitchen sink.

Clinging with both hands to the counter, she panted for a few seconds, her forehead beaded with sweat. His words ran like a newscaster's chyron over and over in her head. *You're a beauty, aren't you? Just like your mother. She was a little Lolita, too. Your thighs could break my neck, I bet, if I put my head right between your legs—you'd like that, wouldn't you? To break my neck?*

And then his hand, snaking across her crotch beneath the dinner table—

She pounded on the sink with her fists, suddenly furious, and cried out, "No!"

"Winter."

Gasping, she whirled around.

Her father stood in the middle of the room, his face blank with shock.

"Baby. What is it?"

He moved carefully toward her, as though she might startle and take off at a run. For an instant, she was tempted to do just that—tear through the cottage door in her pajamas and pound straight past the house where the monster who had laughed and eaten with her lay sleeping, and on out to the end of the dock, where the ocean could swallow her up.

Her father held out his hand. "Sweetie—"

He was whispering. The way she'd talk to a horse, the way she gentled Ardennes when he was frightened by something he didn't understand. The problem was, she understood everything and still she was terrified.

"Daddy," she choked, and her face crumpled as he reached for her. "Daddy, we've got to leave. As soon as we can. Please?"

10 | Santa Claus Comes to Town

ONE OF THE perks of being police chief was the ringside seat Merry Folger commanded for certain critical moments. For instance, this Saturday morning—the first weekend in December, with the sun high in the sky and a brisk, cold wind driving whitecaps across the water as a Coast Guard cutter sailed toward Straight Wharf.

Her white SUV with the distinctive navy and gray police markings was parked where no cars were allowed, within the Christmas Market barricades that blocked the wharf's access to town. She and Peter were lounging against the bumper in their most festive winter gear. Merry's father, John, was inside the car staying warm. They were waiting for Santa Claus to dock.

Nearby was the Town Crier and some of the town's Select-persons who would escort the Man in Red to his island sleigh, a vintage firetruck owned by the Nantucket Hotel. Santa would stand in the back, waving, while the Town Crier walked ahead, ringing his bell, announcing the glad tidings of great joy.

"Look at that guy," Peter muttered in her ear as a man roughly their age walked by, natty in sunglasses, a suit, and a knotted Stroll scarf. Nothing abnormal about that, except that the suit had red and green stripes with white death's-heads and fists stamped all over it.

"Kind of like North-Pole-meets-Venice-Beach-tattoo-parlor," Merry suggested. "You prefer the blonde, I take it?"

The blonde wore a minidress covered in hot pink sequins and thigh-high boots made of fake mink. She had a jingle bell on each boob.

Every third person in the crowd—and there were about ten thousand people in town, jockeying for the best viewing spots— was dressed in ways bizarre or wonderful. The color and noise and exuberance were thrilling after the cheerless quarantine holidays, and Merry was grinning helplessly. She glanced over her shoulder and gave her dad a thumbs-up. John was drinking coffee laced with peppermint schnapps in his passenger seat. He saluted her with his mug.

The sight of him sitting alone jolted her suddenly, as it did whenever she looked for her grandfather, Ralph Waldo Folger, and remembered *he's gone now.* The freshness of loss stunned her each time like a blow to the face.

Merry had known her eighty-nine-year-old grandfather was vulnerable in the pandemic. She and John had talked by phone daily about ways to keep Ralph safe. As a frontline worker exposed for the duration to a germ-laden public, Merry had stayed scrupulously away from her childhood home on Tattle Court throughout the first waves of sickness. Peter arranged for grocery deliveries twice a week and dropped supplies from Marine Home at John's front door. And Ralph was healthy for nearly a year: social distancing on his daily walks, wearing a mask when he ventured into town. He contracted Covid nine days before he was scheduled for his first vaccine.

Nantucket Cottage Hospital had five ventilators; Ralph never made it to one of them. Sickening on a Friday, he was delirious by Sunday and medevacked to Boston in the wee hours of Monday. Intubated, he lingered in a medically induced coma for four days.

What dropped Merry to the floor when they got the news, sobbing and hugging her knees as though she'd been sucker punched, was the fact that her careful distance hadn't mattered a darn. Ralph was alone when he died. And she hadn't seen or touched him for a year before that. Of all the pandemic's cruelties, this was the coldest.

Her father thrust open the car door and stepped out to the paving beside her. "Boat's in," he said.

She linked her arm through his as the cutter drew alongside. A couple of ensigns jumped off with sheets in their hands and moored the steel-gray vessel to the wharf's stanchions. The Town Crier hailed the boat, Santa waved, horns blared, the drum corps drummed. Merry and Peter and John whooped along with everyone else. Despite the logistics and the responsibilities she was nominally handling, despite her underlying grief, joy shot through Merry as she fell into step behind the Selectpersons and jauntered after Santa's firetruck. For the length of Main Street at least, she was uncomplicatedly happy.

It felt like the whole island celebrated with her.

THE MOOD WAS different in town today, Ansel thought, as he stood with his father and Janet in front of The Hub and cheered Santa's parade. There were far more people, for one thing—it was clear a lot had crossed the Sound on the morning boats and would be gone again by bedtime—and with eight square blocks closed to traffic, the historic district felt more than ever like a holiday theme park. Enough outlandish sights screamed for attention that his stepmother was all but invisible, despite the DSS security surrounding her. There were four women dressed as Christmas trees, complete with LED lights, and several people of indeterminate gender disguised as both halves of a pair of reindeer. Ansel's thatch of red and green hair seemed positively tame.

He was dutifully filling the role of stepson today after his brief break for freedom the previous afternoon. He'd put on the khakis and collared pale blue shirt Ron had told him to wear, along with a navy blue boat jacket one of Micheline's people had bought him from ACK 4170. It was, he thought, infantilizing. He hadn't worn this type of clothing since he'd graduated from St. Alban's years ago.

As Santa rolled past and turned right onto Centre Street, the sidewalk throng began to break up. Ron grasped Janet's arm. "Let's head for the car," he said. "You've got a one o'clock back at the house."

Ansel stepped aside as they began to move in a body with the DSS agents, a tight knot of personnel headed for the black Escalade parked a few blocks up Fair Street. His father did not even glance over his shoulder to notice that Ance had fallen behind. This was going to be easy! He held his breath, hands shoved in his pants pockets, his back against The Hub's Federal Street window. They'd figure out he was gone once they reached the car, but by that time, nobody was going to fight their way back through the crowd to collar him.

In another thirty seconds he wheeled, head down, to stride in the opposite direction, toward the bottom of Main and the shuttle stop. He had nearly reached the old fountain filled with holiday greens that stood in the middle of the street when he saw her: Winter Candler. She was standing alone in front of the Pacific Club staring at her phone.

He hesitated, then continued down the street and approached her. His cheeks felt warm and he was conscious of a fluttering sensation in his gut, but what was the worst that could happen? That she'd look through him?

He was used to that.

"Hey," he said.

She glanced up, her eyelids flaring in fear.

For an instant, he thought she might turn and run. Then her expression relaxed as she realized who he was.

"Ansel! Do you have any idea how to get to a place called Ingrid's Gift? It's out this long road in the middle of nowhere, but I have no idea which road, or what the address is. I've been driven here the past two days and I swear to God, I'm too busy looking at my phone to pay attention to where I'm going."

"Ingrid's Gift?" he said stupidly. "That's the name of the house?"

"It's owned by this guy named Mike," she said helpfully. "There's a barn? And a guest cottage? That's where my dad and I are staying."

The description could fit any number of places on Nantucket Island, from Madaket to Tom Nevers. "What happened to your car?" he asked.

"I kind of got separated." She glanced around at the crowds milling haphazardly through the crosswalks and barricades. "We didn't know the streets would be blocked off. Laura—the woman who drove me—had to park, but I just got out and told her I'd find her. Only now my phone's dead and I'm totally SOL."

"Got it." He glanced around. They were an island in a sea of Strollers. "I'd say you could Uber, but nobody's getting a ride here today."

"Laura's gonna be so pissed. She's always saying I'm going to cost her her job. She's probably gone home."

Laura must be the bodyguard who'd stared him down in Lemon Press yesterday. Ansel thought quickly. He hadn't heard of an Ingrid's Gift in the Hulbert Ave. neighborhood. Maybe it was on the Cliff. "Is the house close? Or, like, outside of town?"

"It's that way," she said, turning toward the Ralph Lauren side of Water Street. She waved vaguely. "Way out there."

"Sconset? Surfside?"

"I don't think so." Her fathomless eyes narrowed as she thought, but at least he'd distracted her—she no longer looked terrified.

"Tom Nevers?"

"The name begins with a P. Porpoise? Is that even possible?"

"*Polpis*," he said, relieved.

"Yes!"

"Easy." He grabbed her arm and wove through the crowd another block to the shuttle stop. "We'll take the Polpis bus. It's free. You can use my phone to text your dad for your address."

"You're coming with me?"

To his relief, she was smiling. Not looking through him at all.

"Not exactly *with* you." He stopped and studied her searchingly. Why did it seem natural to tell this girl something he wouldn't dare tell anybody else? "I'm headed out to Polpis myself. My mother lives there."

BY THE TIME they boarded the bus—which was almost empty because everyone wanted to be *in* town today, not leaving it— Ansel had told her more about his situation than he'd ever told anyone except his therapists. Winter simply listened without saying everything would be fine, or trying to one-up him with how crazy her own life was, which suggested she'd learned from her time in rehab, too. She asked the one obvious question that followed from his simple, four-word statement about his mother.

"So where's your dad?"

"By this time? Taking out his anger at me in a phone call with some guy who's totally fucked and working for him on a Saturday."

"What'd you do to make him angry?"

"I showed up for the Santa thing in these clothes—" he gestured to his ridiculous khakis and boat jacket—"and I should have gone back with him to the house. But I ditched him. And my stepmom."

"Okay," Winter said. "But you're not twelve, right? You can walk around Nantucket without holding his hand."

Ansel didn't bother to point out that she had a driver-cum-bodyguard. "Yeah, but . . . it's just . . . my stepmom is kind of important. And they're really sensitive about bad press."

"Ah," she said wisely. "That, I get. Wait—I should totally Google you, shouldn't I?"

She pulled out her phone before remembering the battery was dead.

"Never mind. She's secretary of state. My stepmother."

There was a silence. Ansel wondered if people in California knew what that was.

"You mean, like, of the US?"

"Yeah. So there's this totally suffocating security detail and she's overwhelmed all the time with work and my dad basically lives to service her needs."

Winter giggled. He hadn't intended the sexual innuendo but he let it ride. Ron probably saw it as part of his CV at this point anyway.

"So your stepmom is Janet Brimhold McKay."

"Yep," he said grimly.

"I'm sorry. She looks like a total tool."

"She's not that bad. Or at least, she wasn't. The whole time I was growing up." The shuttle bus entered the Milestone Rotary and dove into the turnoff for Monomoy. He tried to remember how long it had been since Janet had liked him. Or at least, tolerated him. Definitely before rehab. Which meant at least three years ago, now. "I'm kind of an embarrassment to her."

Winter frowned. "Why?"

"I'm twenty-three years old and don't have a real job. I paint."

"You mean, like, houses?"

He laughed out loud. "Canvases. I'm—I'm an artist."

He had never actually said that out loud before.

"Like your mom," Winter prompted.

"Which is the huge problem. My mom ruined my dad's life."

He let the statement sit there between them. It wasn't really fair; he had no idea what his mother had actually done to end her marriage. Just vague references and bitter innuendos.

"But you're going to see her."

"Yeah. Up until about a year ago, I thought she was dead."

"Wait—you *thought?*"

"She left when I was three. Rehab. She was addicted to cocaine." Or at least, that's what his dad had told him. He had long since stopped believing most of what Ron said, so why did he continue to repeat this? What if he asked his mother for *her* side of the story, this afternoon?

Winter touched his hand. Her fingers were cool and light and the dark green nails sparkled.

Ansel swallowed. "I don't know why I said that. It may not even be true. My dad's lied to me a lot."

"My dad doesn't," she said simply. "That's why I love him. But yours told you your mother was dead?"

He nodded.

Winter tucked her phone back in her cross-body. "You're going to have to explain everything fast. I think it's a long story, and there's not much more road ahead."

11 | The Hopeless

"CHRIS, ARE YOU okay?"

Carly Sonnenfeld had ordered a fifteen-minute break and found her lead male actor sitting on a driftwood log staring at his phone while Seth from Makeup dabbed at his forehead. They were having a sudden problem with wind this morning, gusts of about fifty miles an hour whipping her stars' hair as they filmed near the beach end of the Nantucket Field Station.

This was empty of life and approved for the filming permit because it was conservation land—one hundred and ten acres of marsh, hiking paths, a long, swath of wetland bordering the harbor not far from Ingrid's Gift. The Nantucket Conservation Foundation had bought it years ago from the University of Massachusetts, which continued to operate a seasonal program for its marine biology majors on the premises. Locals called it after the family that had originally owned it: Folger's Marsh.

It was a haven for pelagic birds and a favorite place for photographers and walkers of all kinds. Carly had chosen to place her victim's body on the tree-studded plateau above the dunes—a former sheep meadow—that in winter had a bleak and mystic moodiness she hoped the camera operator was capturing.

Chris Candler glanced at her. His eyes were shadowed and a set of marionette lines ran from nostrils to mouth. He looked, she thought, his actual age instead of a carefully preserved ten years younger. He'd been haggard enough at the 7 A.M. call—said he hadn't slept well—but now he was positively haunted.

"Winter's bodyguard lost her," he said flatly. "She was stupid enough to drop her off in town while she looked for parking, and now she can't find her."

"Can't she call Winter?"

"Going straight to voice mail." He waved off Seth and thrust himself to his feet. "I'm sorry, Carly, but I've got to go look for her."

"You can't," she said quickly.

"What?" He took a step toward her, confusion on his face. "This is my daughter we're talking about!"

"Who is not a child. And is roaming alone in the most picturesque town in America, not a war zone. It's broad daylight, Chris! What could possibly happen to a young woman at large on a Christmas weekend in Nantucket? Is she going to drown in hot chocolate? Be trampled by elves? Shop herself to death?"

"You don't—" He paused, a spasm of pain twitching his mouth. "She's more fragile than she seems. She—"

"Went to rehab, I know." Carly sighed in exasperation. "Every other kid in LA is struggling with some kind of disorder, Chris, especially in our business. Winter is *normal* by that standard. You've got to stop treating her like she's made of glass. We've got a film schedule, a budget, only so many hours of daylight we can—"

"It's just that last night something upset her. I found her crying in the kitchen. She wouldn't tell me why, but I'm sorry, Carly, I'm worried."

And it was her job to talk The Talent down off the ledge. Deliberately, Carly laughed. "That's because you're a guy! Girls her age cry all the time. It's probably hormones. Just stop hovering, all right? I'm sure Winter's forgotten it completely. And you've got a scene to do."

She might as well not have spoken. He just stared at his phone distractedly.

Fuck, she thought. *Why can't anything be easy?*

"I know you want and need this project," Carly said in a lowered tone. "Winter told me how much it means to you both—last night, during cocktails. She knows it's critical to reorienting your career. She wouldn't want to be the reason you walk off set. When she's probably completely fine—"

"You're right, you're right." He glanced once more at his phone and stabbed savagely at a button. The bodyguard's hair, presumably, was about to stand on end.

Carly touched his shoulder. Through the layers of costuming she could feel the tautness of his biceps, the tension singing in his frame. "Seriously, she'll be fine. Let Laura do her job. If they're not at the house when we get back, we'll send out the cavalry."

"Okay." He attempted a smile, but it didn't reach his eyes. That's when Carly realized: he, and everyone else on the set, regarded her as The Authority. She was not a friend, not an attractive woman, not even a colleague. She was employing all of them and had power over their lives. What she decided here was law.

She'd wanted this job all her life. Vic had made it possible. So why the stab of regret?

Because it's lonely. Because it's hard to be the new bitch on the block.

And because suddenly, she felt like she had no choice.

Vic had laid it out for her in the clearest possible terms last night while he sipped a cognac in bed, watching her undress. If *The Hopeless* wasn't a blockbuster success, she would never get a second chance. She would never direct a project again. He would certainly never arrange the financing for one.

Unspoken in all of that was a deeper truth: their marriage

would be over if she failed. Vic didn't suffer fools. He basked in her reputation as a rising creative force in the industry—but he wouldn't risk being seen with her if she bombed.

The sex that night was rough, both of them fighting for mastery. He'd enjoyed hurting her. She'd hated submitting. But they'd both gotten off on it.

She'd always known the rules. Vic had to win.

She'd married him anyway.

In her worst moments, she told herself that at least she'd outlive a man thirty years older than she was.

And that, Vic, is the ultimate score.

Carly looked searchingly among the knots of production people for her husband. He'd insisted on watching the first few hours of filming, probably because he knew it unnerved her. She'd forced herself to ignore him and to her wonder, the magic had happened within a few moments of the cameras starting to roll—she'd been so engrossed in her work she'd completely forgot he was there.

Now, when she felt a sudden desire to talk to him—the one person who would *never* view her as his boss—Vic was nowhere to be found.

Probably got bored and went home, she thought. It wasn't far to Ingrid's Gift, and if he hadn't felt like walking the bike path along the Polpis road, somebody would volunteer to drive him.

Seth was just finishing with Marni LeGuin's face, and from the looks of him, gushing over the woman. Carly felt a finger of doubt trail upwards along her spine. What had happened between Vic and Marni yesterday morning? And what had Vic done to Marni's assistant, Theo Patel? He'd looked so quietly triumphant when he'd told her the squalid little story about Theo and a boy, sexual abuse and a suicide, the parents paid off to hush things up—how it was going to destroy the man's career. Then he'd eaten with Theo companionably in the Barn, chatting away as though full-blown disaster wasn't waiting for the guy in the morning tabloids. Carly hadn't seen Theo before she left for the Field Station this morning, but she assumed he'd be gone when she got back to the house.

Marni was looking distracted and strained.

That's okay, Carly told herself. Both Marni and Chris *should* look like hell—they'd just probed the body of a friend, murdered by heroin dealers. If their personal lives provided fodder for some sort of Method Acting, all the better. She wasn't intimate with either of them, really—she didn't have to care. She was their employer, she held their fucking contracts in her hands, and she had a story to film.

"Let's go!" she called out, and immediately the people around her sprang into action.

Her Assistant Director glanced at her, and Carly nodded. "Roll Sound!"

No regrets, she thought. *Only power.*

She was smiling to herself as she turned away from her stars.

12 | Stella Maris, Saturday Afternoon

YESTERDAY, ANSEL'S APPEARANCE out of the blue had brought her nothing but joy.

Today, she felt anxious.

She barely knew her son, and could not predict his behavior. If he mentioned her name to his father, life as she knew it—life as she had carefully constructed it for the past twenty months—would be over.

After the first rush of conversation yesterday, the sheer delight of seeing each other in the flesh, when for years there had been only loss and silence—she had asked him to say nothing about her. To anyone.

And now he was standing at her kitchen door with a girl.

"This is Winter," he said, as he eased into the room, his size diminishing it immediately.

She stepped back until her hands came to rest on the worn oak table behind her. "Winter. What a lovely name. I'm Mary Alice Fillmore."

The girl held out her hand and Mary Alice shook it tentatively. It was probable her unease showed in her face—she could not feel welcoming. She felt invaded.

No one had penetrated her sanctuary at Stella Maris since the first day she'd arrived. To all appearances, the house might still be uninhabited. Even in summer, when the island's population swelled sixfold, the dense vegetation overwhelming the drive suggested desertion, and nobody ventured down it even in Nantucket's rugged rental jeeps. She cultivated shabbiness; it protected her.

Once, last November, she'd watched silently from an upstairs window as a carful of teenagers had pulled up in front of the house and hung out for a while, drinking beer and chattering. They'd left the doors of their Subaru wide open and the radio playing. Two of the boys had poked around the foundations of the house but the fact that most of the front windows were still boarded over discouraged them. A girl had ventured around the back and sat for a time on the kitchen porch, staring out at the thin line of Polpis Harbor in the distance, smoking.

If they had attempted to breach the perimeter of her safe haven she would have scared them witless by revealing herself, but she had been patient, and they were gone soon enough. She discarded the cigarette butt in her cast iron stove but left the beer bottles—from Cisco Brewers, which she'd never visited—lying as the kids had left them in the underbrush. Further evidence, if any was needed, of desolation.

"Winter is staying at a house out here and doesn't know the address," Ansel said. "I thought you might be familiar with it. Ingrid's Gift?"

Despite herself, Mary Alice smiled. "Indeed I do. If you step out on the back porch, you can actually see it from here."

They followed her dutifully outside and turned to gaze north-west, the direction she was pointing. "Those are the roofs of the place."

"Big," Ansel commented.

"The property is around twelve acres," she agreed, "and it has its own dock. Ingrid doesn't live there anymore, of course."

"Ingrid was a real person?" Winter asked, her extraordinary blue eyes widening.

"Oh, yes. An interesting one—a horticulturist. She was a

daffodil expert, one of the people who planted them all over the island in the sixties. That's how the Daffodil Festival came about."

"There's a festival for daffodils?"

"In April. It's just an excuse to welcome spring, really, after the gloom of a Nantucket winter. It can get very gray around here." Mary Alice's anxiety started to subside; the girl was clearly an off-islander if she didn't know her own address, and was probably harmless.

"So you knew her?" Winter asked.

"Ingrid? She was a friend of my mother's. But yes, I knew her. She left the house to her grandchildren—hence the name, Ingrid's Gift—but they couldn't agree on who should pay the property taxes and who was responsible for maintenance." She shrugged. "Half of them lived on the West Coast anyway. So they sold it."

"To Mike Struna," Winter said.

"I wouldn't know. Would you like to sit down? I could make some tea."

"That's okay. I should probably be getting back." Winter glanced at Ansel. "It's not too far to walk, right?"

"Mary Alice has a van." He'd asked if he could call her that, Mary Alice, instead of *Mother* or *Mom*, because the words felt strange to him.

She hadn't earned them, she supposed. But she remembered him saying *Mummah* when he was two and a part of her yearned to hear that again.

"We could drop her off and then come back here to talk," Ansel suggested.

She considered the idea unwillingly. She was afraid of being seen—not by strangers like Winter or random islanders she encountered in her treks around Nantucket for services and supplies. None of them recognized her face or name anymore. She was afraid of being seen with Ansel. Reporters followed Ron's wife, and she could not afford to be photographed by one of them.

But Ansel was looking at Winter with an air of concern, and if she didn't drive the girl back to her house he'd probably walk her there. She'd miss the chance to have another precious hour with her son. He'd told her he was flying back to DC in the morning. And they had twenty years to catch up on.

"All right," she said. "I'd like that."

And went to find her keys.

"Cool van!" Winter said as she climbed into the passenger seat. Ansel threw himself in behind, but leaned forward between the two women, his arms loosely draped across their seatbacks. Mary Alice tried not to feel claustrophobic as she put the van in gear. She'd been alone too long.

"Do you use it as, like, a camper?"

"Sometimes. I drove here from Oregon, where I'd been living before this. I slept in it when I was on the road."

"Mary Alice used to be a photographer for *National Geographic*," Ansel said proudly. "But now she's working on a book."

"What kind of book?"

"About birds. Vanishing species. Climate change. Loss of habitat. It's my pandemic project."

"Wow," Winter said.

"You can follow her on Instagram. That's how I found her."

"Was she lost?" Winter laughed at Ansel.

Mary Alice felt her throat constrict. *Yes*, she wanted to say. *For a long time*. But she listened instead to her son, who simply said, "We were out of touch for a while. But her account is really gorgeous—the images are unbelievable. You'd like them, I think. She's photographed condors in the Sierras."

"I'll have to search for you." Winter pulled out her phone.

"Mary Alice Fillmore, right? Oh, crap—I forgot. Battery's still dead."

"I charge mine in the car," Mary Alice said. "You're welcome to use my cord if it fits. But the Insta account is under Birdwoman59."

"Thanks. I'll look for it."

Mary Alice slowed as she neared the drive to Ingrid's Gift. "What a monstrosity that entry gate is," she said. "Ingrid would have hated it."

"The Barn? Some of the production people are staying there."

"Production people?"

"Winter's father is an actor," Ansel supplied. "That's why she's here. They're filming a streaming series."

There was an electronic gate inside the barn's open archway, and a middle-aged man with a dusting of stubble sitting near it. As the ancient green van approached, he rose and moved toward them.

Mary Alice rolled down her window.

Winter leaned across. "Blake? It's me?"

He peered through the window, a surgical mask over the lower half of his face. It truncated his features into a thatch of salt-and-pepper hair and a pair of gray eyes. These drifted over Mary Alice's face before settling on the girl beside her.

"The prodigal returns," he said, and stepped back.

Mary Alice drove under the barn's open archway and up the immaculate drive. "Film crews! That explains why there were cameras all over Folger's Marsh this morning. I'd never seen anything like it out there."

"You were at the shoot?" Winter turned in her seat to study her.

"Well—not where the chaos was happening, and not for very long. Booms and trucks tend to startle the birds. I got there in the dark—around six A.M.—and when the traffic suddenly showed up, I moved on to Squam Swamp."

"Did you see my dad?"

"I have no idea. What's his name?"

"Chris Candler."

Mary Alice smiled. "If I'd seen him, I'd remember it. Chris Candler! But no—my lens was focused on mergansers, I'm afraid."

"What are they?"

"Ducks. And they don't live in Squam Swamp, so once I left the marsh I had to settle for what I could get. Do I drive straight up to the main house?"

"You can stop here, at the Guest Cottage." Winter opened the van door and flashed a smile at Ansel. "Thank you both. And don't be a stranger, Ance."

He nodded. "Be safe."

"I'll try."

Mary Alice saw the happiness drain suddenly from the girl's face as she stepped down to the quahog-shell drive. Her shoulders came back and her head lifted as she turned toward the cottage door.

"Is she likely to be in danger?" she murmured as her son shifted from back seat to front.

"I'm not sure," he said thoughtfully. "Something has freaked her out. But she doesn't know me well enough yet to tell me."

"How long *has* she known you?"

He glanced at his watch and shrugged. "About two hours? But it feels like forever, Mary Alice. In the best possible way."

LAURA-THE-BODYGUARD WAS WAITING for her when she walked through the door, along with her father's longtime assistant, Carlos. Both of them were sitting in the cottage's main room, the gas fire roaring, with their phones in their hands.

"Winter!" Laura shot off the sofa, relief on her face. Instantly, she spoke into a radio dangling from her chest. "Bullfinch is back safe and sound. Repeat, Bullfinch is back."

Bullfinch was her code name among Chris Candler's body-guards. Laura had chosen it after accompanying Winter to a show jumping event. A bullfinch is a fence surmounted by thick branches of leaves or brush, which the rider encourages a horse to jump *through* rather than over. Chris had told Winter the codename was intended as a compliment: Laura saw her as a per-son willing to plow through tough times, rather than sail over them pretending they didn't exist.

Winter knew he was wrong. She'd heard Laura refer to her too often as "Bullshit" instead of "Bullfinch." *By mistake*, of course.

"I'm sorry," Winter said immediately. "My phone died."

Laura's expression of relief turned to exasperation. "Right. And that nearly cost me my job."

It was a phrase Winter heard far too often. In Laura's estima-tion, Winter was a sulky child who lived to make problems for the staff charged with protecting her, not a nineteen-year-old capable of making her own decisions. That had been true enough, Winter reflected, in the years after she'd found her mother hang-ing from the rafters above Ardenne's loose box. She'd lost her balance, like a horse focused on the water in the ditch she was jumping instead of the fence straddling it. She'd lost her focus, her discipline, and her nerve.

All that had to change.

"Where's my father?" she asked.

It was Carlos who answered. "Up at the main house. He wanted to call the police, file a missing person's report—"

"Then let's go," Winter said. "I'll explain everything to him. This wasn't Laura's fault."

"*Thank* you," the bodyguard said, her lips compressed. "Tak-ing responsibility for a change."

Winter looked at her directly. "I'm about to take more. You're right, Laura, I *should* be responsible for my choices and my life. Even my own safety. I'm too old to rely on other people for that. Maybe you should start job-hunting, in fact. I don't think I need security anymore."

"That's a decision for Chris to make," Carlos broke in.

"Is it?" Winter smiled. "Then let's go talk to him."

13 | Ingrid's Gift, Saturday Night

"HELLO?"

Carly rolled back the boathouse's sliding door and stepped over the threshold. The interior was pitch black, and it was obvious she'd chosen the wrong point of attack. She retreated hurriedly and saw that there was an exterior staircase at the far side of the structure, leading to the second floor. She ran up and knocked at the door.

Mike opened it.

The relief that flooded over her at the sight of his familiar face told her how much anxiety she'd been tamping down. If he'd been out running errands or seeing friends who had nothing to do with the craziness she'd deposited on his doorstep, she'd have cried. But all she said was, "Hey."

"Hey." He stepped backwards, an invitation to enter.

She took it, and the relief deepened when he shut the door behind her, shutting everything else out.

"How'd the shoot go today?"

"Okay. We had to quit early because the wind was too high and my leading man was as distracted as fuck, but I'll know when I watch the dailies down at the Barn tonight whether any of that mattered."

The home theatre at the Barn would be perfect for daily film reviews, and the fact that Trina, her Assistant Director; Marty, the head of the Video Village; and both the A and B camera operators were staying there was perfect. She was planning to walk down as soon as dinner in the main house was over—Brittany had left a menu and call time of 7:30 P.M. on everyone's bedroom door. Except—

"No wind tomorrow," Mike said. He was studying a weather app on his phone. "And sunny. Should be a better day."

"Good," she said. "Every hour we're sitting around your gorgeous house twiddling our thumbs is costing me money."

He glanced at her. "How long have you been back?"

"Since about two-thirty." It was now close to five-forty-five. "I'm wondering whether you've seen Vic?"

"Vic?" Mike's brow furrowed. "Today? No, I'm sorry, I haven't. But I was out myself, catching Stroll. You didn't get downtown today?"

She shook her head.

"You missed something magical."

"Mike—" She walked past him, noticing that Mike had been watching a college football game; the players lunged back and forth on a large screen, the audio muted. A laptop sat open on the coffee table.

"What is it, Carly?"

"Vic isn't picking up his phone, or answering texts."

"You're worried about *him*?"

The incredulity in his voice was momentarily reassuring. After all, Vic had been out of touch only a few hours, and back in LA she wouldn't have given it a thought. It was just weird, here, to be unable to reach him in the isolation of the compound—

"Sit," Mike ordered, and reached for a bottle of wine and a corkscrew.

She sank down on the sofa and watched him, marveling as she did at how little he'd changed. He was still the compact, contained package he'd been when she'd first met him nearly thirty years before, on an elevator in their freshman dorm. They had both been eighteen, moving into Goddard Hall, their parents standing awkwardly in opposite corners of the carriage, an abundance of belongings between them. Mike had held out his hand and introduced himself, a gesture that was way too adult at the time and tracked with his inveterate politeness, his studied formality, which she had learned masked a painful shyness. He wasn't tall. He wasn't broad-shouldered or distinctly handsome. He still combed his plain brown hair straight back and probably had it trimmed like clockwork, every three weeks. Isolating in the pandemic hadn't moved him to sprout facial hair or let himself go. He was predictable, disciplined, competent, and solitary.

And he had never stopped wanting her.

Strangely, that inspired neither guilt nor a sense of obligation in Carly. Neither did it annoy her. She exploited Mike's unspoken devotion because it was a rarity in her life and she was grateful, as she had once been grateful for the unconditional love of her parents. Mike was beyond friend; he was *family*.

He handed her a glass of Daou cabernet and she drank from it gratefully.

"Now, explain why you're worried about your husband."

"I shouldn't be," she countered, for both their benefit. "I mean, he probably just wanted to get away for a while. Caught a rideshare into town and is watching this game"—she gestured at Mike's screen—"at Ventuno's Back Bar."

"But you've called and texted him, and he hasn't responded."

"Nope." She set down her glass. "He's not picking up. For a guy who practically has a chip embedded in his brain, he's so constantly connected, that's . . . odd."

Mike's earnest gaze never wavered. "Does he have a woman here, Carly? Could he have met one?"

She drew a quick breath. "He's always acquiring them, sure."

"When did you last see him?"

"After we struck for the day. He went with me to the location, and watched the first hour or so. Maybe? When I looked around for him later, around one-thirty this afternoon, he was gone."

"But nobody knows when he actually left Folger's Marsh?" Mike frowned again. "That's weird. He's not exactly a low-profile kind of guy."

"There were forty-nine people running around, doing their jobs. Which did not include tracking Vic."

"You have a rental car, right?"

"And it's still here, parked near the main house. We shuttled in the crew bus to the location and back."

Mike glanced at his watch. Carly didn't have to ask why; she knew it was over five hours since she remembered glimpsing her husband. Mike was doing the math.

"Could he have lost his phone?"

"He's more likely to lose his hand."

Mike smiled faintly. He was a tech guy; similarly attached to devices. "Seems like you're going to have to wait for him to turn up. In the meantime, what can I do to help?"

"Tell me I'm overreacting?"

"Carly." Mike took her hand and kissed the back of it, then gently soothed her fingers with his own. "Vic's a grown man. On an island. He can't have gone far. He's getting some time in town on a holiday weekend, like any sane guy would. Yes, you're overreacting."

"It's just—" She rose and began to pace. "He's been *off* ever since we got here."

"I don't know Vic well enough to understand what that means." Mike's voice was carefully neutral. He never reproached Carly for marrying Vic. Never questioned why she had.

"There's been this . . . *suppressed triumph* about him. As though he's got a secret that's giving him immense pleasure, but he's refusing to share it. And I know that mood. It means he's hurting somebody."

There. She'd said it. The ugliest possible thing she could betray about Vic—that he enjoyed inflicting pain.

Mike said nothing for a few seconds. "Not you, I hope?"

"No more than usual." She met his gaze squarely. "I think it's Marni. Or Theo, her assistant. Or both."

"And now he's disappeared. Which is *not* the way a sadist works. He should be right in Marni's face, enjoying the power he has over her."

"Over Theo. Vic despises him."

"Same thing. Threaten Theo, you hurt Marni." Mike handed her the wineglass, studying her face, as though weighing a decision. "Do you know how I made my money?"

She narrowed her eyes. Money was Mike's touchstone. It reassured him that he mattered. He'd grown up in Queens when it was anything but fashionable, the only child of a widowed mother. Mike had fought for his success, his stature in the tech world, his name recognition. But it hadn't filled the hole in his soul. Hadn't answered his need, Carly thought. Because it was money he mentioned when he felt too small.

"Software," she said tiredly.

He picked up her phone. "*Surveillance* software. I can monitor and track anyone without their knowledge, and I can do it remotely. You have Vic's contact info in here, right?"

"Of course."

"So." His brows lifted in challenge. "How badly do you want to find him?"

"I'M GLAD YOU didn't let the prick scare you," Theo Patel said to Marni LeGuin. She had just emerged from her post-shoot shower, and was swathed in a terry robe lined with silk. The bones of her face stood out in sharp relief, beautifully molded; with her wet hair slicked back and her skin free of makeup, she looked every day of her forty-six years. Fine lines radiated from the corners of her mouth and beneath her chin. That she was confident enough in their long friendship to see Theo with a naked face meant everything, suddenly. There was no greater depth of trust in Hollywood, and this evening, it nearly brought him to tears.

"I stopped being scared of Vic years ago," she said. "That doesn't mean I like being around him. But I don't believe any-thing he says."

"Thank you." Theo drew a shaky breath. "Vic's telling lies. About Cameron Duval. Yes, he was a troubled kid who killed himself. But there was never any assault. No payoffs. No coverup."

Marni toweled her wet hair. "Tell me about him."

"For a while I served on the board of a nonprofit that did out-reach to gay teens." Theo smiled faintly. "My rare effort at giving back. Ironic, isn't it?"

"In LA?"

He nodded. "They asked me to speak about my own experi-ence—how I came out, what kind of emotional preparation that took, how to find allies and fight bullies—at a monthly meeting for the kids. I agreed. I'd been donating for years, and figured it was time to put my mouth where my money was."

"Good for you," Marni said. "I should be doing the same thing. For women in the business."

"Cameron came up to me after the talk. He was younger than most of the kids there. Thirteen, like Vic said. Although age doesn't matter—I knew at six I was attracted to other boys. He asked if he could contact me for advice."

"And you let him?"

Theo shrugged. "I figured I could help."

"Uh-oh," Marni said softly.

He moved to her closet and shifted among the hangers. Pulled out a vintage silk top, studied it keenly, then shoved it back. "Too Pucci, not enough Boho. Most of what I packed for you looks simply *wrong*, darling, in this chilly gray backwater. You should find a younger Dresser. With *range*."

"I'll never fire you, Theo. You'll have to quit. But not because Vic says so."

"Bless you." He stared dismally into the closet depths. "You *might* get away with this Vivienne Westwood plaid. Vintage is very Nantucket."

"Only if it's your grandma's cashmere," she said, amused.

"I brought your fuchsia twinset." He dived for a drawer. "You *scream* Grace Kelly in it."

"So what did the thirteen-year-old do?" she persisted.

He stood upright, the folded sweaters in his hands. "Showed up at my condo one night. He'd scored some middle-school coke he thought I'd like. We'd been texting for maybe ten days."

"Oh, Theo."

He placed the cashmere beside her on the sofa. Gently, as though it were a sleeping cat. "I patted him on the head, told him he was a nice boy but barking up the wrong tree, and got him an Uber home." The next words came out in a rush of regret and embarrassment. "Then I blocked him. You should be getting dressed, Sweets. We'll be late for din-din."

"I'd have done the same thing."

"No." Theo shook his head. "You'd have blocked him after day one."

"Yeah. But I've probably had more experience with stalkers."

"Were they thirteen?"

"No, but . . ."

"And did they jump off the fifth level of a parking garage?"

"Theo—"

He heaved a shuddering sigh, and put his face in his hands. This was *his* form of trust: having no words. For decades, Theo had relied on his tongue to defend himself. But Marni's belief could only be met with silence.

She touched the sleek hair at his nape with her fingers. "Hey. That's not your fault."

"Then whose?"

"Not *yours.*" There was an edge of anger in her voice. "Feel sadness, Theo. Feel bad for the kid and everyone who failed him. But not guilt. That's what people like Vic exploit. They make you cop to crimes you never committed."

"I'm not sure how I can face him tonight," Theo muttered.

"Break bread with the man. He's sure to be vile."

"He won't say a word." Marni rose from the sofa and reached for her sweaters. "I made sure of that."

Theo's head came up. "How?"

She smiled. "I threatened to kill him. Now, give me twenty minutes. There's a Cisco Brewers gin downstairs with our names on it."

CARLY AND MIKE were the last two people to reach the main house for dinner.

Chris Candler was sitting in the heart of the great room, on one of the sofas facing the fire, with his arm around his daughter's shoulders. They were both studying something on her phone. Winter was looking happier and more animated than Carly remembered seeing her, and Chris's face was transformed from the worried mask he'd worn all day.

". . . so incredibly cool," Winter was saying. "She backpacked into Denali in January to get these pictures. Can you believe it?"

Marni was arranged on a chaise longue nearby, her blond hair newly refreshed after the long day of work, gazing at the Candlers indulgently. She was wearing jeans, a vivid twin set, and a pair of boots. She looked casually, effortlessly, fabulous. Carly wondered for an instant if she was interested in Chris—that could complicate the production—or if she was simply an idle observer of a domestic drama not her own.

Theo Patel was mixing a drink at the bar, coolly elegant in houndstooth trousers and a black silk jacket. The fact that he hadn't left the island early that morning surprised Carly. Her husband's exultant prediction that Theo's life was over was clearly incorrect.

And Vic, still, was nowhere.

Correction: Vic was almost certainly in bed with a woman whose name she didn't know, in a house she had no interest in finding.

"It's a backdoor exploitation of a standard cell phone vulner-ability," Mike had explained as he opened his app and targeted her husband. "He won't know we've pirated his phone. There will be no trace of our data mining. I promise you."

Sickened, she'd left her wine untouched while she watched his fingers move, saw the code materialize on his laptop, and waited for him to interpret what he'd found.

"He's definitely in Town," Mike told her, a slight line between his brows. "In fact, I can tell you everywhere he's been since two-thirteen this afternoon."

Vic had apparently found a seat at The Proprietors Bar on India Street, known for its craft cocktails. By a few minutes past 4 P.M., however, he'd moved on to an address on Howard Court, a short dead end in the neighborhood of Upper Main and Gar-diner Streets.

"That's residential." Mike was openly frowning, now. There was a map with a red location flag pulled up on his screen. "In fact, the address is a short-term rental property. Owned by a real estate group that manages vacation leasing."

"Vic has a short-term rental?"

"Or he's visiting someone who does."

Carly felt a surge of resentment. Her husband couldn't bother to answer her texts or pick up the phone, even though it was nearly dinner time and he'd been gone all afternoon. This was not what she'd expected—or deserved, Carly thought—when he'd decided to come to Nantucket to *support her.*

"Do you want to jump in the car and drive over there?" Mike asked quietly.

She shook her head, mortified. Vic was deliberately ignoring her, on the Saturday of Stroll Weekend, during the most challenging moment of her career. He probably couldn't stand the fact that she was in the spotlight. He was taunting her with his silence—inviting her to make a scene and humiliate herself in front of the entire cast and crew of *The Hopeless.*

She'd be damned if she'd do it.

"So you make money spying on people. Tracking their sordid little hobbies." There was a taste of bile at the back of her throat.

"I'm sorry," Mike said.

"Don't be." She held out her hand for her phone. "He's not worth it. Are you coming to dinner?"

CHRIS CANDLER GLANCED up as the two of them entered the great room, and smiled at Carly. But his joy was entirely for his daughter.

"We got her back!" he exclaimed, with a gesture at Winter.

"I *told* you she was fine," Carly said, wishing she could feel as certain of Vic. "Did you have fun in Town, Winter?"

"I met the most phenomenal woman," the girl said. "A bird photographer, working on a book. Here's her Insta!"

She held out her phone, and Carly tried to feign interest.

"She lives next door!"

"Next door?" Mike echoed. He leaned around Carly to study Winter's phone.

"Well, as much as anything is next door out here." Winter waved vaguely. "In a house somewhere over there. It's called Stella Maris. She was at the shoot today! Only she left. Because you disturbed her birds. Merg-somethings."

Everyone in the room tried to look interested.

Chris cleared his throat. "This woman and her son dropped Winter off. They're local people, and were familiar with the house."

Mike frowned. "What's her name? I thought I knew everyone who lived around here."

"Mary Alice Fillmore," Winter said promptly. "She said her mom knew Ingrid. As in, Ingrid's Gift? But she's dead now. Ingrid, I mean."

Mike repeated the name under his breath. "Doesn't ring a bell. Which house is it?"

"The really run-down one over there." Again, a vague hand-wave. "I mean, the windows are boarded up and there's no electricity or heat except from a wood stove, but she's *living* there. With a van and a ton of camera equipment."

For an instant, everyone in the room went still, holding themselves. Evaluating Winter's statement.

"Off the grid on Nantucket," Theo said distinctly. "Photo-graphing *birds*. Who knew?"

"And this person was . . . on our set today?" Carly moved closer to Winter, extending her hand for the girl's phone. *We definitely need better security.*

Winter wrinkled her nose. "She got there before any of you did, so I wouldn't really call it *on set*. And she left anyway. For some *swamp*, because it was so noisy."

Mike lifted his head. "Squam Swamp?"

"Yeah!" Winter grinned at him. "She was photographing there all day. I may go look for her tomorrow—if she posts where she's going to be. I'm following her on Insta, now."

"I was hoping you'd come to the Marsh," her father broke in. "I'd like you to watch us film."

But Winter was already absorbed in her phone again, and didn't seem to have heard him. Chris would be worrying about her all day tomorrow, Carly guessed—unless the girl's bodyguard kept better tabs on her.

He could really use Mike's surveillance software, she thought, then flushed guiltily. She wouldn't wish that kind of tracking power on anyone. It didn't help to know where Vic was when he obviously didn't want to tell her.

14 | Stella Maris, Saturday Night

DARKNESS HAD FALLEN, and quiet descended, on the dilapidated old house up the road from Ingrid's Gift. The grackles and whip-poor-wills had ceased their sunset calls; the wind that had tugged at the shifting landscape all day had died; but the gentle and distant murmur of waves lapping at shoreline remained, if one strained to hear it.

She was standing outside on the back kitchen steps, listening, when the nearer grate of wheels on the rutted front drive caught her ear. She froze.

It would not be Ansel returning; he had only left her a few hours before. After dropping Winter Candler at Ingrid's Gift, they had sat over tea together by the kitchen's wood-burning stove. While she boiled the water, Ansel carried two armchairs from the living room closer to the heat. She was quietly astounded at his size, at the shock of seeing him grown, when in memory he was always a toddler with the sweetest of round faces. That child was gone; the cut of this one's nose and the color of his hair reminded her more of her father than of the boy he had been.

Of Ron, she thought, there was little trace. How was that possible? Ron had shaped Ance for twenty years—

She didn't apologize about the lack of alcohol in the house as she handed him a steaming mug. He had found her online almost a year ago while in rehab—or rather, his counselor had.

"Ansel is working through abandonment issues," the woman told Mary Alice. "His father led him to believe you were dead."

She had felt a fist tighten at the very core of her body, where she had once carried him, below her heart. It stopped the breath in her lungs.

"He would like to contact you," the woman had continued, "and I think it would be good for him—offer some closure. But I felt it was important to see if you were open to that before he got in touch. Because . . ."

She didn't have to continue, Mary Alice thought. *Because it would be devastating to be rejected by his mother twice.*

She had written to Ansel that very night, using the email address the counselor had given her. And over the next twelve months, they had exchanged tentative snippets of information. Ance was guarded, but so was she. They kept their conversations online firmly in the realm of the present: Ance's goals in therapy—he was addicted, it seemed, to opioids. *Broke my collar bone in lacrosse in high school,* he'd written, *then found out Oxy-Contin made me fly. It was much more fun to be Superman than Ron MacKay's failed son.*

She suggested a few things that had helped her free herself from cocaine, years before: Getting out alone into the wilderness. Listening to her thoughts until they slowed enough, along with her breathing, to isolate the cravings. She suggested a few books he might read.

I'm starting to paint, he wrote back, and sent her pictures of exuberant canvases. Sharply, she remembered plastic pots of water-based pigments, set out on an old board table in the backyard, red and yellow and green, how she had guided the fat little fist wrapped around the brush and taught him to mix brown. Somewhere between his second and third birthday. Somewhere before she'd plummeted out of his life.

Good, she'd written back. *Keep going.*

They did not talk about the past. And she hadn't told him where she was living. He had figured that out for himself, from pictures she posted on Instagram, and careful questions Ron answered about her parents. There were pictures of Stella Maris in old photo albums in DC, pictures Ron had never destroyed.

Yesterday, Ance had taken a sip of tea, looked at her over the rim with her father's eyes, and finally asked, "Why'd you leave?"

"I wasn't given a choice," she said.

And sat herself down in a chair to explain what she could.

Now, Mary Alice heard the approaching car and knew what had happened—someone had followed Ansel here. A reporter. An aide of Janet Brimhold's.

She turned swiftly back into her house and locked the kitchen door. She doused the flame of her oil lamp and shut the damper on her stove. Smoke was bound to leak into the main floor rooms, but she was forced to risk it. She slipped off her shoes as she crept quietly up the stairs. She would have to hope that her green van, parked in an ell she'd clawed out of the moorland scrub, and surrounded by the humped shapes of overgrown rugosa, was camouflaged by the night.

Once safely on the second floor, she crawled the length of the hallway, keeping below the sashes of the windows, lest the slightest movement register on the retinas of the person standing below. The engine was cut off, but she could feel the eyes of a watcher sweeping the decayed shingle façade of Stella Maris.

When she reached the front bedroom, whose windows like all the others out front were still boarded shut, she rose behind the protective wood covering and set her eye to the spy hole she had bored in the lower panel.

From this, she could see the entire approach from Polpis Road along the derelict drive.

There was a vehicle parked below, ten feet from her front

door. It was long and massive, the color indiscernible in the
darkness, the headlights sweeping into the brush to one side of
the house. A man was standing near the open driver's side, hands
on his hips, staring up at her window.

He can't see you, she thought in panic. *He can't see you, he
doesn't know you're here.* But her heart galloped calliope-fast, the
blood pounded in her ears, because even after all these years, she
knew instantly it was Ron.

She watched the silhouette of his head move as his gaze
swept the house. He was looking for the slightest detail, a
chink in her protective armor, that would betray the house and
herself both.

Then he moved, and leapt out of her limited field of vision.

Anxiety foamed into her throat. Was he probing the front
door, which was still nailed shut? Was he running his gloved
finger along the jagged edge of the side-light's glass, which she'd
deliberately left shattered as though vandals had broken it?
No—he was moving swiftly around the side of the house toward
the back.

Which, though locked, was penetrable.

She crawled frantically back down the hallway to her bedroom, where she had conceded something to her need for light,
her need for the soul-lifting vista across the marsh to Polpis Harbor, and had unboarded the windows to the sun.

She stood at an angle to the glass, her gaze directed downward,
and watched him poke around the foundations of her house.

He tested the stair railing. He set his foot upon the stairs.
He mounted them, his head pivoting upward to study the rear
façade. He would see that this window, alone among all the others, was free of its wooden barricade. Would that recognition
flare in his nostrils, like the scent of blood?

She stopped breathing. Her body turned to stone.

He reached for the handle of her back door.

She closed her eyes. The handle would still be warm from her fingers. He would know, relentlessly, that she was there.

When she opened her eyes again, he was gone.

She drew an unsteady breath, her heart still racing, and listened to the sound of the car as it died away.

Had Ansel told him she was here?

And why did that suddenly feel like the worst possible betrayal?

But no. If Ron had actually known she was in the house, nothing would have stopped him from breaking down the door. He'd have brought the police with him, and watched while they did it.

Why, then, had he driven out Polpis Road to stand in the dark, probing the shambles of his past? Did he need to see the ruined house to convince himself he was free of her?

He's savoring his revenge, Mary Alice thought.

That must be so bad for Ansel. If she could feel Ron's anger and hatred through the walls of this house, what must it be like for their son to live with him?

Unhealthy.

Unfair.

And she was the boy's mother. She had to do something.

She could not approach Ron directly—the cost to herself would be too great—but she could do something for the person he was damaging.

She picked up her phone and called a number she'd memorized years ago, to the summer house of a long-lost friend, who had lived with her grandmother on Hulbert Avenue each July and August.

A woman who would never take her calls if they popped up on her secure cell phone—but who might just pick up a landline. Because only people she trusted knew how to call it.

Janet Brimhold MacKay.

15 | Stella Maris, Sunday Morning

I T   W A S   T H E   first time Howie Seitz had spent Christmas Stroll at a desk instead of on the streets in town, standing mutely in a crosswalk as holiday revelers streamed across the cobblestones. He was used to being in uniform, so official that he was basically invisible, but enjoying the parade and the ranks of decorated trees marching along the brick sidewalks and the huge official one at the top of Main Street that actually talked to people as they walked by. (There was a speaker wired at its base, connected to a hidden manned microphone, but the trick always startled the unwitting and enchanted children, who would linger to ask the tree questions. Only rarely were people rude.)

This year, however, he'd been promoted. To Meredith Folger's old job, of detective. And he'd inherited Merry's small office. She'd inherited the one vacated suddenly by Bob Pocock that had once been her father's, and Ralph Waldo Folger's before that. The office of Nantucket's chief of police.

Pocock had never put art on the walls, but Merry had hung two of Cary Hazelgrove's massive photographs of the textures of curling waves and an oil landscape by David Lazarus that her husband, Peter, had given her for her birthday. She'd told Howie she thought it humanized the department for people who'd never had occasion to enter the chief's office before. A glimpse of the soul behind law enforcement.

She wasn't sitting in her office now—it was after nine on

Sunday of Stroll Weekend, and Merry probably had someplace to be. Or maybe she was still drinking coffee, Howie reflected, in the comfortable farmhouse in the middle of the cranberry bog.

She and Peter had invited him and his girlfriend, Dionis Mather, to a barbecue over the summer, when everyone was safely vaccinated and it was possible to eat good grilled food and fresh corn from Moor's End together in the middle of August with the long rays of the setting sun touching their faces. Tess and Rafe da Silva had been there, too, and a few of Merry's other friends—and the memory of it hit Howie forcibly now, on a cold, bright December morning of similar sun, when the pandemic news was turning uncertain again.

Dionis was gone, back to her teaching job at a private school on the mainland. The station was almost empty. Everything had an end-of-holiday feel to it, even though it was a few weeks before Christmas and he was scheduled to take some leave to spend in Boston with the woman he suspected he might actually love. Howie was lonely. And for the first time in nearly a decade of working on Nantucket, he was questioning why he lived thirty miles out at sea.

He had paperwork to file and could technically have left it until Monday, but the caretaker's apartment over a garage where he lived was too empty this morning, so he'd wandered into his home away from home. He was following football games on a cell phone app. The Patriots weren't playing until Monday night, and he refused to watch the Buccaneers.

"Hey, Seitz."

He glanced up from his screen. Hanameel, the take-no-prisoners Voice of Dispatch, was standing in his doorway.

"You gonna want to know this."

"What, Hana?"

Her expression was apprehensive; usually she was unflappable. "There's a body. Out Polpis way. I just sent a squad."

Involuntarily, Howie felt his thigh twitch beneath his desk. "Unexplained death?"

Hanameel nodded. "Kid who reported it says gunshot."

"Ouch." He thrust back his chair. "Text me the address."

"Okay." Hana lingered. "Another thing, Seitz."

"Yeah?" Howie grabbed his jacket.

"Kid says the victim's his mother."

THE UNIFORMED OFFICERS and the EMTs beat Howie to Stella Maris. By the time he'd followed them up the rutted gravel drive, Ansel MacKay was seated inside at the kitchen table under the concerned eye of a female police officer and the scene out back was cordoned off with yellow tape. Howie left his Toyota near the fire department's ambulance and paused to study the house's exterior.

The front façade's window frames had not been painted in years. Decades, possibly. The paint was not simply peeling—it was gone, and the underlying wood was decayed. All of the front windows were boarded over—not unusual during the offseason, when owners wished to protect a coastal house from storm damage, but distinctly odd when the house was inhabited. From what he could see of the roof, it leaked. A whole section of shingles was missing. Remembering the Cat 3 hurricane that had hit Nantucket a few years before, Howie was astounded that any of the roof was left. His gaze drifted down to the foundation. The latticework running the house's perimeter suggested the storm cellar was original, primitive, and from the look of it, infested with rodents. And the underbrush everywhere was filled with old beer bottles.

Stella Maris, the faded quarter board said; Star of the Sea.

More like crack house, Howie thought, and followed the sound of voices to the backyard.

SHE WAS LYING on the frowsy turf below the kitchen porch in a pair of sweats and a hoodie, staring blindly up at the sky. Her feet were bare and her arms flung out at her sides as though she'd intended to make a snow angel, had there been any snow. The front of the hoodie was ratcheted with holes and stained dark brown with blood that had also soaked into the ground beneath her.

There was no sign of a gun.

So much for suicide.

He put in a call to dispatch and requested Clarence Strangerfield's Scene of Crimes team. Clarence wasn't working this morning as far as Howie knew, but he had a deputy now, Candace Moriarity—a position Meredith Folger had added when she took over the department. Clarence was already well past retirement age, although nobody mentioned this to his face or behind his back. He'd first been hired by Ralph Waldo Folger.

"And Hanameel," Howie added, "get an ME over here."

"Already called, Seitz. It's John Fairborn, and he's on his way."

"Thanks."

Howie walked all the way around the corpse, studying its position near the northern edge of the backyard, just where it merged into scrub, and wondered what had drawn the victim to that point. He crouched down and studied the turf. Nuts and seeds were scattered everywhere—a few had caught in the loose strands of the woman's hair. Howie stared at this, which was gray and wiry, ribboning out from her head like an aureole. He identified sunflower seeds and the halves of peanuts. He rocked back on his heels and looked around for a birdfeeder. There was none.

Weird, he thought, and got to his feet.

"MARY ALICE FILLMORE," said Annie, the policewoman, as she rose from the kitchen table. "This is her son, Ansel MacKay. He found her and identified her."

"Ansel." Howie nodded at the guy, who was a few years younger than himself, but hardly a kid, as Hanameel had suggested. "I'm sorry for your loss."

There were no tears on MacKay's face, just the thousand-mile stare of shock. The man's hair was white-blond at the roots but dyed randomly red and green. Stroll? Howie thought again, *Crack house*.

"I'd like to ask you a few questions," he ventured, "and then you'll have to go to the station with Officer Dowd and make a statement. Are you able to do that?"

"I'll have to call my dad." Ansel rubbed his forehead fretfully and then stared at the scarred wood floor. "He doesn't even know I'm here."

"Okay." Howie glanced at Annie Down. "Where is Mr. Fillmore at the moment?"

"It's Mr. MacKay—Ron MacKay—and he's with my stepmom at Stronghold. That's on Hulbert Avenue."

Hulbert Ave. Definitely *not* a crack house.

"We're supposed to fly back to DC in a few hours," Ansel went on. "Wheels up at one P.M."

"I'm afraid you'll have to stay on Nantucket for a while at least," Howie said. "If not for the next few days. Your parents are divorced?"

Ansel nodded. "My dad is unaware she's here . . . *Was* here. Or that I found her."

"Found her. You mean, this morning? How did that happen, exactly?" Howie slipped his lanky frame into Annie's empty chair and pulled his phone out of his jacket to take notes.

"Found out she was *alive*," Ansel corrected. "And living on Nantucket. My dad told me Mary Alice was dead for as long as I can remember. After the divorce, she was dead to *him*. And now," he concluded, "she really is."

He looked toward the kitchen window, where two people in

white Tyvek evidence collection jumpsuits were ducking under the yellow tape. "This is unbelievable."

The guy seemed disoriented. Was he on something? Could he have killed the woman, and then called it in out of remorse? Howie typed a text into his phone. *Search the house for a weapon.*

Ten seconds later, he got Annie's response. *Drake's on it.* Her partner. Howie could hear him moving around overhead. He hoped the floorboards were stronger than the roof, and that Drake—who was two-fifty if he was a pound—didn't fall through and land on Howie's lap.

"Let's start at the beginning," he suggested. "How did you get here today?"

There had been no bicycle, and no other car on the rutted drive.

"I Ubered, actually."

Good; an Uber ride could be verified. "I'll need to check your app for the driver's contact info," Howie said, "and follow up with that. Roughly what time would you say?"

Obediently, Ansel pulled up his app notifications and displayed them. "I walked into Town and realized there was no shuttle out here until ten A.M. That was too late, so I put in for the car. That was at . . . eight-twenty-seven A.M." He glanced at his watch. "Shit. I've really gotta call my dad."

The drop-off time would also be noted, Howie reflected. "And then?"

"I walked up the drive. The house was really quiet, but she mainly lives—*lived*—in the back, so I didn't think anything. I walked around and saw her lying there."

"Did you touch her?"

Ansel shook his head. "I just screamed. Completely lost it, dude, like I never have before. I mean, you saw her, right?"

Howie nodded.

"Obviously dead. You don't survive that. How many bullets *were* there?"

"It was a shotgun," Howie said gently. "That can do a lot of damage in a single discharge. We've got people searching for the shell casing right now."

"Buckshot?" Ansel looked horrified. "What the fuck?"

"Well . . . it *is* deer-hunting season."

"You mean, you think she was killed by a hunter? By *mistake?*"

"It's a possibility." Howie was deliberately hedging; he knew too little for a firm conclusion. "You're allowed to hunt from sunrise to sunset on Nantucket almost anywhere except conservation land that gets a lot of pedestrian traffic, and those areas are clearly posted. This isn't conservation land. And I'd bet there are deer coming through here all the time."

"Oh my god," Ansel muttered. "Poor Mary Alice. That's just . . . sick."

There were far too many deer on Nantucket. With the deer came ticks, the source of the island's sky-high rates of Lyme disease. Residents were allowed to bow hunt October through Thanksgiving, with shotgun season following for about two weeks after that. The rest of December was reserved for Primitive Firearm hunting, which meant muzzle-loaded black powder guns. Venison tended to surface on the menus of island restaurants from Thanksgiving through New Year—and most hunters were careful around residential areas. They were required to stay five hundred feet away from occupied buildings, but Stella Maris looked deserted.

The only flaw in the explanation, if Howie could call it that, was that hunting was prohibited on Sundays. Violating that part of the provisions—and killing somebody—would explain why a hunter would panic and run. Taking the shotgun with them.

"So you screamed," he said encouragingly. "What next?"

"I ran," Ansel said simply. "Not my finest hour. I ran to Polpis

Road and tried to flag down a car. But only three went by and none of them stopped. I probably looked like a maniac."

And there's the hair, Howie added mentally.

"So I hit 911. They told me to wait for a cop car. I did."

It was all straightforward, Howie thought. He glanced through his notes. "Your mother was expecting you?"

"Yeah, I texted her from the Uber."

Howie glanced up. "Did she respond?"

Ansel frowned slightly. "She did." He fished out his phone again and pulled up the text.

Howie studied the exchange.

Mary Alice. Stopping by to say bye. Be there in fifteen.

Wonderful, Ance. Coffee's brewed.

"She had a cell phone?" Howie asked.

"Yeah. She was an Instagram influencer. Posted all the time."

"Instagram influencer?" Howie couldn't help it. He practically yelped the words back at Ansel. The term simply did not fit with the house or the dead woman lying in the backyard.

"Mary Alice is an amazing person," her son said quietly. "She's—*was*—a major photographer. Traveled all over the world. Working on a book. About birds, and climate change, and Nantucket."

"I see," Howie said. Seeing nothing at all, suddenly.

He glanced around the kitchen. Unlike the exterior of the house, it looked comfortable and neat. A coffee mug was rinsed and draining on the counter. She must have started a fire in the cast-iron stove before she went out into the backyard, because he could see the coals glowing through the small window in the door.

"Do you know why she would have been standing outside in her bare feet early in the morning?"

"She fed the birds," Ansel said. "She posted videos of it online. You can watch them on her account."

He pulled up a clip on his phone and offered it to Howie.

And there it was: An extended palm filled with seeds and nuts, a bird alighting in slow-motion on the fingertips. Howie had no idea what bird—he could only identify the usual robins and cardinals. This one's bright eye assessed the camera lens, then stabbed at a peanut with its beak. An instant later, it lifted its wings. And a second bird alighted.

"That's from Oregon, where she lived before she moved. That's digital video footage. The cameras she used here took real film, and were all manual—because, no power."

"No power," Howie repeated.

"Not in the house."

"You mean, the utilities are turned off?"

Ansel shrugged. "I didn't really ask. She said she charged her phone and laptop in her van."

"Was your mom *squatting* in this house?" Howie demanded. It happened during the pandemic: desperate people, out of jobs, broke into empty buildings and camped there. But they usually didn't have ex-husbands living on Hulbert Ave.

"I wouldn't call it that," Ansel returned defensively. "It's not like she didn't have a *right* to be here. This was her mom's house. And went way back in her family, years before that."

She must have been dirt poor, Howie thought, if she'd never turned on the utilities in her own house. Sad.

"You said you'd only found her lately." He studied Ansel. He had as many questions about the guy as he did about the victim. "When?"

Ansel closed his eyes an instant as he thought. "It would have been the first month of the pandemic. Couple of years ago. I was in rehab. We were going over a lot of stuff from my childhood and one of the docs thought it would help if I could fully process my mother's death. Only when she went looking for it, she discovered Mary Alice was alive."

This was a lot to absorb; Howie took a deep breath. "Rehab?"

Ansel smiled faintly. "I used to have an opioid problem. My dad will tell you it's genetic. And not on his side."

"Okay." Howie added to his notes. "You using now? Your mother using?"

Ansel shook his head. "No. And not that I know of. But you're searching the house. So—"

He'd understood that much, then.

On the table between them, the clip of birds looped quietly, attenuated by the slo-mo. Howie's eyes drifted back to it and he was caught, instantly, by the surreal peace.

"She just held out her hand, and they came?" he asked.

"Like Saint Francis," Ansel said.

16 | Stronghold, Sunday Morning

FRANK WAS ON guard at the gate of the Hulbert Avenue house. Howie was prepped—Ansel had told him who his step-mother was—and he passed his badge to the DSS officer, who studied it and then Howie's face with eyes entirely devoid of emotion. The cold gaze shifted to Ansel. "What does this concern?"

"An unexplained death," Howie said. "I need to speak to Mr. MacKay."

The guard did not reply. His eyes lingered on Ansel, who was sitting in the passenger seat of Howie's ancient Toyota. Then Frank stepped back from the car, ignoring them both, and muttered into his radio. The gate remained closed.

"You're not cleared to enter this facility," the DSS officer said simply. "Mr. MacKay is coming out."

Beside him, Ansel drew a deep breath. Howie could feel the guy's tension filling the available space between them, which consisted of the gearshift console and cupholder. Howie had told him he'd break the news to Ron MacKay rather than allowing Ansel to alert his father by phone or text; he'd wanted to observe the man's reaction to the news. But that meant he'd just set up somebody who was apparently important to be blindsided by the Nantucket police. Anxiety seeped into Howie's clothes and hair and caused his stomach to somersault. He knew nothing about federal officials or their protocols and might already have screwed things up.

Two men suddenly appeared in the courtyard that joined the house and the separate garage—the latter fronted Hulbert Ave., the former ran along the beach—and strode purposefully toward the gate. Ron MacKay and another bodyguard. Howie deduced this from the similarity in the baseball caps and navy windbreakers the DSS guys were wearing.

"Your dad," he said to Ansel.

"Yep."

Howie pulled on his car door handle and swung it open. Ansel followed.

They stood waiting as Ron MacKay and his guard swung beneath the closed wooden gate and came to a halt near Howie's front bumper.

"Mr. MacKay?"

The man nodded. "You are?"

"Howie Seitz of the Nantucket Police. That gentleman"—he ducked his head at Frank—"has my badge if you'd like to inspect it."

MacKay extended his hand. Frank gave him Howie's badge. "What's this about?"

"Your son discovered the body of a deceased woman at a property off the Polpis road roughly an hour ago. Mary Alice Fillmore. I believe she was your ex-wife?"

For the first time, Ron MacKay looked fully at his son. His jaw flexed, and his eyelids flickered. "What the hell. Ansel?"

His son stepped toward him, hands balled in his pockets. "I found out she was alive about a year ago, Dad. We've been in touch, and once I hit Nantucket I went to see her. Only, this morning—she was dead."

"Jesus *Christ*," MacKay said forcefully, and lifted a hand to his eyes. "She's not supposed to be anywhere near Nantucket! What was it, an overdose?"

"She was shot." Howie's eyes drifted to the DSS guards, who stood together near the guardhouse, their hands on their belts.

They were attempting to look uninterested, but he would bet they were drinking in every word.

"Shot?" Ron darted a look at Ansel. "Did she kill herself?"

"Unlikely." Howie reached inside his car and turned off the ignition. "We haven't found a weapon. I need to ask you some questions, sir."

"*Now?*" MacKay flipped his wrist in a display of impatience. "We're about to leave for the airport. Ansel, are you even *packed?*"

"You'll have to delay your flight."

"That's not possible." MacKay stepped in to stare down Howie, but he was a good six inches shorter, which meant he was forced to look up. "Do you know who my wife is?"

"Yes, sir. Your son explained. And I know you're flying on a government jet, which will depart on *your* schedule, not a commercial flight. You'll have to delay your plans."

"This is outrageous! The secretary has a working dinner tonight in Georgetown!"

"If I can take down a verifiable statement about her knowledge of the Deceased and her movements this morning," Howie said, "the secretary is free to go. As are you, sir. Once you answer my questions."

"My wife knows nothing about Mary Alice," MacKay said bitterly. "I kept Janet far away from my nightmares. She was here all morning, working with her staff. I can verify it. Happy?"

"No, sir, I'm afraid that's not adequate."

"You're going to cross-examine every person in this house? There are seven other people staying here!"

Howie waited.

Ron tossed his badge in front of him and caught it in midair. "Who's your boss? I'm calling him."

"Go right ahead, sir." Howie drew his cell from his pocket and punched in Merry's cell number. "Her name is Chief Meredith Folger."

ON ANY OTHER Stroll Sunday, Merry would've been having brunch at Nautilus, wedged into a hightop with Peter and his family. But George and her husband had kept the kids at home this year, worried about the pandemic, and to be honest Merry was feeling *done* with the holiday weekend at this point, after a chic dinner in Sconset with Peter's friend Sky Tate-Jackson and his wife, the clothing designer Mayling Stern, and thirty of their most intimate friends. Tess da Silva had provided the food; for most of the night, Merry had wished she could escape to the kitchen. Ralph Waldo's death had made her acutely aware of Covid's risks, and a variant of the virus was reportedly surging. It didn't matter, Merry thought, that everyone at Sky's house claimed to be vaccinated; she knew they were all vulnerable. Nantucket's public health officials were resigned to a surge in cases following the joyous holiday weekend—inevitable, with ten thousand people roaming downtown, and masks voluntary during Stroll. No one on the Chamber of Commerce had wanted to discourage tourist dollars during the best three days of winter shopping.

Merry's Stroll duties this Sunday were few, as most of the off-island revelers would be departing by boat and plane as the day wore on. Those who remained were congregating out Bartlett Farm Road, at Cisco Brewers, which her uniformed officers informed her by radio was booming with beer garden patrons.

A bit past noon she found herself standing on a windy, deserted hillside off Quaker Road, toward the western end of the island, in what had once been a sheep meadow. Now Prospect Hill was a cemetery.

She reached out and touched the letters etched into the granite on Ralph's headstone. He wasn't really lying here, in the grave with his wife, Sylvie; he'd been cremated in Boston, and his ashes sent back to Nantucket. Merry, her father, and Peter had taken Ralph out in John Folger's boat, and scattered his ashes just past the Jetties. Merry had tossed a penny in after him, so that wherever Ralph drifted, he'd always come back to the island.

That was a Nantucket thing.

She gazed toward the south, where a fine rime of cloud was advancing across the sea. It was a completely gorgeous day and she missed her grandpa acutely. "Love you, Ralph," she whispered, and patted the top of the headstone.

Her cell phone vibrated in her coat pocket.

The number was not one she recognized. Spam, probably; but on Stroll weekend, it was her duty to answer.

"Meredith Folger," she said.

"Merry? This is Brittany Novak. I used to work with Tess da Silva? I catered your wedding?"

"Of course," Merry said. "Brittany! What can I do for you?"

"Oh, you're so kind to remember!" the girl cried. In her mind's eye, Merry pictured pleasant features, hazel eyes, long red hair drawn back in a neat bun. Freckles. She'd pulled perfect lamb out of her hat in the middle of a hurricane, and plated it flawlessly.

"It's not me, actually, but the man I work for. Mike Struna? He's got kind of a problem, and he wanted to talk to somebody about it. I thought of you."

People always thought of Merry when there was a problem.

Mike Struna. Her mind raced through a mental index of island names. He was one of the famous ones, a dot-commer who'd relocated to sit out the pandemic on Nantucket. Big estate on the Polpis road. Ingrid's Gift.

"When did you start working for him?" she asked.

"Nearly two years ago. I'm personal-cheffing."

"Got it."

"Actually, could you talk to him? Mike? He's right here."

"Of course."

Merry walked briskly toward her car. The wind had dropped from yesterday, but was still buffeting her earphones and whipping up static. She'd take this call on Bluetooth, driving back to Mason Farms.

"Chief Folger?"

"Mr. Struna. How are you today, sir?"

"Fine, just fine." The man's tone was distracted. "I don't know if you're aware, but there's a film production going on out here near my place?"

Oh, God, Merry thought. He's actually calling the chief of police to complain about traffic. And using his chef to do it.

"Yes, sir. We issued a permit for it months ago. How can I help you?"

"Well—it may be nothing. But I thought I should check with somebody who knows the ropes, to be sure."

"Uh-huh," she said encouragingly.

"One of my houseguests. I'm hosting the actors and some of the production crew here at the house—actually, at the *houses*, because there are several on my property."

Merry suppressed a sigh. She knew Ingrid's Gift—she'd known Ingrid herself, an old friend of Ralph's who was lying quietly not far from the Folger headstone in this same cemetery. The building and remodeling and landscaping and *terrain sculpting* that had gone on at the property for three years after it sold for twenty million dollars had actually pained her. Ingrid was an off-islander, sure—a German war bride who'd come home with a GI in the '50s and visited her summer house at most two months a year—but over the decades she'd woven herself into the fabric of Nantucket. Funded chamber orchestras and educational programs and taught classes in horticulture at the Atheneum. Mike Struna, on the other hand, was dedicated to building solely his own assets.

"Yes?" she prompted.

"Well, one of my guests is missing."

"Really." There was a question mark in her voice, Merry knew. It was tough to truly go missing on Nantucket; the island was ten miles by fifteen.

"Vic Sonnenfeld. He's the CEO and founder of CMI—Creative Management International. That's a talent agency."

"Okay," Merry said.

"He was at the shoot yesterday morning over at the Field Station—his wife's the director, Carly Simpson, we were at NYU together—but he never came back to the house. It was one thing last evening, we thought he'd just gone into town and got caught up in Stroll, but he's nowhere to be found this morning."

Merry stopped short. *Hollywood people.* She couldn't help it—her mind immediately went back to a famous incident on Nantucket from a few years before, when a notable actor at the height of his career had made the mistake of propositioning a busboy at a local restaurant. The object of his affection was underage. There were texts. And a lawsuit. And the star's career had abruptly tanked, amid a fanfare of lawsuits and negative press coverage.

"Has his wife attempted to reach him?" she asked.

"She has." Struna's voice dropped. "Yesterday, he never picked up. Today, the calls go straight to voice mail."

Because his battery has died, Merry thought.

"If you or your guest would like to file a Missing Person's Report," she said carefully, "you're welcome to stop by the station. That's off the Fairgrounds road, as I'm sure you know."

Struna cleared his throat. "Look—I'll be honest. Carly's really worked up, but trying to hide it from her cast and crew. She has a lot riding on this production, and she doesn't want to upset anybody or anything. If she files a report, it could leak to the press.

I'm trying to help. She's . . . a very good and very old friend. Isn't there something you can do? On an informal basis?"

Merry hesitated. "Where and when was the gentleman last seen?"

"At the Field Station. Folger's Marsh. Around one-thirty yesterday afternoon. Carly tried to ask casually last night at dinner whether anybody else had seen him leave, but it was hard to pin people down without giving everyone an explanation for why she was asking."

"This morning, however, her husband's absence must be obvious."

"Everybody is back out at the Marsh, filming again today. Vic—Mr. Sonnenfeld—wouldn't normally be there. So I'm betting nobody's noticed. But Carly's nervous. Keeps texting me to see if her husband has turned up. Hence my call."

"I understand," Merry said. "But there's not much I can do until you file a report. Private citizens resent being tracked by the police if they're minding their own business, off on their own adventures. There has to be an official reason for individual surveillance."

"Oh, believe me, I know," Struna said. There was a slight pause on the line. "By talking to you, I was probably just trying to make myself feel better."

"If he's not back by tonight, file a report."

"We will. Thank you."

17 | Stronghold, Sunday afternoon

"SHE MANAGED TO screw up our lives to the last, didn't she?" Janet said. "Typical."

Ron shoved his fingers through his hair. He looked distracted, which was unusual, and angry, which was not. Janet suspected the latter emotion was divided equally between his ex-wife and his son. As it had been for the past twenty years.

"I cannot believe Ance went behind my back." Ron paced across the worn rag rug that covered the living room's mahogany floor. "He's been communicating with that woman for a year! And never told me!"

Janet tried to look sympathetic. But most of her attention was elsewhere, running through her schedule for the remainder of the day and the adjustments that would have to be made. Micheline was making calls and sending out emails now, informing various interlocuters of the secretary's unavoidable delay on family business; Janet figured she could spare fifteen minutes to soothe her husband's fury.

"Incredibly selfish," she offered. "Ansel has never given a flying fuck for anyone's feelings but his own. You simply can't trust him. Did the cop say when we'd be cleared to leave?"

"He wants to ask us questions. Take *statements*. I told him, 'No way, Bud! I want to talk to your *superior*.'"

Janet frowned. "This has nothing to do with us, Ron. What

can we possibly contribute to an investigation? We didn't even know Mary Alice was on the island."

"But Ansel found her body."

If the press got hold of this . . .

Ron turned to stare at Janet in frustration. "And that's another thing! She was in that house in violation of *the law*. She was trespassing. *Squatting*. And now it's *our* fault she's dead?"

"It's not. Our fault, I mean. *Obviously*," Janet said. She rose from the faded chintz club chair where she'd been sitting near the hearth—no fire in it, because they were supposed to be leaving the island. Should already have left, in fact. "I'll tell Mick to call the police. Pull rank. Explain how impossible this is."

"You can try," Ron retorted. "I called the chief's direct line and got voice mail. She's some woman. Never heard of her."

Janet paused in midstride and glanced at him. "What does being a *woman* have to do with it, Ron?"

"Oh, you know—I mean . . ." He waggled his fingers dismissively. "Out here in the middle of nowhere. She *can't* be that experienced. Or very senior. The police probably park people on the beach who can't make it anywhere else."

"What's her name?" Janet asked. She was remembering something suddenly, an afternoon from a vanished summer, the cries of children drifting down from Jetties, and Granny Brimhold handing someone a glass of iced tea. Tall and genial and kind, with his hand resting on Janet's shoulder. She could only have been, what? Eight? Seven? . . . *so grateful to you, Chief Folger. Janet knows she's not supposed to ride her bicycle alone* . . .

She had been lost. Turned around in the bewildering maze of streets that ran off Centre, ending up somewhere off Mill Hill and the wide, unfamiliar expanse of Quaker Road. She had intended to bike out to her friend Mary Alice's house, only she hadn't known the way. She was terrified and pedaling doggedly on, far from Brant Point, and although she was thirsty and her legs were tired, she knew that she must never, ever, ask a *stranger* for help or she'd never see her grandmother again. Afraid to admit that she was in trouble. She would be spanked if she didn't get home soon . . .

And then the car had pulled up slowly alongside her, and the gentle voice had asked her name . . .

"Meredith Folger," Ron said.

"Ah." Janet resumed her walk to the living room door. "Never mind Micheline. I'll call *the woman* myself."

ANSEL SAW THE official SUV arrive through his bedroom dormer window, which overlooked the front courtyard of the house. He had retreated upstairs once the detective, Howie Seitz, had left, but not before his father had grabbed him by the shoulder and shouted, "What in the *hell* were you thinking?"

"That I wanted to know my mother," Ansel had retorted. "What were *you* thinking when you told me she was dead?"

His father had paused in mid-tirade, his mouth slack and hanging open. "I was thinking of *you*," he sputtered. "Of your well-being, as a three-year-old abandoned by an addict. She walked away from us, Ance. *She walked away.* And when I saw the damage she'd done to both our lives, I determined she was never coming back."

"That's not quite what she told me."

Your father gave me an ultimatum, Mary Alice had said yesterday, sinking into her armchair. *He'd pay for me to go to rehab, give myself a chance to get clean and have a new start at life—if I gave up all custody of you.*

Or I could go to prison.

He had people willing to testify that I was dealing cocaine.

Were you? Ance had asked.

She had smiled wistfully. *Oh, yes. Yes, Ansel, I was.*

She hadn't need to explain anything more. He knew, from

everything he'd observed about her remarkable life, that Mary Alice would have died in prison as swiftly as a caged wild bird.

"You *lied*," he said to Ron furiously, now. "For most of my life. You raised me in a *lie*." Ansel turned his back on his father and walked to the stairs. "No wonder I've been medicating myself for years."

"Don't blame that on *me*, buddy!" Irate, his father charged after him. "I did everything humanly possible to keep you on the straight and narrow! It's not my fault you have lousy genes. None of this came from *my* side of the family."

Ansel stopped dead, refusing to look at the man behind him. "I hope that makes you happy, Dad. Being better than everyone else. I just want you to know that I felt more at home in an hour with Mary Alice than I've ever felt in twenty years with you."

"Oh, *fine*," Ron said. "Play the Mommy card. After everything I've given you. I'm done with you, Ansel. You hear me? I'm *done*."

WHEN HE TURNED once more into the rutted drive leading to Stella Maris, bare twigs scratching the sides of his Toyota as he bucketed through the bayberry and rugosa, Howie spied another car pulled up before the front of the house. A battered and ancient Jeep Wrangler in olive Army green. It belonged to the Medical Examiner on call today, John Fairborn. The Doc was a legend on Nantucket, a throwback to a less conventional time, a bit of a renegade. Howie would rather have worked with Summer Hughes, a Cottage Hospital doc who traded medical examiner duties with Fairborn, but on Stroll Weekend, he'd take what he could get.

Confronted with the hauteur of Official Washington and an immoveable wooden gate he could arguably have busted through with his Japanese front end, Howie had decided the better part of valor lay in retreat. He'd clapped Ansel MacKay on the back and left the secretary of state to Meredith Folger's tender mercies. He'd phoned in a précis of the unexplained death to the chief's voice mail, promised a full report via email, and had driven immediately back out the Polpis road.

Questioning bigwigs could wait; he had a scene to investigate. This was his first Suspicious Death as a police detective, and Howie was alive enough to his prospects for career advancement to take that very seriously indeed.

Two images cycled through his mind: the video Ansel MacKay had shown him, of Mary Alice's palm extended to the gentle and trusting birds; and her sightless eyes, staring at a perfectly clear Nantucket winter sky.

"Doctor John," Howie called as he walked around the back end of Stella Maris. "What can you tell me, my friend?"

"Howie!"

The Doc shambled forward, clad in a white Tyvek evidence collection jumpsuit, and ducked under the yellow police barrier tape. He met Howie near the railing of the kitchen porch, and they stood there, three feet apart, conscious not to cross-contaminate.

"This is your first scene as detective, isn't it?" Fairborn asked.

Howie ducked his head in admission.

"And you're thinking—"

Fairborn paused. Howie realized the medical examiner was conducting a bit of field training.

"Not suicide, since there's no weapon at the scene," he said, to humor him. "Has Candy found a gun, by the way?"

"Not that she'll admit," Fairborn said.

Howie's eyes strayed to the corpse, which was still lying as he'd first seen it, arms flung wide and visage pointed at the sky. He had to think of Mary Alice in official terms—the Corpse, the Victim, the Deceased—in order to do his job. Thinking of her as Ansel's mom was too much.

"So she was clearly killed by persons unknown, and the weapon is not yet located," Howie recited. "The wound is from a shotgun shell. That means one of two things: Accidental discharge of a hunting rifle, possibly by someone stalking a deer; or a deliberate murder, with a similar weapon."

"And how would we distinguish between the two?" Fairborn asked.

Howie thought for a moment. "If the Victim was shot by a deer hunter, the hunter must have mistaken her movements for wildlife. Which suggests the hunter fired from a distance."

"Nice if you can get it," the ME observed, "but not possible in this case, with this tight a dispersal pattern."

"Explain," Howie said.

"You don't hunt, do you?"

He shook his head.

Fairborn's wrinkled countenance jack-knifed in a grin. His canines, Howie noticed, were as sharp and pointed as a vampire's. "The farther you fire a shotgun from your target, the less likely you are to hit anything, because the pellets—in this case, buckshot—scatter pretty widely. Effective range for penetration is between twenty-five and fifty yards. That's usually the distance a deer hunter has from his target."

"Makes sense."

Fairborn took Howie's elbow and led him over to the corpse. "See how tight that wound pattern is here? I pulled a pellet from the chest—it looks like pretty standard #00 buckshot to me— but most of the pellets penetrated the entire torso."

Howie swallowed. "So you're saying she was shot at pretty close range."

"Hell, yeah. There's powder stipple on her sweatshirt if you look past the blood. I'd say she was shot from within three feet." Fairborn's tone was smug; he believed he held all the knowledge the police needed, for every crime imaginable.

Point-blank range. Howie shuddered involuntarily.

"She saw the trigger pulled," Fairborn declared.

"You've got a murder on your hands, Seitz."

MERRY WAITED RESIGNEDLY while the security agents ran her driver's license through their database for possible criminal violations, her Nantucket Police vehicle idling in front of the closed barrier on Hulbert Ave. She could have told the DSS guys that as a Town of Nantucket official who had coordinated on the secretary of state's security needs prior to this Stroll visit, not to mention the president's before that, her background checks had already been run. She could have added that her presence had been requested by the secretary of state herself, on a personal phone call patched through by Hanameel in Dispatch. But she understood protocols, and the need individuals felt to check off all the boxes, particularly when local jurisdictions ran afoul of federal ones; so she said nothing, and let the Diplomatic Security Service do their jobs. She figured she was only losing ten minutes, give or take, either way.

Frank walked out of the makeshift guardhouse—it looked hastily erected to Merry, like a toy soldier's shelter—and returned her license and badge through her open car window.

"Pull through," he said; the wooden guardrail rose.

She drove into the courtyard and turned off her car.

It was impossible not to admire Stronghold, the home Janet Brimhold MacKay had inherited. Merry was well-enough-versed in island history to understand that she had set foot on Old Money. The Brimholds were Brahmin Boston, not quite the Lowells and Cabots, but close enough. Generations had ruled Massachusetts in a way that Folgers only dreamed of. Stronghold, the house, was a Hulbert Ave. fixture, handed down in unbroken line since the 1880s, when it was built.

It was a rambling shingle-style house of no particular

architectural distinction, fronting on the sheltered rim of sand wedged between the stone harbor jetty and Brant Point. An eight-foot-tall hedge screened the home from the street, and white-painted latticework supported the roses that climbed its front walls. There was no ostentation, no obvious éclat. *Unassuming*, most observers would label it. Yet the location was worth a fortune and the house was beyond the reach of most humans on the planet. That was the magic of Nantucket beachfront. It was, as the credit card ads liked to say, *Priceless*.

Her cell phone vibrated.

"Seitz. I'm at the secretary of state's house. What do you have for me?"

"Mary Alice Fillmore was murdered," Howie said. "Fairborn found powder marks around the entry wounds. She was shot at point-blank range. Her killer could not have mistaken her for a deer."

There was a silence between them for an instant.

"And I'm about to talk to her ex-husband," Merry articulated, "who has a lot invested in keeping scandal at bay."

"As does his second wife," Seitz observed. "And the victim's son found her body."

"So the whole family's involved. Better and better," Merry said.

She stared through her windshield at Stronghold's mild-looking front entry: A six-paneled door, no sidelights, with a shingled dormer shielding it from the elements. An exuberant wreath of winter conifer greens, beach heather, scallop shells and red velvet bows dangled from the lintel. The Norway spruce to the left of the door was garlanded with white lights, unlit at this hour of the morning. She wondered idly if the secretary of state had inherited a trust from her grandmother to provide for the house's maintenance, or if that came out of taxpayers' pockets. She assumed a trust; these kinds of people always had one.

It was the trust or an LLC that transferred the properties, usually for the token price of a dollar, when death evicted one generation in favor of another.

"Seitz," she said. "When you're finished at the scene, meet me back at the station for a conference. Got it?"

"Yeah, Mer," he said. "Thanks. Glad you're on it."

Howie, Merry reflected as she clicked off her phone and grabbed a face mask, was one of the few people left who still called her by something other than her title.

JANET BRIMHOLD MACKAY received Nantucket's chief of police in her large living room, which ran from the front of the house straight back to the water, the harbor curling gently on her beach.

She was dressed in what must be, for the secretary of state, casual clothes: slate gray wool trousers, a V-neck sweater in a lighter gray shade, and low-heeled pumps. A surgical mask covered her nose and mouth, and there were pearls at her throat, which was starting to evidence her age. She had tucked unruly brown hair behind her ears. Her visible makeup was of the slapdash sort that suggested concern for her looks took up only minimal headspace.

Merry had searched the woman's vital statistics quickly on her phone after the patched-in call, and knew the secretary was fifty-four years old. She also learned that Janet was a political moderate (to Merry, this suggested calculation and prudence rather than passion or conviction), and had received only lukewarm praise for her performance thus far. It was the most attention Merry had paid to national affairs since the last election. Merry was supposed to address Janet as "Madam Secretary."

Merry had pulled up what she could find on the spouse and stepson, too. The latter was absent from the living room, but the former, also masked, stood by the fireplace that punctuated

the long outer wall of the house. Ron MacKay, political consultant, met his wife when he took over her first Senate campaign.
He was sixty-one, his dark hair neither thinning nor grayed.
Inside-the-Beltway sources described him as disciplined, razor-
sharp, meticulous in his attention to detail. A careful man
who betrayed very little emotion when he laid down his poker
stakes.

All in all, Merry thought, that was a perfect skill set for
murder.

Neither of the MacKays had the slightest whiff of a police
record, although Janet had been cited for speeding years ago.
Merry suspected she'd enjoyed the services of a paid chauffeur
ever since.

"Chief Folger," the secretary said, rising from the chintz club
chair where she'd tidily arranged herself. "Thank you for answering my call."

The language rang falsely epic, as though Meredith was being
sent into battle.

"Thank you for answering my questions," Merry returned.

The secretary held up her right fist, mute welcome in the pandemic era; Merry bumped it gingerly.

"I'll try to be as efficient as possible. I know you're pressed for
time."

"Finally, someone who gets it." Ron stepped away from the
mantle.

"My husband, Ron MacKay," Janet said.

Merry nodded. "Sir. It was your son, Ansel, who found the
Deceased, I'm told?"

He spread his arms wide in exasperation. "We're working
from the same information, Ms. Folger. If your source was that
poor guy who ran Ance back to the house, God knows what the
true facts are."

"That's what I'm here to establish." Merry set down her tote bag and drew out her laptop. If MacKay intended to antagonize her, she was determined not to reward him.

"Please—sit down." Janet resumed her seat.

Ron remained standing.

Merry glanced around the room and drew forth a hard-backed side chair, placing it ten feet from the secretary.

"Are you any relation to the Chief Folger who ran the force when I was a girl?" Janet asked, her voice warm.

Merry met her gaze as she settled herself. "Both my grandfather and father have served in the post."

"This would have been—oh, twenty or thirty years ago, at least."

At least, Merry thought with amusement. If Janet had been a girl, more like forty. "Then you probably met my grandfather. May I ask, Madam Secretary, when you arrived on Nantucket?"

"Thursday afternoon," she said. "We just came for Stroll. A bit of . . . family time."

Merry would solicit the official flight records of the government jet later. "How many people traveled with you?"

"Oh . . ." Janet looked around vaguely.

"Eight," Ron MacKay said. "The three of us—the secretary, my son, and myself—Janet's chief of staff, Micheline Tran; her deputy, Josh Stein; and three members of the Diplomatic Security Staff. Frank Delgado, agent-in-charge; Ian Swift, and Sasha Rubin."

Succinct and precise. As scripted.

"There's a DSS person at the front gate at all times?"

Ron's eyebrows rose. "I'm impressed, Ms. Folger. Most people mistake the DSS for Secret Service."

"I was informed of the difference when the Service cleared me, as police chief, to liaise on preparations for your visit," Merry said. So much for the guy's condescension. "Individual movements in and out of this household are therefore logged?"

"Yes." Again, from Ron.

"I'll need those timesheets later."

"Is this really necessary?" he shot back. "There's no connection whatsoever between this household and the death you're investigating. Your dedication is appreciated, Ms. Folger, but it's completely misplaced. We have no idea why that woman died, and nothing to do with her death. So if you could get this over with, and let us board our plane back to DC, the secretary and I would be *deeply grateful*."

The last two words dripped with acid; it was clear Ron MacKay felt contempt, not gratitude.

Merry ignored him. Fixing her gaze on Janet Brimhold MacKay, she said, "Someone killed Mary Alice Fillmore this morning at a house off Polpis Road, owned, according to local title records, by your husband, Ronald Graham MacKay. The victim is Mr. MacKay's former wife, whom he divorced twenty years ago."

"I know who Mary Alice is," she said. "In fact, we were friends once, long ago. We both grew up here during the summers, and met at the yacht club. Her father owned a boat in the Rainbow fleet. She let me sail it once, and I tipped it over. Mary Alice got the boat righted while I screamed—she was that sort of person."

It was a long and unexpected speech. Ron MacKay looked as though he felt a hundred years old; Merry was tempted to ask which wife had introduced him to the other.

"Did you know Mary Alice was on the island, Madam Secretary?" Merry asked.

Janet shook her head. "I haven't spoken to her since we were both about seventeen."

"Where were you this morning?"

"Here, in the house, with my staff," she said. "There was breakfast, the usual intel briefing afterward, and an Undersecretaries' video teleconference after that."

"Who makes breakfast?"

Janet smiled, and glanced at her husband. "The ninth member of the household. Miranda Stephenson, my housekeeper. Randi's always been a part of Stronghold. You may know her as a painter in oils—she's a backbone of the Artists Association. But she's also a great cook."

Merry had heard the name; and as always when a member of the AAN—the Artists Association of Nantucket—came up, she felt a flare of angst. Her mother, long gone but never quite forgotten, had been a painter.

She made a mental note to crosscheck everything the MacKays said with Miranda Stephenson. The woman might owe the Brimhold family decades of loyalty, but she was unrelated to Washington, and that might encourage her to talk.

"You never left the house?" she asked.

"I did not," Janet said.

"I hope you got to enjoy *something* of Stroll."

"Oh, I mean, I never left *today*," the secretary clarified. "I was out and about on Main Street yesterday. Saw Santa arrive. It's wonderful to be back. The island is so festive this time of year!"

Is it? "I'll need to verify this morning's movements with the staff in question," Merry said. "Your verification will also serve as theirs, of course."

"I understand." Janet nodded regally. "I should say that I have a body person—Sasha Rubin—who is almost always with me. I asked her to step away during this interview, because I assumed it was my husband's private business, not a governmental matter."

"Correct." Merry's fingers paused, and her gaze drifted to Ron MacKay. "And you, Mr. MacKay. Where were you this morning?"

He hesitated, wordless for the first time since Meredith had entered Stronghold. Of all questions, this ought to have been the one he anticipated, Merry thought; and his cluelessness surprised her.

He ran the fingers of his right hand through his hair. "Jesus. It's all a blur. I feel like everything has been upended since—"

"Since you heard about the death of your wife?" Merry said.

"Ex-wife."

"Right," she amended. "My bad."

She stared at him benignly.

His arm dropped to his side. "I knew nothing about Mary Alice being on Nantucket until Ansel—my son—told me this morning. And that cop, by the way, was useless!"

"Detective," Merry amended. "Detective Seitz."

"Whatever." Ron glanced away, out toward the ocean. "He just . . . sat out at the gate like the Grim Reaper, demanding to come in and ask questions. With Ansel beside him. 'A woman's dead,' he said, 'and your son found her.' I mean, what the hell happened?"

"Your son went to see his mother at roughly eight-thirty this morning. He hailed a rideshare, and texted Ms. Fillmore, who responded. We have time and date stamps on both texts to verify this."

"I can't believe Ance hid her from us," Ron muttered.

"His rideshare app shows that he was dropped off at the end of the house's driveway at eight-fifty-three," Merry continued. "According to Ansel's statement, taken down by Detective Seitz and signed by Ansel at ten-eighteen this morning, your son walked up the drive, intending to knock on the back door. When he reached the backyard, however, he found Mary Alice lying near the northern perimeter of the yard, on her back, dead. She had been shot at close range by a shotgun, armed in all likelihood with buckshot."

"Surprised it didn't happen years ago."

MacKay still stared out at the sea. It was difficult to read his expression above his mask.

"Really?" Merry studied the man. "And why is that?"

"Mary Alice was a cocaine addict. Everyone she knew was either using or dealing. I've been expecting her to die for the past two decades."

"We've found no drugs in Stella Maris," Merry said.

"Keep looking."

"Okay." She paused, her eyes shifting to Janet Brimhold MacKay. The woman's expression was concerned and her hands were clenched in her lap. Because her husband's behavior was unusual? Or because he was having difficulty controlling it?

"From Ansel's message and app notifications," Merry went on, "we believe your ex-wife died between the time she texted your son and the time he found her body at her house."

"It's *my* house, Ms. Folger, not hers. She lost it in the divorce."

Merry's eyes flicked to MacKay's face. "Really? Ansel told Detective Seitz it had been in his mother's family for generations."

He shrugged. "Not for the past twenty years, it hasn't."

"I see. Ansel suggested Mary Alice had been living at Stella Maris for the past two years or so. Since the start of the pandemic, at least. Did you tell her she could live there, Mr. MacKay?"

"She was expressly forbidden by court order to come within five hundred feet of the place."

"So you would say . . ." Merry hesitated. "Her presence was unauthorized."

"Damn right."

"I understand all utilities were shut off at the property. And that it appears to be in some disrepair." She let the statements hang between them, interested in MacKay's reaction.

He laughed abruptly, the sound muffled by the surgical mask. "I'm surprised the place hasn't fallen down around her!"

"Was that your intention? For the house to collapse?"

"I'd crack open a bottle of champagne at the news, Ms. Folger."

This made very little sense. Island real estate was a gold mine; allowing a place to deliberately decay was foolishness.

"Mr. MacKay," she persisted. "Tell me about your morning."

"I got up as I always do around six A.M. Made a pot of coffee. I caught up on email, read the digital edition of the *Washington Post*, *The Wall Street Journal*, the *CipherBrief*, *The Hill*, and *The New York Times*; then I showered, dressed, and drove into town."

Drove, from Brant Point to Main. Surprising, given that the heart of Nantucket was only a short walk away. But perhaps off-islanders got in the habit of driving everywhere.

"Were you alone?"

"Yes." At last, he turned to face Meredith.

"What time would this have been?"

Again he shrugged. "While Janet had her intel briefing."

"About eight A.M.," the secretary supplied. "We did it earlier today because of the travel plans."

"I see." Merry typed as she listened. "And what did you do in town, sir?"

"Parked and walked around town, like everyone else during Stroll Weekend."

"Around?"

He sighed audibly. "I went up Broad, across Centre—I like to look at the Congregational Church—and over to Fair Street. Walked all the way out to Eagle Lane and came back Pine. It was a nice morning. Everyone's window boxes are decorated for Christmas. It was good to have time alone."

"Did you stop anywhere? Talk to anybody?"

He shook his head.

"And what time did you return to this house?"

"*Exactly*? I have no idea."

"If you had to guess?" Merry said patiently.

"Probably . . . nine or so? I was aware of packing, and the plane flight ahead."

"I see." So his movements were completely unverifiable. The only times Merry could corroborate were his exit and return to Stronghold—which the DSS officer at the gate would have noted.

Merry thought quickly. MacKay could easily have skipped town and driven straight out the Polpis road to kill his ex-wife. A house as old as Stronghold might have a shotgun stored in its attic or garage. He could have wiped it clean of fingerprints and replaced it, or ditched the gun somewhere on the moors during his ride home.

Were there tire tread marks on Stella Maris's drive? It had rained Thursday night, but it was now Sunday . . . Would it be possible to compare any marks at this late date with the tires of the car MacKay had driven?

Questions, Merry thought, for Seitz.

She asked MacKay, "When did you last communicate with Mary Alice Fillmore?"

"The day the judge granted my decree of divorce."

"She had no share in the custody of your son?"

"None."

"And no alimony?"

He shook his head. "She was lucky to get off scot-free. I took her precious house and all her unsettled debts. I walked away and never looked back. And by God, I made sure my son walked with me."

So much anger and bitterness. Deep, Merry thought; corrosive, and unresolved.

"Thank you for your time." She closed her laptop and rose from her chair. "Madam Secretary, I appreciate your time as well. I'd like to speak to Ansel now."

"Oh, my *God*," Ron MacKay burst out. "The kid already signed a statement! What more could you possibly need? Ance isn't the one who killed her. He doesn't own a gun."

"Do you, Mr. MacKay?" Merry asked.

"Of *course* I don't. You'll be asking if Janet packs an AR-15 next!"

"Oh, Ron." Janet MacKay sprang up from her chair and went to her husband. "Calm down, darling. Chief Folger is only doing her job."

"She'd be doing it a hell of a lot better if she were out on the Polpis road, not wasting our time here!" he retorted.

Either Mary Alice Fillmore's death has freaked him out, Merry thought, *or he fears for his son.*

She would know better when she interviewed Ansel.

BUT WHEN RON MacKay called up the steps to his son's bedroom, Ansel failed to answer. Further inspection revealed his bedroom to be empty. While Meredith had distracted his father and stepmother, Ansel had walked out of the house.

It was anybody's guess, now, where he'd gone.

18 | Ingrid's Gift, Sunday Afternoon

"I FOUND MY mom, too," Winter said matter-of-factly.

She was walking beside Ansel along the clipped swath of lawn that led through semi-feral mounds of rugosa and bay-berry to Polpis Harbor. They had their hands in their jacket pockets and their eyes were trained on the dead grass at their feet, but by mutual and completely silent agreement they were avoiding the indoors and everyone connected to *The Hopeless* production.

This time, Ansel had taken the free shuttle bus from down-town, bailing in front of the arched barn entrance to Ingrid's Gift. The guard at the gate had no intention of allowing him through, but he'd texted Winter and she'd come down the drive at a run.

"I'll be responsible for him, Blake," she'd said crisply, and slid her arm through Ance's as they turned back up the drive. "Sorry I'm surrounded by dicks," she said. "Tell me what happened to your mother."

"Someone killed her. With a shotgun."

"Oh, my God," Winter said. She had stopped short on the drive, staring at him, her beautiful eyes wide with shock. "Not Mary Alice! Why would someone do that?"

Ansel shrugged in bewilderment. "I don't think she even knew anybody here."

"And she was *so* amazing!" Winter pressed her hands against her cheeks, cradling her own face in disbelief. "The pictures she took! No one could possibly want to hurt her."

Except my dad, he thought, but did not say. *Except my dad.*

Winter glanced over at him apprehensively. "But you didn't really know her, did you?"

"No," he agreed. "I didn't know at her all."

That was when they'd turned and walked resolutely toward the water, both of them thinking.

He was glad she didn't offer the stupid things people feel obliged to say in the face of violent loss. She seemed to take it in stride that horrible things happened all the time, and it was enough to survive them.

The grass path ended and the dock came into view. It was a beautiful day, Ansel realized, the sky cloudless and deep blue, the water of the harbor still as glass. Cold and bright, the very best of an island December.

He'd found Mary Alice too late. In so many ways.

"She was feeding the birds," he said.

"From her hand?"

He nodded.

Winter drew a quick breath. "I watched those videos on her Insta last night. They're amazing. The way the birds trust her . . . the way they interact . . . She was *so cool,* Ance. Whatever happened."

"I know."

"I was going to go look for her today, watch her photograph. I was totally fan-girling about Mary Alice to anyone who would listen last night."

They ignored the boathouse and walked straight out the dock, their footfalls resounding hollowly on the boards.

"She didn't kill *herself,* did she?" Winter asked.

"No." He hadn't even thought of that as a possibility. But then it hit him: "There was no gun by her body. I guess it could have been an accident . . . ? And the person panicked? Ran off without reporting it?"

"Maybe."

They reached the end of the dock and stood there an instant, heads turning slowly to survey the outcrops of marsh and sand punctuating the water. Beyond the narrow channel of Polpis Harbor, the barrier beach of Coatue looked almost close enough to touch. Then Winter sat down on the dock and let her legs dangle over the water. She was wearing black leggings embroidered with enormous scrolls of lipstick-colored flowers and a pair of ankle boots with sheepskin cuffs, her dark hair spilling over her shoulders. She had very little makeup on today and she looked much more approachable. Young.

"Thanks for letting me bother you," Ansel said. "I couldn't stay in the house any longer. I had to talk to somebody."

"Not your dad?"

He shook his head. "He's really pissed."

"That somebody killed your mom?"

Ansel laughed. "God, no. That I got him *involved*. I'm not supposed to even know she existed."

"I'm sorry, that's just so fucked up."

"Yep. It is." He hesitated, then said, "What did you mean when you said you found your mother, too?"

"When she killed herself."

"I . . . didn't realize."

Winter glanced at him sidelong. "You mean, you didn't do an internet search on my entire life history the minute after I met you?"

"Well . . . not an *exhaustive* one. I saw the paparazzi and the bikini shots, but other than that . . ."

Winter choked a little in her throat, as though she were swallowing a laugh. "Thank you for being honest."

"What happened?"

She shifted her shoulders slightly, then knotted her fingers in the sleeves of her jacket. It was black quilted silk, probably not warm enough for the East Coast in winter, Ansel thought. He resisted the impulse to put his arm around her.

"She had a drinking problem. Actually, more than a problem. It was really, really bad. She used to knock back handle after handle until she hit blackout, then wander around the house or the barn or, like, the entirety of Santa Monica, totally awake but staggering and unable to remember a thing the next day. A couple of times she took the car out in that state. Until my dad started hiding the keys whenever he had to leave the house."

"I met people like that in rehab. Did she ever go?"

Winter shook her head. "It terrified her. I think she was afraid she'd never come back."

Ansel sighed. "Me, too, but I didn't have a choice. I was still a minor when my dad intervened. He got to do what he liked."

"That's what happened to me."

"But yours wasn't substance abuse."

"Unless the substance is food." Winter's smile was slightly twisted. "Or my own body. I've abused that enough, lemme tell you."

Ansel considered it; how a person spun off-balance might turn, in desperation, to rules and rituals so disciplined they bordered on insanity. His father would understand that.

"How did your dad deal with it?" he asked curiously. "The drinking, I mean, and . . . her death?"

"I'm not sure he has." Winter's right leg swung back and forth, carving the space between the water and the dock. "He really loved my mother. Even when I was a little kid I knew that—the two of them floated in this charmed bubble, you know? Totally jonesed on each other. Which, believe me, is *not* Hollywood. Until something happened."

"What was that?"

Winter lifted her hands in a gesture of futility. "I have no idea. And my father has never said. Maybe *he* doesn't know. It's like this massive sinkhole opened in her life and alcohol filled it. She went from blissed-out to haunted. Things were never the same."

"Trauma can do that," Ansel said. "There must have been trauma."

"I hope so." Winter snorted. "Because if it wasn't that, she was just batshit crazy, and I've inherited her genes! I'm sure my dad thinks so."

"I'm sure he doesn't," Ansel said automatically.

Her sense of guilt was too much like his own.

"He went from worrying about Mom to worrying about me," she continued. "Chris Candler's an international idol, Ance, but the guy can't catch a break. I've decided to change that."

"What do you mean?"

"It's time to let him go. Let him be happy and live his own life again. Which means I'm going to have to live mine."

Ansel nodded. It was the same conclusion he'd been working toward, himself. He'd been tentative since rehab, figuring out a new set of rules. His parents wanted him to get his degree; he wanted to paint. The pandemic had made it easy to avoid going back to college, all that remote learning. He realized he'd been acting like Mary Alice: hiding in plain sight, concentrating on what only he could see. She used a lens to hyperfocus; he used a brush. Both of them missed what went on outside their careful frames. That felt safe to Ansel. But it wasn't a life.

"What are you going to do?" he asked Winter.

"Move to Normandy and train horses," she said unexpectedly.

"No way." Ansel's eyes widened. "You could do that?"

"I've spent most of my life learning how. I was a top amateur show jumper in every age group—until I decided to stop eating."

"Do you have pictures?"

She smiled a little sadly and fished out her phone. "Oh, sure. This is Ardennes—my competition horse."

The photograph she offered him was a revelation. Not just of the massive, muscled creature vaulting over a five-foot high fence, but of the taut, disciplined figure holding the reins. Winter, as he'd never seen her: poised above the saddle, leaning forward into challenge and risk. Her hair was hidden beneath an equestrian helmet, her lips compressed, her gaze focused between her horse's ears. The frailty Ansel usually sensed in her was completely absent; she was a coiled steel spring, as powerful as the animal she commanded.

"How beautiful," he whispered.

"Yeah, he's a cutie," Winter said fondly.

Ansel hadn't been talking about the horse. "Why Normandy?" he asked.

"Some of the best show jumpers in the world train in France. I don't want to compete anymore, but I'd love to work in a good equine athlete program. The family that bred Ardennes have a spot open. They let me know."

"That's amazing," Ansel said. "I'm happy for you. Have you told your dad?"

"Not yet. I'm going to tell him when this shoot is over." Again, that wobbly smile. "He'll worry. He thinks every time he lets me out of his sight, I relapse."

So Chris Candler was hyperfocused, too.

"Is that why somebody tails you all the time?"

"Laura? The woman needs to find a new job. She's not even *vegan*."

Speaking of Laura, she was nowhere in sight. Ansel looked around. They appeared to be alone in Ingrid's Gift; the compound's numerous buildings looked completely unoccupied. "Are they out filming today?"

"Sure. Time is money, in this world. You don't take Sundays off."

It seemed incredible to him, that other people's lives had gone on like normal, as though Mary Alice Fillmore had never lived or died.

He thrust himself to his feet. "Thanks for talking. You helped."

Winter stood up and opened her arms. "Hug?"

He reached for her, aware that the gesture was one of sympathy and friendship, not seduction. They clasped briefly; he could feel all her bones through her layers of clothing. He could feel her heartbeat, too, and the breath as it entered and left her body, and for reasons he could not name this simple proof of life brought tears to his eyes.

"Are you allowed to leave?" she asked. "—Nantucket, I mean?"

"I don't know." He hadn't thought about logistics or the police since he'd left Brant Point. But his phone had been vibrating continuously in his pocket. "Either way, I'm sure my dad's furious. I didn't tell him I was leaving the house."

"You'd better get back."

"I will. But I have to do something first. Come with me?"

19 | Stella Maris, Sunday Afternoon

"THERE'S NO EVIDENCE of illicit drug use." Howie led Meredith Folger through the hallway from Mary Alice Fillmore's kitchen to the front door. The interior of this side of Stella Maris was dim and aqueous with filtered gray light; the front windows of the house were still boarded over. The woman who'd repossessed the property had opened up only the back windows that faced toward the sea.

Which suggested, Merry thought, that Mary Alice Fillmore had not expected a frontal assault. She was not on high alert, prepared for mortal threat.

On either side of the front hall were rooms: one for living, with faded and sagging curtains, the other for dining. Plaster had fallen from the ceilings into each, powdering the wood floors with chalky dust; there was a strong smell of mildew. Both rooms looked desolate and freezing.

"She was only using part of the house," Howie said.

"The kitchen?"

"And the main bedroom. She was flushing the toilet with seawater."

"Yikes."

Merry followed him up the creaking stairs, which were high, narrow, and covered with a threadbare rag runner tacked to the risers. Stella Maris reminded her of so many houses she'd known as a child. It was a Nantucket classic, from the unconsidered

nonchalance of its haphazard additions to the low ceilings that
minimized the need for heat and emphasized snugness. It had
a central chimney and an off-center door. It probably dated,
like her husband Peter's house on Cliff Road, from the early
decades of the 19th century, but this was the home of a Quaker
sheep farmer, sturdy and plain, not the trophy Greek Revival
of a wealthy sea captain. She could feel the long succession of
women who'd grasped the banister over hundreds of years in the
satin of the oak beneath her palm.

"The roof leaks," Howie said briefly.

Damage was obvious upstairs, where the cold was penetrat-
ing. In the front bedroom, Merry could see through the ceiling
to the attic, and through the attic roof to the blue sky above.
The floorboards in this room were buckled and heaving where
snow and rain had warped the wood. Yellow patches of damp
discolored the fabrics and the 1950s-era wallpaper of pink rambling roses.

Merry wrinkled her nose. "This is so sad. Ron MacKay deliberately took this house from his wife and let it fall to pieces."

"Seriously? This part of Polpis—hell, any part of Polpis—is
worth a mint."

"No kidding. I get the feeling he did it for revenge."

Howie snorted. "Must have money to burn, then."

Merry followed his retreating back down the upper hall to the
room Mary Alice had occupied.

It was large, running the entire width of the house's rear,
with broad windows overlooking the marshland surrounding
Polpis Harbor. The vista was breathtaking on such a brilliant
day, and must have compensated the woman who'd lived here
for the difficulties of squatting in a derelict house. A four-poster
bed was neatly made up with an old, pieced quilt, and several
books sat on a neighboring table, beside an oil lamp with a
glass hurricane of a kind Merry remembered her grandmother

Sylvie lighting during nor'easters. A box of matches completed the still life.

A desk had been tucked under a dormer, companionably sheltered by the slope of the roof. This was covered with camera equipment, and as she glanced at it, Merry drew a sudden, gasping, breath.

"Somebody's trashed it!"

"Yep," Howie agreed. "Whoever shot her, I'm thinking. Must have killed her outside, then come upstairs to look for something."

Two cameras, both Nikons, were lying on the floor. They had been savagely battered with a heavy object—probably one of the tripods lying nearby, Merry thought. Canisters of 35 millimeter Fujichrome film were strewn around the desk, and spools of something Merry didn't recognize—Ilford HP5—lay twisted and snarled underfoot. Lenses, too, had been vandalized. Merry touched one carefully with a latex-gloved hand, and saw that the glass was starred with fractures.

"But they didn't turn over the rest of the room." She glanced around. "So the search must have been limited to camera equipment, or . . ."

". . . Ansel MacKay interrupted the killer. The time lapse between the victim's last text and MacKay's arrival was pretty brief, remember. Maybe half an hour."

Merry's eyes narrowed as she bent closer to look, conscious not to touch anything. "Has Clarence seen this?"

"It's Candace Moriarity this morning. She's working out back—still searching for shell casings—but I've asked her to collect any fibers up here and dust for fingerprints."

"You interviewed Ansel down in the kitchen, right?"

Howie nodded.

"You should have kept everybody out of the house and dusted that room, too."

"What, she gave the guy coffee before he shot her?"

Howie wasn't wisecracking; his expression was mortified. This was his first investigation. He was going to make mistakes. Merry remembered how she'd tried to hide her gaping inexperience as she'd interviewed Peter, years ago now, about the murder of his brother.

"You think she knew her killer?" Seitz asked.

"Most women who die by violence in the United States are murdered by someone they know," Merry recited mechanically. In the previous year alone, 92 percent of women who'd been killed by men, in fact, had known their murderers. "Mary Alice's killer came right up to this bedroom without hunting through the rest of the house. Which means he knew what he was looking for, and where it could be found."

"Ansel?" Howie asked.

Merry's eyelids flickered. "Could be. Or maybe Ron MacKay lied about not knowing his ex-wife was here."

"Seems kinda odd he wouldn't know."

Merry walked carefully around the debris of what had once been Mary Alice's camera table. "This damage looks fast, desperate, and uncontrolled. You might be right that the killer was interrupted."

"Here's the thing, Mer," Howie said. "If Ansel surprised him, how'd he get away? I mean, the front door's boarded shut. He had to have gone out the back. Which is where Ansel says he was standing over his mom's body. So . . ."

"Either the killer exited like a bat out of hell the minute he saw Ansel walking up the drive—"

"Which he couldn't have done, because all the front windows are blocked—"

"Or Ansel's . . . prevaricating."

Howie lifted his brows.

Neither he nor Merry liked the idea of the diffident young man shooting his mother. But such things were known.

"Why would he hurt her?" Merry said.

"Because she abandoned him as a child."

"I don't know, Seitz. It seems . . ."

"Odd that he wouldn't have killed her the first time he visited? Unless he needed to plan for today. Find a gun, find a ride, get off the island on his stepmother's jet."

"We have only Ansel's word that he came out here Friday and Saturday."

"His word, and a series of texts between the two of them."

Ah. Merry had forgotten those.

Wish I'd been able to talk to him myself.

She'd issued an all-points bulletin for Ansel as soon as she left his parents' house on Brant Point. "Wanted for questioning" was a simple enough reason to bring someone in, and the Nantucket force was bound to come across him. They were watching the ferries and the airport; there were only so many places on the island he could go.

Ruminating, Merry drifted toward the bedroom windows and stared down at the crime scene. The fire department's EMTs had taken Mary Alice Fillmore's body to the Cottage Hospital morgue; it would be flown to the Barnstable County medical examiner's office on Cape Cod, in Bourne, for the official postmortem. But as Seitz had said, Candace Moriarity was still combing the brush at the edge of the property, bent-backed in her white Tyvek jumpsuit and hood, in search of evidence.

"Seitz," Merry said suddenly. "We have company."

He joined her at the window. Below them, a young man and woman had approached the yellow police barrier and were gazing at it respectfully.

Candace Moriarity straightened up and spoke to them.

"Ansel," Howie said. "And he's brought a date."

CONSCIOUS OF THE evidence collection going on all around them, Merry decided to talk to the newcomers where she found them—on Stella Maris's kitchen steps.

"Ansel MacKay?" she asked as she opened the back door.

He looked slightly startled. "That's me."

"Meredith Folger, chief of Nantucket Police. I just met with your father and stepmother at your home on Brant Point."

"It's Janet's place, not ours," he said. "This is Winter Candler," he added, with a glance at the girl beside him. "She's a friend."

"Hello, Winter." Merry stepped outside. Howie followed, shutting the kitchen door behind him. The two of them stood on the steps, a human barrier to the house. "Mind if I ask you a few questions?"

"Not at all." Ansel looked at Howie. "Detective Seitz took down a statement from me earlier, though."

"And that's great," Merry agreed. "I just wanted to follow up. Did you go inside the house for any reason after you found your mother's body?"

"Not until the police arrived. I completely freaked out when I found her and ran down the drive to the road. I already told him that."

Meaning Seitz.

"Okay," Merry said. "Was there anyone else here when you arrived?"

"What?" Ansel frowned. "No. There was never anyone else around when I visited Mary Alice."

"Not on the property, and not in the house?"

"You mean, like, the person who shot her? I think I'd have noticed if somebody was running around with a gun."

"Right. Since arriving on Nantucket, you've come here daily to see your mother?"

"Starting Friday afternoon, yeah."

"How did you get here?"

"Well, I've already told *him* this, but . . . I took the Polpis road shuttle the past two days. This morning, I Ubered."

"And just now?"

"I walked. From Winter's place. She's nearby, at Ingrid's Gift."

Twice in one morning, Merry thought. Coincidence? She smiled at Winter. "Ingrid's Gift! So you must know Mike Struna."

"Yeah, he's a nice guy. He's hosting us this week."

"You're here for the television production?"

"My dad is. Chris Candler? He's an actor."

"Ah." Merry knew the name, had difficulty summoning a face to mind. There were a lot of Chrises starring in films these days. "How do you know Ansel?"

Winter glanced at him. "We just sort of . . . got to know each other. While we were here. During Stroll."

"I see."

"Winter met my mother yesterday," Ansel supplied. "So I thought I should tell her that Mary Alice was . . . that she had passed away."

"I was planning to watch her photograph birds over at Squam Swamp," Winter offered. "She was going back today. My dad's film shoot ruined the marsh she'd planned to be in."

Merry made a noncommittal noise. "Why'd you come back here this afternoon, Ansel?"

Involuntarily, he turned to look at the turf where he'd found Mary Alice's corpse. "My mother was working on a book. About birds. A photo study, I mean. That's why she was taking so many pictures here. She's a famous photographer. Or was."

"Just birds?" Merry asked.

"Right now, yeah. In the past, it's been everything. She used to work for *NatGeo.*"

"Okay . . ."

"I came back because . . ." Ansel drew a deep breath. "There's nobody to take care of her things. Her pictures, and stuff. My dad would never do it. He doesn't care. I wanted Detective Seitz to know that if you need a point of contact—a next of kin—I'm it. I want to be responsible."

There was a short silence. The notion of personal effects was complicated, Merry reflected, by the fact that Mary Alice Fillmore was occupying a house that did not legally belong to her. Which meant that whatever she'd left behind in the house probably belonged to Ron MacKay. "You may have to take that up with your father," she said, "or the executor of Ms. Fillmore's will. If she had one."

"Right," Ansel said. "I just don't want her research for the book to be thrown away."

It could be a thoughtful request from a son who cared. Or an attempt to find something among Mary Alice's things—an attempt cut short this morning.

Merry studied Ansel. His expression was open, but his eyes had a bruised look about them. "Did Mary Alice show you what she was working on?"

"Just her portfolio of prints."

Merry glanced at Howie. They hadn't found anything like a portfolio.

"She was shooting actual film, not digital, because, no electricity," Ansel explained. "Sometimes she posted images from her phone on Instagram, but the real photographs—the ones she was curating for her book—she kept here."

"What did the portfolio look like?" Howie asked.

Ansel shrugged. "The usual. Black archival corrugated plastic, maybe two feet by three. With a closure flap and a handle. Why?"

"She didn't have a dark room here," Merry said.

"Again," Ansel said, "no water or electricity. She got her film developed in town."

"That has to have been tough. For a photographer, I mean. To give up control of her negatives and prints."

"Sure. The prints were disposable. It was the negatives and slides that were important."

This last sentence echoed in Meredith's mind. In her limited experience, photographers stored their negatives and slides in archival acid-free sleeves and waterproof boxes. She hadn't seen any of those in the upstairs bedroom, either.

"So I guess I really came for her keys," Ansel added.

"Her keys?"

The house was wide open.

"To the van." Ansel was trying to be patient.

"What van?" Merry interjected.

Together, the four of them walked around the house to the front drive. Stella Maris had no garage; Mary Alice Fillmore's ancient green Volkswagen sat quietly parked in a tiny clearing completely camouflaged by the surrounding brush. The van was invisible from the drive. The keys were dangling from the ignition.

Before Ansel could touch a door, Merry stepped in front of him with a plastic glove on her hand. She kept them in her pockets for emergencies.

"Just in case there are fingerprints," she said.

The van, too, was unlocked. Mary Alice's phone lay innocently on the console, connected to a charging cord. And in the van's cargo area was a large black plastic art portfolio. Matching boxes—presumably for slides and negatives—rested nearby.

"Ansel," Merry said, "We'd like to go through her phone and images before we turn them over to you. Or whoever is authorized to have them."

"Why?" he asked.

She looked at him. His complete transparency regarding his mother's art suggested he was not the person who had been frantically searching for something among the smashed camera equipment upstairs. He'd known where to find Mary Alice's negatives and slides. Clearly, her killer had not.

"Someone shot your mother. The reason for that, or some link to the shooter, may be right here among her things."

"I get that."

"Do you know why someone would want her dead, Ansel?"

"Of course not." He shook his head. "But the truth is, I didn't know her well. I'd only really talked to her . . . for a few days."

His voice caught on the words.

"Look at her stuff if it'll help. I just don't want her images . . . to be lost."

"I understand."

"And call *me*, please, when you're done. I'm an artist, too," he persisted. "My dad isn't. He'll probably throw away everything Mary Alice owned. I mean, look what he did to her house." Ansel stepped back and surveyed the blind façade of Stella Maris. "She loved this place so much. It was her refuge. He took it away and let it fall apart."

It was nothing Merry hadn't concluded for herself. But she was interested to know how Ansel explained his father's motives. "Why do you think he did that?" she asked.

"He wanted to hurt her," the son said. "As badly as she hurt him."

20 | Squam Swamp, Sunday Afternoon

It was Kennedy Quinn's last real day on Nantucket—she'd be taking the fast ferry back to the Cape in the morning, after a quick Stroll visit with her parents at the family summer home in Siasconset. She had driven up to Hyannis Thursday night from Providence, where she worked as a postdoc in English Lit, with her golden retriever, Charlie, and crossed the Sound in torrential rain. Fortunately Susan and Bob, her Boston-based parents, had already opened up the house on Morey Lane that they'd dubbed, thirty-three years before, Quinntucket. There was a boxwood wreath on the Brewster Green door and lights strung on a passable tree.

The old whaling village on the southern tip of the island was absolutely dead in winter, with Chanticleer and the Casino and the Sconset Market shuttered. All the bright umbrellas by the Summerhouse Hotel's beachside bar were collapsed and stored, and the hotel itself closed. Few people walked the narrow, one-way streets that ran between the seventeenth-century fishing shacks, reclaimed as rose-covered cottages. The rugosa canes that overwhelmed the roof trellises were almost leafless and purple-tinged with cold.

Kennedy didn't mind. She liked Sconset best when it was empty, and completely hers. Charlie chased tennis balls they filched from behind the Casino's courts and lost them in the surf of Low Beach. Her mother, Susan, made a huge pot of cioppino they ate scalding hot with charred bread and garlic oil. They played dominoes and Crazy Eights at night by the driftwood fire, and drove into Nantucket Saturday for the obligatory Stroll. Kennedy met up with college friends later at Cisco Brewers, where they stood in the endless line snaking through the beer garden and made the most of the dinner choices once they got a table inside.

Sunday morning, Susan and Bob caught their Cape Air flight back to Boston. Kennedy was slightly hungover, and glad to sleep late in the big old house that was as quiet as a tomb. Even Charlie the dog snoozed on the end of her bed without a whiffle.

By two o'clock, however, she was recovered and Charlie was restless. Darkness would start to fall by 4:15, but right now the weather was too perfect to waste. Kennedy loaded the retriever into the backseat of her Mini Coope and drove through Sconset toward Wauwinet.

She knew the stylish hotel of the same name was closed for the season. The Mini's clearance was no match for driving over sand, so trekking out to Great Point was a nonstarter. She turned the wheel instead into the tiny parking lot halfway up the Wau-winet Road, discreetly posted with the Nantucket Conservation Foundation sign.

Hers was the only car in the lot. She took that, and the general air of desertion, as a sign from the Dog Walk Gods. Charlie could run off-leash. She tucked his lead in the pocket of her woven poncho just in case, and the two of them set off down the Squam Swamp trail. Charlie bounded ahead with his tongue out and flanks rolling, his ears perked to *ecstatic*.

It was one of her favorite trails on Nantucket, and in this season, one of the least traveled. Squam Swamp was a misleading name, Kennedy thought, as the five hundred acres of adjoin-ing conservation lands contained hardwood forest, grasslands, and freshwater bogs. The neat paths wound through oaks and cinnamon ferns, past American beech and mockernut hickory and sweet pepperbush. Impossibly tame deer wandered among the oaks' spiraled limbs, which hung low and mystic over the leaf-strewn paths. The trails were punctuated by sudden pools of fresh water, unusual on a sandy island, where the deer came to drink.

Charlie liked to drink in them, too.

He nosed ahead of her excitedly and circled back with his whole face grinning, glad to know that she was enjoying herself as hugely as he was. She called to him from time to time as they walked, mostly to know that she had company. This was the foundation of their relationship: parallel and absorbing experiences of the world, shared without a common language.

There were fifty-four wooden interpretive markers on the Squam Swamp trail noting environmental features—mostly flora and fauna—that could be found on the hike. Each numbered marker correlated with printed information in a free guide left helpfully in a box in the lot at the trailhead. Kennedy hadn't bothered to take a pamphlet—she knew the trail backwards and forwards—but the numbered signposts helped her later, when she found the body, to call in her location to the 911 dispatcher.

She was totally oblivious to everything but the startling beauty of the day when she came upon Charlie, standing off the trail near a vernal pool, bowed over the man with his tail drooping, his muzzle thrust into the fabric of the stranger's jacket. The figure was face down, slightly hunched, and unmoving. Kennedy stepped toward her dog tentatively and said, "Charlie. Come!"

The dog looked up at her, then gamboled over. She caught his collar and snapped on his lead.

The man still hadn't moved.

He was silver haired, burly, in charcoal-colored corduroys and a shearling coat. His legs were splayed at odd angles, just as he'd fallen. He was frighteningly still.

A sick feeling curled in Kennedy's gut and she felt, suddenly, the isolation of the surrounding woods, the fundamental loneliness. Nevertheless, she approached the still form, leaning toward him.

"Sir?" she said loudly. "*Sir?* Are you . . . okay?"

No answer. No movement. Of course he wasn't okay.

She considered feeling for a pulse, and her stomach turned over. It was off-season; who knew how long he'd been there? She backed away, eyes fixed on the body, and reached for her phone.

Charlie barked. Maybe he sensed her tension. Maybe he could smell something wrong.

Kennedy dialed 911.

She had just passed the trail's Marker 13. Its description in the Nantucket Conservation Foundation guide was curiously apt.

13. The water in this stream is usually tan to dark reddish brown in color, due to decaying vegetation such as dead aquatic plants, fallen leaves, and branches that lie within the stream and along its margins. As this matter decomposes, it releases tannins—darkly colored organic compounds that are the by-products of plant metabolism and decay.[1]

---

1 Text by Karen C. Beattie, NCF Science and Stewardship Department, from "Information and Trails: Squam Swamp," Nantucket Conservation Foundation, no date.

21 | Squam Swamp, Sunday Evening

HANAMEEL CAUGHT HOWIE as he was warming his hands at one of Foggy Nantucket's tall propane heaters, waiting for his barbecue takeout. The gas towers flared like beacon fires in the profound December darkness, casting the faces of the loitering clients in a dappled orange glow. The food place off Orange Street was primarily a professional catering kitchen, with proprietors who handed to-go orders through the door. Their pizza consistently made the island's "Best of" lists, but Howie craved their pulled pork dinners. A woman named Toni, in an apron and white cap, was flipping dough in the air. He found it oddly soothing to watch her.

"What's up?" he asked the dispatcher, turning his back on the exhausted-looking woman waiting near the opposite heater with a three-year-old sacked out on her shoulder.

"Another victim, Seitz, killed with a shotgun."

"Shit," he muttered. "In Polpis?"

"Squam."

As the gull flies, roughly the same neighborhood.

"Fire department responded to a 911 call for EMTs out the Wauwinet road. Girl was hiking, dog found the body. Soon as the Med Techs got there, they saw it was a gunshot death. They made sure the victim was dead—said he's stiff, in fact—and called it in to us."

Stiff could mean a lot of things in this weather. Cold temps,

Howie knew, slowed the onset and passing off of rigor mortis. Time of death would be difficult to gauge.

"Victim is an elderly white male. No ID yet. EMTs did not search for one—"

"Whereabouts in Squam?" Howie asked.

"The swamp off Wauwinet Road. NCF land." The sound of Hanameel shuffling paper came down the line. "There are numbered markers on the trail. Body's near thirteen."

Because the killer has a sense of humor.

"One of the EMTs was on the Polpis call this morning," Hanameel continued. "Recognized that both victims had similar wounds."

"Is he still there?"

"*She* is. Rachel Tompkins. Fire department stayed on-scene, pending law enforcement response."

"Try to raise Candace," Howie said, "and let the chief know."

"She knows. She's en route to the scene, and wants you there ASAP." Hanameel's voice shaded skeptical. "She said she thinks she knows who the victim is."

"Order for Seitz!" Toni called through Foggy's back door.

Howie stepped forward and took the paper bag she proffered. The mingled smells of smoked pork and mac 'n' cheese were mouthwatering, and it seemed completely unfair that he'd be eating dinner behind the wheel of his car.

Two bodies in one day, linked by manner of death. How could Mer possibly know who the victim was? Did she think it was a case of murder-suicide?

"I'm on my way," he said.

MARNI LeGUIN KNOCKED tentatively on the bedroom door next to hers. "Theo? Theo, darling, are you decent?"

Footsteps, muffled by excellent carpeting, and then the door drew back.

"Never ask me that," he said. "The range of possible answers, from the mundane to the scatological, is too tempting."

He stood aside, hand still on the door, and closed it behind her as she joined him. Theo's room mirrored her own—both overlooked the back of the house, with mesmerizing views down to the harbor. "How'd it go today?"

"Better. We're all starting to hit our stride."

"That means you're happy with your own work."

"Do I look smug?"

"No. But you're only generous when you can afford to be. How's Chris doing?"

Marni's expression turned thoughtful. "He's trying. It's hard to reach deep when you've phoned in so many action turns. He tends to rely too much on raised eyebrows and quirky smiles. His heartthrob stock-in-trade. I'd like to see some *pain* there."

"Lord! Hasn't he had enough of that in real life?"

"Yes. Which makes it odd he's got so little to draw on."

"Meow," Theo said comfortably. "But when you're catty, you're happy. We're celebrating, I take it. Would you like a drink? I've some bourbon in a flask."

She threw herself down on the sofa in front of the broad windows and smiled up at him. He took that as a yes, and went into his bathroom in search of tumblers.

"Dear Theo. Thank God you're still here."

"I echo the sentiment," he called back. "And as my survival is *all* down to you—"

He returned and handed her two inches of bourbon. "Cheers." They clicked glasses.

"Have you been bored here, alone all day?" Marni asked.

"I'm catching up on my knitting. How's Carly managing?"

"Well enough, once we're filming. She's got a definite vision for the script—I only wish Chris took direction better. Carly wants to see more pain, too."

"Sadists," Theo tsked. "When one is as gorgeous as Chris, pain is superfluous."

"I think he'd concentrate better if that girl weren't around."

"His daughter, you mean? She's not even on set."

"I know—but he's distracted. Constantly worrying. So is Carly, if it comes to that. Vic still hasn't surfaced."

Theo met her eyes, then sipped his drink. "Boo. *Hoo*. No one else misses him."

"The first thing Carly asked tonight is whether he'd shown up. She tried to do it discreetly—but I heard the guard at the Barn tell her there'd been no sign of Mr. Sonnenfeld."

"Probably reveling in her brief window of freedom! Let's hope he stays lost." Theo collected their glasses and went to refill them. "The world is a much happier place without Victor Sonnenfeld."

HOWIE REACHED TRAIL Marker 13 after about fifteen minutes of walking. He'd pulled a flashlight out of his glove compartment, but the batteries were old and the beam was wavering. From the vehicles parked in the Squam Swamp lot, he knew Meredith had already arrived. So had John Fairborn and Candace from Crime Scene Collection Unit. She had probably been the closest to the scene—coming straight from Stella Maris to Wauwinet Road. Her van was pulled up next to the Fire Department ambulance.

Candy, he suspected, would have pulled battery-powered floodlights from her van.

A few minutes' farther walk down the trail, and he could see them: a fluorescent glare that threw everything into stark black and white, the outlines of his colleagues silhouetted against the tangled limbs of the surrounding trees.

A form detached itself as his weak beam approached.

"Seitz," Merry said. "Want to see the victim? The EMT's are just about ready to go."

He walked with her to the gurney where the body bag lay.

"Victor Sonnenfeld, age seventy-three, according to the California driver's license in his wallet," Merry told him as he peered at the dead face. It was not a peaceful sight; the body must have been prone, lying facedown, because the features were purple with lividity. "He's one of the Hollywood people staying nearby at Mike Struna's property, Ingrid's Gift."

"Wait—isn't that where the girl said *she* was staying this afternoon? Ansel's friend?"

"Winter Candler. Yes." Merry stood back, and a female Med Tech—Rachel Tompkins, Howie thought—zipped the bag closed.

"Hanameel said you guessed who he was."

"Mike Struna called me this morning. Told me one of his guests had gone missing—but the wife didn't want to file a report."

"Interesting," Seitz said. "Concerned, but not concerned enough. Think this guy was shot with the same gun that killed Mary Alice Fillmore?"

"It's possible. But you know yourself that even two people killed in the same room can be shot with different weapons."

Howie had been the one to figure that out during the last murder he'd worked with Merry. Only in that case, the room had been a boat.

"Sonnenfeld was definitely killed by a shotgun, however. He bled out right where he fell," she added.

"And no weapon found?"

"Nope."

"Did Fairborn look at him?"

"He just finished. The shot dispersal wasn't as tight, he says, as our Polpis victim, and the pellets didn't penetrate as deeply, so it's probable Sonnenfeld was shot from a greater distance."

"I don't think we can blame a deer hunter, even so."

"Had this been the only body we found today, Seitz, maybe we would have. Maybe we'd have called this a fluke accident in a part of the island known for deer. That would have been convenient for the murderer. But given that these deaths came within hours of each other . . ."

"Did they?" Howie asked. "Does Doctor John have a time of death?"

"The cold makes it tricky. Could be as recent as six hours ago, as long as thirty-six."

Howie took his promotion to detective seriously. In his less busy hours during the past year, he had reviewed his Northeastern textbooks on crime scene investigation, against the time when he might have to investigate a murder. He knew that rigor mortis normally set in two to four hours after death. It began to dissipate eight to twelve hours later—when a corpse was at room temperature, roughly seventy degrees. In hot weather the entire process sped up; in cold weather—and it had been in the forties all day—the process slowed to a crawl. The victim could have been killed at noon—or noon the previous day . . .

"Did Mike Struna say when Sonnenfeld went missing?"

"Sometime during yesterday's filming. Which isn't terribly helpful. If you can, pin down the exact time when you question the widow."

Howie felt a surge of emotions—trepidation, relief. The chief was letting him keep the case. After the debacle at the secretary of state's house, the contamination of the Stella Maris kitchen by a possible suspect (Ansel), and the way he'd been forced to call an audible—bring Meredith in on a Sunday—he'd assumed nothing.

Seitz followed her over to the trampled area off the trail where the body had lain. Candace was working there with a junior officer in a white jumpsuit; Howie greeted them briefly, but he and

Merry stayed on the far side of Candy's barrier tape. "Hana said a hiker found him?"

"Woman named Kennedy Quinn. I took her contact info and sent her home. She stated she was walking her dog, saw the body, didn't touch anything, called 911. We can check whether there's any connection between Quinn and the victim, but given the presence of the dog and the lack of powder residue on her hands, I doubt she was perping a murder today."

It was a bit more straightforward than Ansel's story, Howie thought. He crouched down to peer at the ground where Victor Sonnenfeld had lain, but truth be told, the glare of the lights caused ghost images to dance on his eyelids, and from this distance behind the perimeter he could discern very little. He'd have to come back in daylight.

"Why, Seitz?" Merry murmured.

"Why, what?"

"Why would this guy be killed out here, in the middle of the Squam Swamp Trail? Who drew him here, straight into their sights? And how?"

"A text, maybe?" Howie got to his feet. "Meet me at Marker Thirteen?"

Candace spoke up. "No phone in the victim's pockets."

"And no piece of paper helpfully signed by the person he met?"

She shook her head. "It's possible he dropped his phone when he was shot. We may still find it."

Or possible that his killer—knowing the phone would lead police straight to them—had taken it from Vic Sonnenfeld's body.

Howie stood up. "What's the connection, Mer? Between our two victims?"

"Between politics and Hollywood? Off the top of my head— Ansel MacKay and Winter Candler."

"—Who told us they just 'sort of met' during Stroll. I wonder."

"Seitz, you read my mind." Merry turned away from the floodlights, back toward the head of the trail. "Let's go ask them."

22 | Ingrid's Gift, Sunday Evening

"I NEED YOU to hold back dinner," Mike Struna said, his voice lowered.

Brittany paused in the act of removing baked brie from the main house's oven. The kitchen was open to the great room, where Marni LeGuin and Chris Candler were already standing by a crackling fire. The first night she'd cooked for them, the pair's star power had made her ridiculously nervous. But she'd grown used to it now, and was able to greet each of them with professional insouciance. She was proud of this. If she still studied the way Marni styled her eyeliner and privately swooned over Chris's cheekbones, she managed to hide it from everyone else.

She set down the sheet pan of puff pastry and cheese near a platter of native bay scallops, homemade bluefish paté, and roasted venison lollipops in a blueberry-balsamic glaze. "We're okay to pass hors d'oeuvres, though?" she asked, with a glance at the great room.

"I'd hold off on those, too." Mike's voice dropped even lower. "I just heard from your friend Meredith Folger. The police have found Vic. They're on their way here, now."

IT WAS HOWIE who got the job of questioning the widow.

Merry had asked Mike Struna to bring everyone together in the main house before her detective arrived. This included the production people staying in the Barn and the security people on the front gate. There were nineteen individuals assembled in the great room within a few minutes of the chief of police's phone call, and Mike had escorted Carly down to the Barn gate to meet the police there. For speed and privacy, he drove her himself in his Maserati Levante.

"What's going on, Mike?" she'd asked when he knocked on her bedroom door. Her cap of brown hair was tousled and she was wrapped in a terry robe.

This was normally *his* bedroom door; he'd placed the Sonnenfelds in the main house's principal bedroom. He stood awkwardly in the hallway, wanting to reach for her and enfold her in his arms, and aware that every wall had ears. "I need you to throw on some clothes and come with me to the gate," he said. "Quickly. Please."

She had asked no further questions, even when he walked her to the marine blue SUV pulled up to the door. Once he'd turned the ignition and pointed the Maserati toward the gate, however, she said, "Tell me."

"Vic's dead." His fingers flexed on the black leather steering wheel.

"*What?*" She turned in her seat to stare at him, her face aghast. "What are you telling me? Where is he?"

"At Cottage Hospital. The police called. They're meeting us at the gate—they need you to make a formal identification."

"*Mike!*" There was a rising note of hysteria in her voice.

He pulled the car to the side of the drive and threw it into park. "Carly, I'm so sorry."

He held out his arms then, and she leaned into him over the car's middle console, her whole body tense with shock.

"What happened to him?" The words came on a half-whisper.

"I don't know. Somebody found him in the woods."

"Heart attack?"

"He'd been shot. That's all they said."

"Shot?" Utter bewilderment, now, and he didn't blame her. This was Nantucket, not East LA. "My God! *When?*"

"Carly, I have no idea."

"Who would *do* that to Vic?"

"I don't know. Maybe it was an accident."

"An *accident?*"

She kept repeating everything he said, as though mouthing the words herself would make them more comprehensible.

"He's been lying out there all this time? Since he disappeared?"

"I doubt it. We traced his phone to Town, remember?" Mike released her, but kept hold of her shoulders. "It's a terrible thing. I know. It's . . . a shock. Carly, are you going to be okay?"

She was still staring dazedly at him, without, Mike thought, actually focusing on his face.

"Are you going to be *okay?*"

"Shit," she said. "What will this do to my financing?"

HOWIE FOLLOWED THE Maserati through the gate and up to the entrance of the main house. He had never seen Ingrid's Gift, even before it changed hands and turned from an old island summer house to a tech billionaire's compound. He glimpsed groomed landscaping and specimen trees through the darkness, newly shingled outbuildings lit warmly with yellow interior lights. There were sparkling garlands in every doorway and LED Christmas bulbs glowing on a large conifer near the main house. It would look even more idyllic by day, he guessed, when the waters of Polpis Harbor were visible on the horizon.

A greater contrast to the house he'd seen that morning— Stella Maris—could not be imagined. And yet something linked them.

Violent death.

He had driven Carly Simpson and Mike Struna to Cottage Hospital, where an attendant had shown Carly the body

retrieved from Squam Swamp's nature trail. The woman had
nodded mutely at her dead husband's face, then turned and
stumbled into Struna's arms. She had not wept, and neither
had he.

Howie hoped that someone would mourn him a bit more
deeply when his own time came.

Carly asked for his personal effects, and was told they were
being retained as evidence.

"Even his phone?"

"We didn't find one," Howie told her.

"Impossible." She stared at him, then at Mike. "He was never
without it. Vic lived and died by that phone!"

"Maybe that's why you couldn't reach him," Struna suggested.

"Jesus," said the redheaded young woman in the passenger
seat beside Howie now. "How is it possible there's so much
money in the world, Seitz?"

He'd brought Tori Ambrose along for the ride. Like Howie,
she'd started her career on the island on the back of a bike—as
part of the summer seasonal hires. Despite finding the restaurants exorbitant and her bed in a group house impossibly small,
she'd fallen in love with Nantucket and decided to stay. Tori was
only twenty-four years old, and had spent the past year on the
NPD in a uniform, which was the way she was still most comfortable with her job. Merry had suggested Howie ease her into a
bit more responsibility. Show her the ropes while she had time,
off-season, to learn them.

Mike Struna and Carly Simpson-Sonnenfeld were waiting for
them at the house's front entrance. There were elaborate wreaths
on the double doors, twined with metallic gold fishermen's nets
and green-and-gold mermaids who clasped glittering baubles in
their hands. Posed against them, the owner of the house was
underwhelming, Howie thought. A trim figure in his forties, simply dressed in a suede baseball jacket and jeans. Medium height,

medium brown hair, unremarkable features. It must be the brain that was outsized and extraordinary, the brain that had gotten Mike Struna all this.

The widow beside him did not seem to merit the word. When he'd broken the news of her husband's probable murder at the property's gate, Howie had been surprised at Carly Simpson's discipline. She neither cried out nor wept, needed no one's hand to hold, and had told Howie crisply, "I ought to have reported him missing. Vic went AWOL all the time, but not without answering his phone." Howie assumed Struna had told her why the police were there, and this was a studied reaction.

He reminded himself he was dealing with Hollywood people. They were good at assembling fake pictures of the truth, and selling them with the utmost sincerity.

"I asked everybody who's currently staying on the property to gather in the great room," Struna said. "That includes Carly's top production people, her lead actors, and their friends or family. I thought if might simplify matters if you could make a statement, get everyone's contact info, and ask some general questions."

"Thanks," Howie said, "but we'll want to talk to few people individually as well. Mrs. Sonnenfeld, for instance."

"Of course," Carly said.

"You're welcome to use my office for interviews," Struna said. "It's separate from the great room—has a desk and a door."

He led them into the house.

The immediate impression Howie received was of crashing a party. It was clear that no one who'd walked up from the guest quarters in the Barn understood the reason for the summons; they were laughing and talking in scattered groups, some ranged on the seating around the fire, others collected on the kitchen island's barstools.

"No masks," Howie observed.

"Well, everybody's vaccinated," Mike Struna returned. "It was a stipulation for the production."

Great platters of food had been set out on the kitchen island, and everyone held a glass. Howie tried to pick out the two stars he knew were there—Marni LeGuin and Chris Candler—and saw only the young woman he'd met earlier that day instead. Winter was standing with a dark-haired man in a black turtleneck who looked elegant enough for a movie star, but was unrecognizable. Winter glimpsed Howie and looked immediately apprehensive. She clutched the dark-haired man's wrist, muttered something, and set down her wine glass.

Only one person looked like she was working—the woman darting from refrigerator to kitchen stove. Howie recognized Brittany Novak. She was one of Tess da Silva's people from The Greengage.

"Hey, everybody," Mike Struna called out.

Some faces turned toward him; most continued their conversations. He clapped his hands peremptorily and the noise gradually stilled.

Even Brittany came to a halt behind the kitchen island, her hands resting on the counter and her gaze fixed on Mike.

"I'm afraid we have some difficult and tragic news to share," he said. "I'd like to introduce Detective Seitz of the Nantucket Police Department."

Struna stepped back and Howie forward. Tori stayed well to the rear, a notebook in her hands and her expression challenging.

"Good evening." He nodded to the room, and as the guests looked at him expectantly, did a swift headcount: roughly twenty or so people, including Brittany and the two standing beside him. A man who'd been perched on the sofa near the fire got to his feet, and Howie registered the famous rugged face of Chris Candler. *Shorter than I expected*, he thought. *And older*.

"I regret to have to inform you that Victor Sonnenfeld, one of your fellow guests, has passed away."

A few people gasped; a few set down their plates or drinks.

"Oh, Carly!" exclaimed a woman who'd turned her head to stare over the sofa back. Howie recognized Marni LeGuin.

"Mr. Sonnenfeld was found by a member of the public earlier today, and as his manner of death is unexplained, it is now the subject of an investigation by the Nantucket police."

A low murmur; then one man on a barstool called out, "What do you mean, *found?*"

Howie ignored the question. "It's our understanding that Mr. Sonnenfeld was last seen on the set of his wife's film production, yesterday afternoon, at the UMass Field Station. Firstly, if any of you actually saw Mr. Sonnenfeld *leave*, noticed the *time* he left, or has any knowledge of his intended *purpose* for leaving the area of Folger's Marsh, please come forward and speak to me. Secondly," Howie held up his hand as the conversational level rose—"please write your name, position with the production, cell phone number and email on the piece of paper my colleague, Officer Ambrose, is circulating now. Finally, if any one of you knows of another individual connected to the production who is staying *elsewhere* on the island, but who might have observed Mr. Sonnenfeld yesterday at the film location, please come forward with that information now. Thank you."

Howie stepped back, but before Tori could start circulating with the contact list, Carly Simpson-Sonnenfeld held up her hand.

Instantly, the room fell quiet.

"I just want to say that I know this news is disturbing and unexpected. Obviously, I'm personally torn apart. I also know, however, that Vic would have wanted *The Hopeless* to go on at full strength, regardless of what happened to him. He believed in this project, he believed in each of you, and he believed in me.

The work we did these past two days is great, and nobody's pulling the plug. While the Nantucket police do their jobs, let's do ours. That's the best possible way to honor Vic."

The dark-haired man next to Winter Candler started to clap, and as he walked up to Carly and hugged her, the whole room joined in applause.

"Thanks, Theo," she murmured. "Your support means so much."

"You've always had it, darling," he said, then held out his hand to Howie. "Theo Patel. I'm Marni LeGuin's Gal Friday. I wasn't on the set yesterday and have no idea what poor Victor did to himself, but if you ever wish to chat, here's my card."

Howie pocketed it, wondering what exactly Patel's job title entailed as the man slid away. Winter Candler was standing before him, now, her mouth set and lines of strain around her eyes. "Another deer hunter?" she demanded.

"That's what it looks like," he agreed. "I need to talk to you, Winter. Please stay available here in the house until I do."

She nodded and turned back to the seating around the fireplace. But it was Marni LeGuin Winter huddled with, Howie noticed, not her father.

23 | Stronghold, Sunday Evening

"You're dining with the secretary of state?" Peter Mason said into his cell phone. "I'm impressed! But not surprised. Ney and I will fight for leftovers in front of the TV. Maybe you'll make the local news."

Merry had laughed at him, but was rethinking that impulse now as she halted her police SUV at Stronghold's gate. A tight knot of press people—maybe seven men and women variously encumbered with big boom microphones and video cameras propped on shoulders—circled her car as she offered the DSS officer on duty her badge.

"Chief Folger! How did Ron MacKay's ex-wife die? Is MacKay a suspect in her death? Did Ansel MacKay kill his mother? Chief Folger! Will Janet Brimhold MacKay be forced to resign?"

The guard gave back her badge, the gate went up, and she drove into the courtyard.

Ron MacKay was not going to be happy about this.

Nor, she thought, would he be thrilled when the first people she asked to speak to were his family's security staff. Ron MacKay was a control freak, and being left out of the room where things happened would be an exquisite form of torture.

"I don't think you appreciate what this delay does to the secretary's schedule," Micheline Tran said pointedly to Meredith as the two waited in the living room for the MacKays to appear.

The couple had ordered dinner on trays in their bedroom, as far as possible from the gaggle of media. "I've had to formally apologize to counterparts in Taiwan and South Korea. Not to mention Ukraine—"

"I'm sorry," Merry told the poised, expressionless woman, whose hands were folded neatly across her black trousers. The wool was heavy, draped, with knife-edge pleats; despite being the same trousers Meredith had glimpsed that morning, they looked freshly pressed and just off the hanger. Merry's khakis, thrown on to visit Ralph's grave, were soiled with leaf mold where she'd knelt in Squam Swamp.

"It is not an exaggeration to say that the United States may face an international crisis if Madam Secretary is not back in Washington by noon tomorrow."

"No danger of that, Mick," Ron MacKay broke in easily as he walked into the room. "We're thinking of flying out tonight, regardless of the hour, if Chief Folger will just release us. Chief? You've got news, I hope?"

"Mr. MacKay." Merry nodded to him. "Madam Secretary."

They were all masked, which made reading faces quite difficult. Merry was reduced to scrutinizing foreheads and eyes, which were never as revealing as entire faces.

"Have you found the deer hunter who shot Mary Alice?"

"No. But we *have* found another victim, sir. A man named Victor Sonnenfeld. Does the name mean anything to you?"

"Vic Sonnenfeld?" Janet Brimhold MacKay turned to stare at Micheline. "He's something in Hollywood. Contributed to our last Senate campaign, didn't he? I remember a fundraising dinner at his place in Brentwood—two, three years ago?"

"You gave a speech about gender equality. I'll check the dates," Micheline said, and rose from her seat.

"Are you saying he's dead?" Ron interjected.

"He was found near a hiking trail not far from Stella Maris

this afternoon. He'd been shot in much the way your ex-wife was, with a shotgun to the chest."

"Somebody is really lousy at hitting deer!" Ron sank into a chair and gestured to Merry. "Please. Sit down."

"Thank you, but no. Madam Secretary, I'd like to speak to your DSS security officers, please. In private. Afterward, I'd like to speak to Ansel, to you, and to Ms. Tran, in that order."

"Oh, my God—we're still not allowed to leave the island?" Ron demanded.

"Not tonight, sir. I may have better news for you in the morning."

"I hope so, Chief," he said, rising from his chair. "Or you'll find your job is on the line."

THE DSS OFFICERS—FRANK Delgado, Ian Swift, and Sasha Rubin—represented a brief history of the service, Merry realized. Frank was nearing retirement age and had served as an RSO—a regional security officer—in embassies abroad; he was a member of the Foreign Service as well as Diplomatic Security, and had been named the head of Janet Brimhold MacKay's detail in recognition of his distinguished career. Ian was a former cop who'd transferred laterally into Dip Security after seven years with the NYPD. Sasha was a direct hire, trained to protect dignitaries from the day she'd entered on duty.

The younger two treated Merry cordially, as a fellow law enforcement officer; Frank was inclined to be dismissive.

"Punching a bit above your weight, aren't you, Chief?" he'd said when she'd informed him no one would be leaving Stronghold that night, much less Nantucket.

Merry could name the chips on his shoulder, one by one: she was younger than he was, worked for a local force instead of the federal government, and was completely ignorant of the diplomatic service or life in a foreign country.

Also, she was female. Frank's generation thought women had no business running police departments.

She decided to nip his attitude in the bud.

"Thanks for agreeing to answer my questions," she said, as the three agents took chairs around the desk in Stronghold's library, which she'd commandeered for her interviews. "I know you want to get back to DC as soon as possible. But the secretary's stepson found his mother dead this morning, and is obviously a person of interest in our investigation of her death. So is everyone in this household, including yourselves."

"The woman was murdered, I take it?" Frank said.

"She was shot at point-blank range," Merry replied, "with buckshot. There's powder stipple on her clothes, so our best guess is she was within a yard of the muzzle. The sooner we get your statements, the sooner you get off this island. Understood?"

"Understood," Ian said immediately.

"I'd like copies of your shift rotations, with exact times you each manned the front gate, and all notations of individuals entering or leaving this house."

"I'm not sure you're cleared for that," Frank said.

Merry offered him the screen of her laptop. Displayed was an email from the office of the Principal Deputy Assistant Secretary for Diplomatic Security. "Your boss just gave me clearance."

Frank sighed gustily. "Forward that email to me, please. I'll need the paper trail to wipe my ass when this all hits the fan."

"Certainly. Now, did any of you drive out with the secretary during your time here?"

"I did, obviously," Sasha said. "I'm her principal body person."

"When was this?"

"Yesterday—we watched Santa arrive downtown and visited a couple of local shops."

"Were you driving?"

"Mr. MacKay insisted on doing so. The secretary sat in the back—it's safer."

"And you had tabs on her at all times?"

Sasha smiled faintly. "That's my job."

"What about Mr. MacKay? Did he remain with you at all times?"

"In Town?" The bodywoman swept back her long hair, her gaze fixed on the ceiling molding as she considered the question. "He browsed with us at the bookstore, but stood outside of another place. He was taking a phone call."

"Were you separated very long?"

"A few minutes. The secretary wasn't seriously shopping— just sort of showing the flag. We weren't in any one place for very long. That's good operational security—keep the target moving."

"So the secretary never left this house, by car or on foot, without one of you in attendance?"

The three DSS agents glanced among themselves. "That would be a violation of everything we stand for," Frank said dryly.

"What about other members of the household?"

"Ansel MacKay comes and goes at will." This from Ian. "He likes to leave by a side door onto the beach, so his movements aren't always recorded."

"You're not manning that door?"

"This was supposed to be a quick, private vacay for the secretary and her family," Frank said. "We're a reduced detail. We've got somebody in the house, somebody on the beachfront, and somebody on the gate at all times. That's the best we can do."

Merry looked at him. "When do you sleep?"

He shrugged slightly. "We're taking it in turns to work nights. We're all sleeping here in any case, but we've got one person officially on call each night inside the house. We leave the gate unmanned, but closed, after ten P.M. We're back on duty out front and on the beach at six A.M."

"Long hours," Merry observed.

"And not much to do," Sasha agreed. "Other than yesterday's Santa parade, the secretary's been housebound."

Merry thought of the simple wooden barrier at Stronghold's gate. Anyone on foot could slip under it at night; anyone on foot could approach the house from the Sound side during the same period.

And anyone could leave.

That meant Ansel, Ron, or the secretary could have walked in or out of Stronghold at night largely unobserved, if they chose. Then taken a rideshare or taxi out to Polpis. It was not too much of a stretch to think one of them might even have managed it during manned daylight hours—Ansel's wanderings over the holiday weekend demonstrated that.

The least likely person to escape DSS vigilance was Janet; but what if she'd told Sasha she was resting in her room, then slipped out of the house?

And there was always Micheline Tran to run errands for her boss. Merry found it hard to believe these might include murder.

"Mr. Delgado," she said, "does the secretary or anyone in her household own a gun?"

He shook his head. "Not that I'm aware. No firearms are registered to anyone in the family; we would know if that were the case."

An unregistered gun, though . . . Merry sat back in the desk chair and studied the DSS agent. "What is your impression of Ansel MacKay?"

"He's got his issues." Frank's voice was heavy with contempt, but he went no further.

"I've found a number of them on the internet," Merry said mildly. "Substance abuse, petty theft to support his habit, dropping out of college, rehab for six months and a halfway house after that. But I've also searched criminal databases, and there's no record of violence. What do you think?"

"Is Ance violent?" Ian clarified. "Not in the slightest, that

I've observed. But we've only been assigned to this detail since the secretary took the oath of office, less than a year ago. I've got no idea what he was capable of before that."

"Understood," Merry said. She was typing as the others talked. "Sasha?"

"He's a nice person," she said hesitantly. "I like Ansel. He's sensitive and thoughtful. Just beaten down by his dad's constant criticism and the fact that he's forced to live under a microscope right now. He'd be better off in his own place, leading his own life, I think."

"None of you is expected to babysit him, are you?"

"Now *that*," Frank interjected, "is definitely *not* in our job description."

The others laughed.

"But to be precise," Merry continued, "your protective duties don't extend to the secretary's family members, per se?"

Frank shook his head. "Only when they're with the secretary."

"So, for example, Ron MacKay can come and go from this house—including in his car—without one of you tagging along?"

"Of course. He's a private citizen."

"Got it," Merry said. "But if he took the car out, it would be noted among your front gate records?"

"Between the hours of six A.M. and ten P.M., sure," Ian said.

"Can the MacKays raise the gate themselves?"

"Absolutely," Ian said. "When we're not manning it, the gate is worked by transponder. There's one in the car."

This, Merry reflected, meant that anyone with the keys to the secretary's vehicle could drive it anywhere on the island they liked, at night.

Mary Alice Fillmore had died between 8:30 and 8:50 that morning; but Vic Sonnenfeld's time of death was impossible to pin down.

Anyone from Stronghold might have shot the man. The question remained, however, *why*.

24 | Ingrid's Gift, Sunday evening

"I UNDERSTAND THIS is a difficult time," Howie said, "but the sooner we can document what you recall, the better."

Carly Simpson-Sonnenfeld nodded. "Where should I start?"

"Does the name Mary Alice Fillmore mean anything to you?"

It was not the question she'd expected, he saw; she'd been waiting for him to ask about filming at Folger's Marsh. Her memory of events, yesterday and today, and when she'd last seen her husband. Her expression was bewildered.

"Not a thing. Should it?"

"Not necessarily. Is it possible your husband might have known her?"

"I have no idea. Vic knew a lot of people, and not all of them were mutual acquaintances." Now her expression was guarded. Howie wondered why.

"Who would have a better sense of Mr. Sonnenfeld's contacts?" he asked. "Did he have a personal assistant? A secretary?"

"Julia Waters," Carly said immediately. "She runs his office in LA. I can give you her contact information."

"Thank you. Tell me about your husband, Mrs. Sonnenfeld. What was he like?"

She shifted in her chair in Mike Struna's office, her face side-lit by a desk lamp. "Vic was . . . a powerhouse of a guy. One of the most successful people in Hollywood. He built the top agency in the business over the past forty years, and practically invented the talent-packaging approach to filmmaking. He knew everyone, and his name alone was enough to greenlight a project. The film world revered him."

It was, Howie thought, a resumé, not a character description. The lack of personal insight or emotion was, in itself, telling.

"How long have you known him?" he asked.

He was lounging comfortably in his chair, not obviously taking notes, to place his subjects at ease. He'd watched Meredith Folger do this, and was glad he had Tori Ambrose with him to record the conversation. She was seated on the edge of the room, out of Carly Simpson-Sonnenfeld's line of sight, scribbling with pad and pen.

"My goodness, most of my life," she said ingenuously. "Or at least, for the majority of my career. But we only got serious about a decade ago. We've been married a little over six years."

Howie had seen Carly's birthdate on her identification; she must have married Vic Sonnenfeld when she was thirty-nine. He would have been sixty-seven. Howie found this disconcerting, but did his best to subdue his personal reaction. No one truly understood a relationship except the two people in it.

"You describe Mr. Sonnenfeld as 'revered,' but he sounds like a pretty powerful guy—and men like that sometimes make enemies." Particularly, Howie thought, the ones killed by shotguns. "Was your husband worried about anything lately? Had he received any threats, that you know of, to his person or his business?"

"Vic?" She looked bemused. "Nobody would threaten Vic. That had a way of ending badly."

"Meaning?" Howie asked.

"A word from him could destroy your career."

"That's a pretty strong statement." Not to mention a perfect reason to kill him.

Carly shrugged. "He'd fought his way to the top. You don't do that without building a lot of influential networks."

And pissing off a lot of people, Howie thought.

"Those networks become your armor," Carly added. "You use them to defend and protect your interests. Vic was adept at that. He shut down anyone who tried to threaten him. But similarly, he could open doors—or the entire world—if you were on his team."

"As you were," Howie suggested.

She met his eyes squarely. "I still am. I will always be Team Sonnenfeld. Vic has been the basis of all my success."

"Well—I imagine talent has something to do with it, too."

"Of course. I'm not selling myself short—Vic never backed losers. But I would be lying if I failed to acknowledge that much more than simply talent is necessary to thrive in Hollywood."

Was she a cynic, Howie wondered, or a realist? He was too unfamiliar with the film business to know. But he recognized the subtle message she was offering. If he was investigating a murder, Carly Simpson had every reason to want Vic Sonnenfeld *alive*.

"Will your career suffer now that your husband is dead? Will this project, for example, continue without him?"

Her head came up at that. "Of course the project continues. As I said a few minutes ago to the crew—filming is the best way to honor my husband."

"Mrs. Sonnenfeld, could you take me through your time on the island? When did you and Mr. Sonnenfeld arrive?"

"Thursday afternoon. We were the first to land—by private jet—a little after two P.M. Mike met us at the airport."

"Mr. Struna?"

"Yes. He and I went to school together. Years ago."

"This would be college?"

"NYU."

Howie nodded. "Did you come straight to the house?"

"We did. Mike showed us over the property—he's very proud of it—and we got settled in our rooms. The Candlers were the next to arrive—Chris Candler and his daughter, Winter—and then Marni LeGuin."

"Were you acquainted with any of them prior to this production?"

"Marni and Chris? Of course. We've known them for years. They're CMI clients."

"CMI?"

"Creative Management International—Vic's talent agency."

So it was incestuous, Howie thought—the stars and the director all represented by the same guy. Or his employees. That must be what Carly meant by *packaging.* "And you all got along?"

"Oh, beautifully. This is very much a family production."

"Roughly how many people are in your 'family?'"

"Right now . . . about eighty, all told. We don't have the entire crew here, of course—that runs to about five hundred people, mainly based in Toronto. We're just filming key outdoor scenes on Nantucket, so only certain people were involved."

Howie was surprised. "Eighty people are staying on this property?"

"Oh, God, no. Most of them are farmed out in rentals and hotels. Just the principal production people were invited to Ingrid's Gift. That made the whole week . . . more intimate."

"I see. And Mike Struna?"

"Definitely family. Or as good as."

"Did your husband view him that way?"

Carly shrugged slightly. "Vic only met Mike Thursday. We don't live in each other's pockets as spouses, you know—*didn't* live . . ." Her voice trailed away, then picked up again with greater force. "Vic was very much a tagalong here. My project, my crew, my friend as host. I was simply glad to have his support."

If Carly was to be believed, murder had nothing in common with her wholesome, happy life—which made her husband's violent death all the more incomprehensible.

Howie smiled encouragingly. "So much for Thursday. What happened Friday morning?"

"An easy day. We did a table reading of the script. Everyone gathered for dinner at the Barn, which was truly festive—Mike's chef is fabulous. Then yesterday we had an early call sheet out at the Marsh."

"How early?"

"Some of the crew started at six-thirty A.M. Our call was seven-thirty."

"Must have been chilly." There'd been gusty winds the previous day. It felt to Howie like a month had passed since then.

"It was. We quit early, in fact, because of the weather. Today was better . . ." She faltered, fell silent.

"Mr. Sonnenfeld was on the set yesterday, you said?"

"He came with me, Chris, and Marni, yes. He wanted to watch me direct—really sweet of him."

"Until he decided to leave? When was that, exactly?"

"I don't know. I wish I did." The brown hair slid forward along her chin as she ducked her head, making it difficult for Howie to read her expression; and he wondered if she was prevaricating. "I looked around for him when we broke for fifteen minutes, a little before noon—the time'll be in the Continuity notes. Everyone was roaming then, it was a bit chaotic, but I didn't see Vic. Once we resumed filming, I'm afraid I put him out of my mind. Creative work is like that—it's all-consuming."

"Did you leave Folger's Marsh yourself, Ms. Simpson, at any time yesterday?"

She frowned. "Did I? No, of course not. Anyone can tell you I was there."

"And you quit working for the day at . . ."

"A bit after three. Vic was certainly gone at that point; we came back to the house without him. I assumed he'd come home early—any one of the younger crew might have given him a ride back, there are people designated as Runners. But he wasn't here. And Theo—"

She broke off.

"And Theo?" Howie remembered the elegantly groomed man clapping as he approached Carly to offer an embrace. He fished out the business card in his pocket. "Theo . . . Patel, is it?"

"Yes. Marni's personal assistant."

"What about him?"

Carly shrugged. "Vic had an argument with Theo and suggested to me that he'd be leaving yesterday. But he didn't. I was just . . . surprised Theo was still here, that's all."

"And you didn't see your husband again, after yesterday morning?"

She shook her head. "Not until you took me to the morgue. Although—" She hesitated, her fingers turning a stack of rings on her third left finger. "I think—I think he must have been in Town most of yesterday afternoon."

Howie straightened slightly in his chair. "Why?"

She moistened her lips with her tongue. "Mike—he works in software."

"I know." The entire world—at least, the world Howie's age—knew that.

"He . . . there's this program Mike invented. It can track cell phones."

"Okay . . . " Howie kept his voice deliberately neutral.

"Mike tracked Vic's phone for me yesterday." She was unable to meet his eyes. "He could tell Vic had been to The Proprietors, mid-afternoon, but a little after four o'clock he was in a private home somewhere."

"Still in Town?"

"Yes. Mike says it's a rental property. I've forgotten the address. It didn't mean anything to me."

Howie drew a deep breath. "He did this with your permission?" Or had Struna spied on Sonnenfeld for his own reasons?

"Yes." She looked at him squarely, then. "I was worried because Vic wasn't answering my texts or picking up. But when Mike offered just to see where he was . . ."

"Right. You were curious."

"I was relieved." Her tightening mouth belied the words. "I knew I could leave Vic alone. He certainly wasn't in trouble."

"When did your feeling about that change?"

"This afternoon, when we got back from the Marsh."

Howie nodded. "Did you ask Mr. Struna to try tracking him again?"

She shook her head. "Before I could, you arrived."

The bearer of bad news. Howie's thoughts leapt ahead: Mike Struna would have the address of the house where he'd tracked Sonnenfeld.

"Detective . . ."

"Yes?"

"What's going to happen to Vic?" Carly asked. "Will there be an autopsy?"

"I'm afraid so. The body will be sent to the Medical Examiner's office in Bourne, on the mainland, tomorrow. Once the postmortem is complete, we can release the remains."

Clinical language, and hardly comforting, but Carly Sonnenfeld nodded as if relieved.

"How long do you plan to remain on Nantucket?" Howie asked.

"Through the end of this week. Longer, if need be."

"Good," he said. "That's all I have to discuss at the moment. Would you send Winter Candler in to me, please?"

WINTER LOOKED TOO small for her voluminous ivory sweater, which was knitted in a ragged and wildly oversized pattern that seemed deliberately cartoonish to Howie. She huddled in the office chair, glancing apprehensively at Tori Ambrose and her notepad. Howie tried to look unthreatening.

"Is there a serial killer on the loose?" she asked as soon as she sat down.

"It's possible."

Winter folded her arms across her chest. "You said it was a deer hunter this morning."

"I said it was possible." Howie leaned toward her. "Ms. Candler, do you know of any connection between Mary Alice Fillmore and Victor Sonnenfeld?"

She shook her head. "You'd have to ask Ansel. I only met his mom once, yesterday afternoon, for about half an hour."

"But she drove you back here to Ingrid's Gift, right? Did she seem interested in the group you're staying with? Did she ask any questions about them—about Mr. Sonnenfeld, for instance?"

"Not at all!" The immense blue eyes widened. "I'm not sure Mary Alice even knew who my *dad* is, and that's pretty unusual. But maybe she was just being nice, and not going all weird about it. Ansel was that way, too. Deliberately cool."

Howie sighed. "How did you meet Ansel?"

She told him about Friday's breakfast at Lemon Press. The casual conversation, picked up again Saturday on the shuttle to Polpis. The impromptu visit to Stella Maris.

"He came here looking for you this afternoon," Howie noted. "Were you surprised by that?"

"He texted me first. Told me his mother had died. I was blown away, but said if he wanted to talk . . ."

"You didn't think it was strange that he reached out to an almost-stranger?"

Her head ducked. "Ance isn't a stranger," she said in a subdued voice. "And why are you asking all these questions about *him*? Shouldn't you be investigating Vic's death?"

Howie changed tack. "Did you call him that? Vic?"

Her eyes drifted to Tori. She shrugged. "Everyone did."

"So he was friendly? Someone you felt comfortable talking to?"

"Shit, *no*." Her gaze came immediately back to him. "Vic gave me the creeps. He was a dirty old man! Has nobody told you that?"

Startled, Howie glanced over at Tori Ambrose. The policewoman's pen had stilled over her notebook. "I'm interested in what *you* have to say, Ms. Candler. Sonnenfeld came on to you?"

"He put his hand up my skirt at the dinner table Friday night, and groped my crotch," she said bluntly. "After saying things earlier in the day that were so filthy I thought I'd puke. Vic was sick, detective, and he was triggering. I relapsed that night . . ."

"Relapsed?"

"Got sick. Binge ate, then vomited." Anxiety flooded over her face. "It's an old problem. Then my dad found me, and *he* got all worried . . ."

"Did you tell him what happened?" Howie asked. "What Vic did?"

"God, no. He'd have freaked out, gone straight to Vic in the middle of the night and grabbed him by the throat. You don't mess with Chris Candler's women."

Yet she was telling Howie openly about the incidents now. Was it easier to talk about it, knowing Vic Sonnenfeld was dead?

"Did he threaten you?" Howie asked. "Sonnenfeld, I mean? If you told anyone?"

Winter hesitated. Now, she glanced at Tori. "Is that woman writing everything down?"

"Yes," Howie said. "This is a murder investigation, Ms. Candler. Someone shot Vic Sonnenfeld with a shotgun, and we need to know why."

"Because he was a prick," she said. "No, he didn't threaten me explicitly, but the threat was always implied where Vic was concerned. Ask Marni. Ask Theo. Ask his *wife*, for fuck's sake. I didn't want to be the reason my dad's career reboot bombed from the start. I didn't want to be the reason he left the production 'due to creative differences.' I wanted to get through the week and get on with my life."

Howie had a sudden inspiration. *Ance isn't a stranger.* "Did you happen to tell anyone else about what happened?"

"I told Marni." Winter was toying with the fringe of her sweater, plaiting the long strands between her thin fingers. "She's had to deal with Vic in the past. She said what Vic did wasn't my fault, and that I hadn't invited him to abuse me. She told me to confront him, because the one thing Vic Sonnenfeld couldn't deal with was a woman who fought back. I wasn't willing to do that here, while my dad was working. It helped, though, to know that Marni thought I *could.* She calmed me down. And that stopped . . . the relapse."

A woman who fought back. He would definitely have to question Marni. "Did you tell Ansel MacKay about Friday night?" Howie asked. The thought of Winter assaulted and vulnerable might have spurred MacKay to attack Sonnenfeld. It seemed like an extreme reaction for a relatively new acquaintance— but murder was, by definition, extreme. That motive explained nothing, however, about the murder of Ansel MacKay's mother.

Winter wrinkled her nose. "Eww. *No.* Way too much sharing, thank you very much."

"Okay." Howie sat back. "Please ask Marni LeGuin to come talk to us."

HOWIE WAS SURPRISED, again, to notice how much older Marni LeGuin looked than she did on screen. Perhaps it was the office's lighting, or the stresses of the day and the relative lateness of the hour—the actor had been on call since 7:30 A.M. and was probably exhausted, he reminded himself.

He rose from his seat when she entered, and gestured to the other chair. But Marni paused for a second—aware of her effect, Howie thought—and allowed her eyes to roam the room.

"So *this* is where the magic happens," she said.

"Magic?"

"Mike Struna's billions. I assume he makes them here."

"I've never been quite sure what he does," Howie said vaguely. "Or exactly what he's invented."

"Surveillance software," she immediately replied. "Golden-Eye. It's the best thing at cracking cell phone encryption outside of Israeli intelligence. The FBI uses it, although no one's supposed to know."

"How do *you*?" Howie inquired, fascinated.

She yawned, and took the chair he'd indicated. "I read a script. Spy thriller. Written by an adoring Struna fan, who thinks his genius will save the earth and mankind from extinction. I passed on the project. Software might be threatening, but is it *sexy*? Hell, no."

Marni LeGuin cast as a spy might be, Howie thought, particularly when it was her agent who was dead—but all he said was, "I see."

"You didn't call me in here to talk about that, though, did you?"

She had succeeded, he realized, in taking control of the interview. He decided immediately to take it back.

"No. I wanted to ask you about Vic Sonnenfeld and sexual harassment."

She barely reacted; the slightest flicker of her eyelids was all he saw. "Was that one of his things, do you mean?"

"I understand that it was. Were you a victim of it?"

"Who wasn't?"

"Ms. LeGuin, we're investigating a murder. It would help us greatly if you could answer our questions in a straightforward way."

"I am, detective." She smiled. "Vic Sonnenfeld was a shit. When I was young and stupid, I let him use me for sex in order to advance my career. Twenty-five years ago when I started out in Hollywood, that was how the business worked. When I got smarter and older and more capable of choosing my own roles, I found better representation—a woman who has my back—and together we met with Vic. We assured him we'd out him to the press and our lawyers if he didn't play nice. I've had no problems with Vic since then, and the liberation has been satisfying."

Howie studied her for an instant. The speech seemed a little too rehearsed, a bit too pat. "And this week, you agreed to stay here in the same house with somebody who'd sexually abused you?"

Again, her eyelids flickered. "Yes. For Carly. I'd have preferred the guest cottage, but Chris got that."

"Does Carly know, then, about your history with her husband?"

Marni hesitated. "I'm not sure what Carly knows. Or what she prefers to ignore. I only know that when a woman offers me a starring dramatic role on a project she gets to direct, I'm going to do everything in my power to support her—because it's a win for both of us."

"I see," Howie said. "How did Sonnenfeld treat you, the first few days?"

"Did his hands wander, do you mean? No—although he said something shitty to me Friday morning when he got the chance. I told him to fuck off and went out for a walk. After that, he left me alone."

Or concentrated on Winter Candler, instead.

"Do you remember Mr. Sonnenfeld at Folger's Marsh yesterday?"

"Oh, yes—he was breathing down Carly's neck. He shouldn't have bothered her on the set, but he liked her to feel and see his power."

Howie frowned slightly. "She told me she was happy to have his support."

"*Right.*" Marni grinned hugely. "When it's financial. I wouldn't be surprised if she was doing a delicate balancing act—between massaging Vic's ego and following her own instincts. He'd use his control of the purse to keep her in line."

Is that enough reason to want him dead? Howie wondered. *What if he was threatening to withdraw his "support?" Would Carly Simpson-Sonnenfeld have killed him before he pulled the plug on her production?*

But what did Mary Alice Fillmore have to do with that?

"Yesterday," Howie resumed. "Can you pinpoint when and where you last saw Sonnenfeld?"

"Well, at the Marsh."

"Did you speak to him?"

"No—I avoided that, whenever possible. Plus, I was working. I shut out peripherals when I can. I concentrate on the other actors in the scene, the emotional load I'm supposed to be carrying. The direction. In this case, Carly's direction."

"But you noticed Sonnenfeld enough to remember him there."

She closed her eyes briefly as though summoning a scene in her mind. "He was sitting in a sort of camp chair—one of those collapsible canvas things—right behind Carly. Hovering, like a predator."

Howie wondered if the choice of word was unconscious, or deliberate. "She mentioned a short break, then a longer one for lunch, then calling it a day around three. Any idea when Sonnenfeld was no longer in his chair?"

"After the break."

"Before lunch?"

"Yeah. I was having a hair and makeup fix with Seth—one of the Continuity people. I saw Vic walking toward the parking lot—I remember thinking, *We've seen the back of him for the day.*"

This correlated, Howie thought, with Carly's timing.

"He wasn't at the production's lunch."

Marni shook her head. "Not that I recall."

"You never saw him again?"

"And if there's a God, I never will," she concluded.

"I gather you've known both Sonnenfelds for some time," Howie said.

Marni inclined her head. "I have."

"What was your impression of their marriage?"

"It was a practical arrangement. Vic, as you've probably gathered, could make projects happen in Hollywood—and happen for Carly. On the other hand, Carly gave him cred—meaning, she was a much younger woman, and a professional one, whose presence at Vic's side was a visual statement that a) he wasn't past it; and b) he must be a good guy, if this rising female director trusted him."

"What do you think the impact of his death will be on the production you're currently filming?"

"Hopefully, nothing. Carly has signed contracts. I assume the funding will continue."

That was the impression Vic Sonnenfeld's widow wanted to leave, as well. Howie would give a lot to see the terms of one of those financing contracts. He might learn whether Sonnenfeld was more useful to Carly alive—or whether his manipulation of her money made her want him dead.

25 | Stronghold, Sunday Evening

MEREDITH HAD DONE only a cursory background search on Micheline Tran before sitting down with her in the library. But she had scanned the DSS gate logs, which Frank had brought to her, and noticed the secretary's chief of staff had left Stronghold on three verified occasions in as many days. Twice, she had been alone; once, her deputy, Josh Stein, had accompanied her.

"Ms. Tran," she said, "I appreciate your time."

"Anything I can do to get the secretary back to Washington faster," Micheline returned, "I'm happy, of course, to do."

Merry took the veiled barb in stride.

"How long have you known Janet Brimhold MacKay?"

The other woman's eyes softened above her facemask; a sign, Merry thought, that she was smiling. "Since before she was MacKay. I volunteered for her first campaign—for Massachusetts AG—when I was still at Smith."

"And never left?"

"Well—I worked a stint on the Hill right after college. But I went back for Janet's congressional campaign, as a hired staffer— that would have been the 2000 race—and yes, I've been with her in some capacity, ever since."

So you know her as well, or better, than her husband. And might feel a similar degree of loyalty.

That bond, Merry reflected, could run both ways: Janet MacKay might do a great deal to shield Micheline. There were all sorts of relationships influencing the people at Stronghold—those of friendship and work, of marriage and parenthood. Any one person might attempt to protect any number of others. She could assume nothing, must doubt every answer, and would have to tread lightly.

"Before I forget—could you describe the secretary's past relationship with Victor Sonnenfeld?"

"Oh, there was none," Micheline said. "He's simply a donor. *Was*, I mean. A lot of people in Hollywood like to support politicians. It's a novelty for them to be seen as influential in Washington—a different kind of power than they're used to."

"So he wasn't . . . how to put this . . . soliciting any favor in particular?"

"Bribing the then-senator for a quid pro quo, do you mean?" Micheline's brow—which was basically all Merry could see above her mask—furrowed. "Absolutely not. Mr. Sonnenfeld liked to associate his name, and that of his talent agency, with popular causes—and promoting women looked good around then. He hosted a fundraiser; Janet gave a speech about gender equality. Together they raised a lot of cash and helped keep Janet in the Senate to further the role of women in politics. It's as simple as that."

"When was this?"

"April seventeenth, three years back. I checked the date once you mentioned Mr. Sonnenfeld's name."

"Did you have any personal interaction with him on that occasion yourself?"

Something shifted in the woman's gaze. Merry detected calculation, a withdrawal of confidence. "As little as possible. I find that too much intimacy with donors presents a warped picture to the press, and encourages the donors in question to imagine access that was never there."

A careful answer, as with every word Micheline uttered.

"Did he ever contact you afterwards?"

"Once or twice."

"Which was it? Once, or twice?" Merry lifted a brow inquiringly.

"His wife was denied a film permit by the Town of Nantucket a few years ago," Micheline explained. "I gather she wanted to shoot a production here during the summer, and the town vetoed her request. Mr. Sonnenfeld thought then-Senator MacKay might pull some strings. I told him politely that filming here in the height of the season was more hassle than it was worth, and to try for a winter permit. I suspect that's why Mr. Sonnenfeld was here this year in December."

But not, presumably, why he was shot to death. "Has he contacted anyone associated with the secretary since she was sworn into that office?"

"No," Micheline said.

"Ms. Tran, according to the DSS front-gate logs, you left the house each morning on foot at six-fifteen A.M., returning on two occasions roughly an hour later, and on one occasion—in company with your deputy, Mr. Stein—an hour and half later. That was this morning. Why did you leave?"

"For my morning run. Friday and Saturday I was alone. Today Josh came with me."

"Where'd you go?"

"Out along Cliff Road."

"That's pretty hilly!" Merry exclaimed admiringly.

"It's a challenge, yes. We got lost on some of the side streets, but eventually turned ourselves around. We stopped at a coffee place afterward."

"Which one?" Merry asked. "There's a bit of rivalry among the coffee places."

"Handlebar," Micheline replied. "Janet recommended it."

"But she didn't join you there?"

"Not this visit. Too many logistical headaches."

"I notice," Merry made a show of consulting the gate log, "you also *drove* out on one occasion—Saturday night, eight o'clock in the evening. You took the household car, which the secretary leaves parked in her garage here, rather than an official one."

Micheline sighed. "I just wanted to get out. My job sounds glamorous—all that travel!—but I never see much of the places we visit. This was supposed to be a working vacation—but the fuss over Janet's appearance at the Santa parade made it all seem too much."

"Fuss?"

"The streets were blocked off downtown. Which meant parking was a problem. So the secretary had to be moved from a side street to the parade route on foot. The DSS folks and Ron—Mr. MacKay—were bunched around Janet so tightly she could barely breathe. It drew public attention instead of deflecting it, which is what official cars always do. So when I got back and had some free time in the evening, I asked Janet if I could just borrow her personal car. It seemed easier to fly under the radar."

This was the longest answer Micheline had given. Which brought Merry's antennae up.

"Bet she envied you," she said sympathetically. "She must wish she could do the same thing. Where'd you go?"

"I went looking for Christmas lights."

"Ah." Merry nodded. "You drove around town?"

"Too crowded," Micheline said quickly. "The streets were a madhouse Saturday night. And they're so narrow . . . I just took that long road off the rotary until it dead-ended in the ocean."

"Milestone Road? To Siasconset?"

"Maybe." The aide's voice was cautious.

"Did you see a lighthouse?"

"I saw the arc of one. Flashing. I sat looking at the beach for a while—there were some great stars—until the car got too cold. Then I drove back."

If not Milestone, maybe it was the Polpis road, Merry thought. For such a detail-oriented woman, Micheline was remarkably vague on this point.

Merry let a silence settle between them.

"Ms. Tran, do you ever take calls that come to the house phone—Stronghold's landline?"

The woman tensed slightly, then deliberately eased back in her chair. "What do you mean?"

"Exactly what I said. Do you ever answer the phone?"

Micheline hesitated. "Sometimes."

"Did you receive a call—" Merry glanced at her notes—"at seven-fifty-six Saturday evening?"

"I'm not sure. Possibly."

Merry glanced up. "We have records that suggest a call was placed to this house number at that time. It lasted approximately one minute, seven seconds."

A call from Mary Alice Fillmore's cell phone. She had definitely spoken to someone at Stronghold the night before she died.

A few minutes later, Micheline Tran had left the house in Janet Brimhold MacKay's car. And driven in the direction of Polpis.

"I can't help you, I'm afraid," Micheline said.

Can't—or won't?

Merry decided to probe the woman's vulnerability—her dedication to her boss. "Maybe one of the MacKays answered it, then. I'll have to ask the secretary. Do you think it bothers her to be under house arrest?"

Micheline's eyes widened. "*Arrest?* What do you mean?"

"—Unable to come and go freely from her lifelong vacation home?"

"She has certainly never said so." Micheline paused, then appeared to relent. "But yes, I think she feels a lot of the security restrictions on her life right now are onerous."

"Ever help her make a jailbreak, Ms. Tran?"

"Not this weekend, not here," Micheline replied. "Is there anything else? I have to return some emails—"

"I think we're done, for now," Merry said. "Could you send Mr. Ansel MacKay to me?"

HER QUESTIONS FOR Ansel were brief.

"Victor Sonnenfeld?" he repeated. "Never heard of him."

"He threw a fundraiser for your stepmother about three years ago. Out in California."

"Ah," Ansel said. "I was in college then. Missed that campaign."

"He was also staying with your friend Winter Candler at Ingrid's Gift."

Ansel still looked bewildered. He wasn't wearing a surgical mask, and his emotions were transparent. "Weird. The coincidence, I mean. So this guy's connected to Hollywood?"

"He represented Winter's father, and his wife is directing this production."

"*The Hopeless*. I looked it up—it seems like a pretty big deal."

"Did Winter mention Mr. Sonnenfeld to you?"

Again, the look of confusion, as though Ansel were feeling his way in the dark. "Should she have?"

"Mr. Sonnenfeld was found this afternoon in a hiking area not far from your mother's house. He was killed by a shotgun."

"Jesus." Ansel ran his fingers through his festive hair. It stood on end in a startled way. "That's way too much of a coincidence."

"Did your mother, Mary Alice, ever mention his name?"

"—during the two times I visited her house? Nope. Why would she?"

Merry shrugged. "As you say. Too much of a coincidence."

"I get it. But no."

"She knew Ingrid's Gift, though. And drove you there with Winter."

"Because I suggested it! I'm pretty sure she didn't know anything about Hollywood, or this guy Sonnenfeld."

Merry sighed. "And you're sure you don't either, Ansel?"

He ran his eyes over her face in a worried fashion. "I swear to God, I never heard the man's name. Why would I lie?"

Because two people are dead, Merry thought.

But she simply thanked him for his time, and let him go.

26 | Ingrid's Gift, Sunday Evening

"You placed Vic Sonnenfeld at The Proprietors," Howie Seitz said to Mike Struna, "through your surveillance software—which I believe is called GoldenEye?"

Struna laughed. Again, today, he was wearing no mask. "Very good, detective. You've been doing your homework. Carly told you?"

"She said it calmed her down to know Vic was fine."

Struna's mouth screwed into a knot. "Well, she's being noble about that. Which is very Carly—loyal to a fault. She was probably relieved Vic wasn't lying in a ditch somewhere, but she hated thinking he was shacked up with some woman at an Airbnb he'd booked on the side."

"Is that what you think he did?"

"I think Vic Sonnenfeld made sure to have a comfortable port in every storm." Struna's eyes crinkled, again, with amusement. "He was a conceited old bastard. If the attention wasn't firmly on him, he'd go off in a huff and console himself with all kinds of trouble. Then, self-esteem in place, he'd sweep back like a king. Carly expected him to do that this morning. When he didn't, she shrugged and went on with her day."

"But you didn't?" Howie asked.

The humor leeched out of his face. "GoldenEye told me Vic hadn't moved from the house on Howard Court, twenty hours after he'd arrived. I found that hard to believe. Like a shark, Vic never stops moving."

And when he does, he dies. "Is the program still telling you where he is?"

"I can't access the phone anymore. Which means, it's dead."

Howie nodded. As well as missing. "And when did you determine this?"

"Around noon today."

Which didn't particularly help them with time of death, Howie thought; the phone might, or might not, have run out of power at the same moment its owner did. This morning, yesterday afternoon . . .

"What's the address on Howard Court, Mr. Struna?"

"Number Four."

Howie drummed his fingers on the sleek black desktop, wondering how far to push the tech giant. "Mrs. Sonnenfeld tells us you only met her husband a few days ago. Yet, from what you've said, you formed a distinct impression of his character."

Mike bared his teeth. "I didn't like him, if that's what you're asking. I don't think anyone did."

"Even his wife?"

"As I said—she's loyal. To a fault."

"Thank you. That's all we need, for now."

Mike rose from his seat, slightly awkward at being dismissed from his own office. "You'll keep me apprised?"

It was more of a command than a request.

"When I can," Howie agreed.

Then, as Mike closed the door softly behind him, Howie said, "Tori, call the station and get Candy and her people to Howard Court. We'll need the chief to request a search warrant. Find out who owns Number Four. And who rented it this weekend."

FOR A GAL Friday, Theo Patel had a great deal of assurance. The ease of his entrance reminded Howie of the way Marni LeGuin seized control of her first moments in Mike Struna's

office, and it rankled him. Theo had rehearsed for his time in
the side chair, and Howie wanted to know why. With his first
words, Theo threw down bait, which was usually the way people
diverted attention. From what, exactly?

"Let's hope Carly's not fibbing," he said as he took his seat,
"and that the show really *will* go on. I'd hate to learn that Vic
offed himself because he was bankrupt, and couldn't produce
Carly's cash. That *would* put a damper on the festive film week.
However lovely the food service and linens, one does like to be
paid for one's toil."

The ingenuousness of this speech—with its side wink to suicide, its implication of a wife's motive for murder, and all the
relish of a bystander reveling in schadenfreude—ought to have
both charmed and confused Howie. Instead he asked mildly,
"How do you know the man didn't have a heart attack?"

"You said *unexplained* death. At home in Sussex that's police-
speak for a violent end."

"Here, it just means the autopsy's pending," Howie said.
"Why did Mr. Sonnenfeld tell his wife you'd be leaving Nantucket yesterday?"

Theo mimed jazz hands. "I haven't the foggiest."

"Did you threaten him?"

"Did *I?* Threaten *him?*"

Howie leapt on the point. "So he threatened *you*. What was
it, Mr. Patel? Exposing some sort of misconduct? Financial—or
sexual? Something that would end your career?"

Theo rolled his eyes. "Lord! You're supposed to be a plodding
rural policeman! That's what Central Casting delivers for a cozy
little plot like this. How is it you can read minds?"

Howie tried not to scowl. "I've been told Sonnenfeld was
good at shafting people he didn't like."

"Oh, he even shafted people he *loved*, Mr. Detective. And I
am certainly not one of *those*."

"What happened?"

Theo pressed his palms together like a devout choirboy. "I cannot tell a lie, particularly to the police. Vic was angry when I told him off for his nasty whisper in Marni's ear Friday. He threatened to have me torched. But Marni has her own form of leverage over Mr. Sonnenfeld, and handled him nicely. Vic withdrew from the field, bloodied but unbowed, and I remained on Nantucket. End of story."

Nothing to see here, Howie thought. *Move along, Mr. Detective.* He made a mental note to check Theo's story with Marni LeGuin later.

"Did you watch the filming at Folger's Marsh?"

"No. I make it a point never to interfere with a production's Costuming department; cat fights are so dreary. My genius is worked after hours—my subject being Marni's *real* life."

"How did you spend your time yesterday and today, then?"

"I had a Runner drive me into town Saturday—there was a quaint Christmas market near the harbor, as you may know, all sorts of twee nautical tchotchkes, which I absolutely *adored* and purchased for friends back home. Then I visited Erica Wilson for a few needlepoint canvases to work on the plane"—Theo was ticking off his fingers—"and stopped into an antiques store whose name I *cannot* remember on one of the side streets, where I examined those cunning baskets with the *masses* of actual ivory on top, that you cannot get for love or money anymore. I thought my husband might covet one."

"When did you return to this house?"

"Oh, around drinks time, although I will admit I had a *teensy* champagne cocktail at Ventuno before I summoned my car." He stared at Howie limpidly. "You may check the times with various and sundry Runners, bartenders, etcetera, if you desire."

"And today?"

Theo stifled a yawn. "I lounged, I'm afraid. In bed over the

breakfast tray—Brittany is *such* a love, I'm putting on pounds—
and then with a book by the fireside. Reading is terribly
underrated. Particularly in my profession."

Patel could easily have lured Sonnenfeld to Squam, Howie
thought, on Saturday afternoon, and might have slipped away
from his lounging to shoot Mary Alice Fillmore this morning.
But why kill the latter? And was he likely to have procured a
shotgun out of thin air?

"Did you see anyone? Or did anyone see you?"

He meant today, but Theo took the question generally.

"Well, yesterday morning I waved to Mike as he whooshed
past in his posh car," he said. "We left this place around the
same time. But I didn't run into him or anyone else. The deli-
cious Winter files her nails in peace at the Cottage, and Mike's
immured in his boathouse for the duration. I couldn't begin
to say what he does there. Although he jets out in that divine
wooden dinghy of his from time to time."

This was, Howie conceded, a valid point. Mike Struna could
come and go on his own property unremarked by his security
people, whose salaries he paid. How *had* the inventor of surveillance software occupied his time, while Hollywood took over his
pandemic refuge?

But the question would have to wait. There was a soft knock
on the library door, and as Howie nodded, Tori Ambrose rose to
answer it. She stepped back immediately, a look of awe on her
face.

"I'm sorry to disturb you," Chris Candler said, poking his head
around the door, "but I've got an early call tomorrow and I'd like
to get to bed. If you're planning to question me, detective, would
you make time for me next?"

HOWIE WAS GROWING tired, and the various threads of
the conversations he'd had during the past hour were getting

tangled in his mind. It seemed clear that Victor Sonnenfeld had
wielded power over people's lives; that he enjoyed using it; and
that both his instincts and behavior were predatory. All reason
enough to trigger violence. What his murder had to do with the
death of Mary Alice Fillmore remained a mystery. Before Howie
lost sight of the woman entirely, he decided to ask Chris Candler
the simplest of questions.

"Does the name Mary Alice Fillmore mean anything to you?"

Candler's eyes widened slightly; this was not the question
he'd been expecting. "Mary Alice Fillmore . . . do you mean the
legendary *National Geographic* photographer? I love her work.
Why?"

"You know who she is?" Howie glanced at Tori Ambrose,
whose fascination at being in the same room with a leading Hollywood heartthrob was temporarily affecting her notes. She felt
Howie's gaze on her, smiled apologetically, and leaned down to
retrieve the pen she'd dropped on the carpet.

"I met her a few years back. Maybe . . . five years ago? Six? She
served as a consultant on a documentary a friend of mine was
shooting, on mass extinctions."

"And you remembered her name? After all that time?"

"Well—I had a long conversation with her at a party the
night the documentary debuted. A slideshow of her photographs
was playing that night, and they were pretty mesmerizing. Why?"

"Did you know she was killed this morning, at a house not far
from this?"

"Oh, my God—you mean the woman Winter met yesterday?
My daughter—Winter—she was pretty shaken up this afternoon
when I got back from the set. Told me a friend's mother was
dead, and that she'd talked to the police. Was that *you?*"

"It was."

"Mary Alice Fillmore," Candler said wonderingly. "Dead.
What a small world. Winter showed me her Instagram account

yesterday but the name on it is different, and I didn't put two and two together."

What had the girl said to Howie this afternoon? *I was totally fan-girling about Mary Alice to anyone who would listen last night.* "Did she show the account just to you? Or were there other people in the room?"

"It was right before dinner, so we were all pretty much there, I think—in the great room of this house."

"*All* of you, meaning . . ."

Candler squinted slightly, as though trying to see something at a distance. "Me, Winter, Carly. Theo and Marni. Mike Struna. And the chef, of course—Brittany. Vic was absent, which in retrospect was strange—except that Carly never mentioned it. So neither did we." He paused. "Winter told me that the woman she met yesterday—Mary Alice Fillmore, I guess—was accidentally killed by a random deer hunter. Is that what happened to Vic?"

"It's one possibility we're investigating."

"Jesus, there are way too many guns in the world."

Howie changed tack. Chris Candler was the first person at Ingrid's Gift, other than his daughter, who'd admitted to knowing both victims. Which gave rise to inevitable lines of inquiry. "What time did you arrive at Folger's Marsh this morning, Mr. Candler?"

He smiled faintly at the formal address. "Around nine. I had a later call time today."

Which meant that Candler could certainly have nipped next door to Stella Maris, renewed his acquaintance with Mary Alice Fillmore and her birds, and shot her in the chest before reporting to his film set.

"Do you remember seeing Vic Sonnenfeld at the Marsh yesterday?"

"We rode over in the same car."

"Did you happen to notice when he left?"

"Yes. He came up to me, in fact, and told me he was going back to the house."

"He did? When was this?"

"Right before we broke for lunch." Candler pulled his phone from his jeans pocket and scrolled through his messages. "I can tell you the approximate time, because I was texting my daughter's bodyguard. Laura had lost Winter at Stroll, and I was really pissed off, because Winter's been a bit unsettled lately, and . . ." He stopped, and displayed his screen to Howie. "There. Twelve-forty-two P.M."

"Did you actually see him leave?"

Candler shook his head. "I was more focused on my kid. Sorry. I actually left the set instead of eating lunch, and got a Runner to take me into town. I thought I could look for her. But of course—she was long gone."

Howie's entire body tensed. *Candler left the set at roughly the same time Sonnenfeld had. And Sonnenfeld had molested his daughter. What was it Winter said? "You don't mess with Chris Candler's women."*

"Do you remember the Runner's name?" Howie asked.

"I don't think . . . I ever knew it!" Candler ran his fingers through his black hair. "God, that's awful, isn't it? Am I just another Hollywood shit, detective?"

"Was the Runner a woman? A man?"

"Definitely a guy. One of the Continuity people, doing double duty, I think."

Marni had mentioned a man named Seth. Howie made a mental note. He hoped Tori was making an actual one.

"How long have you known Mr. Sonnenfeld?"

"Forever," Candler said, his facial muscles relaxing. "I realize that's imprecise. Let's say . . . about twenty, twenty-five years."

"Did he seem like himself this week?"

Candler rubbed his square chin with one hand. "Yes and no. Vic's always been a force of nature, but he was getting more abrasive as he aged. Or maybe I'm just getting less tolerant. I don't know."

"Can you give me an example?"

"Well . . ." He hesitated, his eyes shifting to Tori Ambrose in much the way his daughter's had done. "Is all this being written down?"

"You'll have a chance to read it over, fix any mistakes, and sign it," Howie told him. "It's your witness statement."

"I see. I guess that's okay. It's just . . . this is about someone else, and it's a total rumor so I'd hate for it to get out."

"The investigation file is completely confidential," Howie said.

"Vic was practically gloating all the way to the Marsh yesterday about what he'd done to Theo. Theo Patel—you were just talking to him, weren't you?"

Howie nodded.

"Vic said Theo's career and maybe his life and certainly his marriage were over. Because of something Vic had leaked to the press, or was giving to the tabloids."

"Really?" Howie kept his tone neutral.

Candler sighed. "I hate that kind of shit, because whatever the truth of the matter, tabloids are victimizing and you can't fight back. My late wife had that kind of trouble and I . . . Anyway, Vic insinuated that Theo had sex with a minor and the minor killed himself, or something equally horrible. Vic was practically crowing about Theo never working in Hollywood again. The homophobia was obvious and off-putting, frankly. I don't know if any of it's true, but I was pretty shocked at how openly Vic was enjoying himself." He lifted his hands futilely in the air. "Vic's represented me forever and his wife's shooting my latest project, so . . . But it made me feel sick. To my stomach. That he would do that."

Theo's career and maybe his life and certainly his marriage were over . . . Howie remembered Carly saying obliquely: *Vic suggested he'd be leaving yesterday . . .*

Did she know exactly what her husband had done?

"Who else heard this conversation?" he asked.

"I suppose Carly and Marni might have—they were in the seats in front of Vic and me in the SUV—but I'd expect Marni to react, and not in a good way, so maybe I'm wrong. Theo is not only Marni's assistant, he's her best friend. They've worked together for years."

Vic threatens Theo and takes obvious pleasure in it, then Vic dies; and Theo remains happily on Nantucket, secure in his job and his world. Howie could see how it made sense. He could even see how Marni and Theo might have cooked up a murder between them. He just couldn't quite see how it was done—or what Theo Patel's security had to do with the death of an isolated woman in a deserted old house on Polpis Harbor.

He eyed Chris Candler, unsure how much to disclose. Winter had made it clear she had kept Sonnenfeld's assault from her father. "Were you aware that Mr. Sonnenfeld had a habit of sexually harassing women?"

The star shifted in his seat. "There have always been rumors," he said, "but that's true for a lot of men of Vic's generation in Hollywood. That doesn't excuse it. Just a statement of fact."

Howie considered Winter Candler's allegations, and decided they were hers to share with her father. He knew of them, however; knew of Sonnenfeld's history with Marni LeGuin; and now, this story about Theo. Strong motives, all, for violence.

"Thank you, Mr. Candler," he said. "Go home and get some rest."

IT WAS AS Howie was leaving Ingrid's Gift for the night that the one person he'd meant to speak to and hadn't dropped right into his lap.

So to speak.

Brittany Novak, done with all the serving of food and drink to a group of bemused and speculative film production folk, had washed and dried her last dish. She approached Howie and Tori as they stood by the front door, pulling on their jackets before heading once more into the dark. It was nearly ten o'clock, and she had started work that day at 6 A.M. Because she was merely twenty-five years old, her exhaustion did not show on her face. Her auburn hair was a trifle mussed, but her expression was alert and her attitude friendly.

"Hey!" she said to Howie. "You two wouldn't by any chance be heading back toward town?"

"Well—" Tori looked uncertainly at her superior officer.

"Could you give me a lift?"

Brittany glanced from one cop to the other. "What? You didn't come here in a *patrol* car, did you?"

Everyone on Nantucket was familiar with the white, navy and gray-wrapped Nantucket police SUVs.

"Sure," Howie relented. "I can give you a lift. Where're you headed?"

"Oh, my God—after *this* day? Straight to bed with a mug of chamomile tea. But you can drop me at Stop & Shop and I'll get my sister to pick me up. Nora borrowed my car today. Doctor's appointments."

"She okay?" Howie asked.

"Yeah. It's routine, not Covid. We're vaxxed." Brittany beamed at him. "Appreciate it. I'm Brittany, by the way."

"I know," Howie said. "You catered Chief Folger's wedding."

"Wait," Tori interjected. "You went to the *wedding?*"

"I did," Howie said, wondering why he felt both privileged and embarrassed. "It was pretty sweet. You guys did a great job, Brittany."

"Although, right after the hurricane," she reminded him,

as they exited the main house and crunched across the quahog
shell drive to Howie's ancient hatchback, "I wasn't sure we'd pull
it off. If that storm had been twelve hours later—"

"You'd still have pulled something incredible out of your ass,"
Howie said. "That's what you guys at The Greengage do. Take
the front seat, Brittany—Tori's good in the back."

As Tori walked past him, slightly crushed, Howie whispered
to her, "*Notes*, Ambrose."

"Right," she mouthed back, her flaming eyebrows soaring.

Howie slid behind the driver's seat and turned his key.

"So, Brittany," he began as he turned the Toyota toward the
Polpis road gate. "How's life with the Tech Giant?"

27 | Mason's Farm, Sunday Evening

"It's important," Peter Mason said, "to remember that none of these people owns a dog. Or even a cat. I'm not sure you can trust any one of them."

"I don't own a dog," said Howie, disgruntled.

"But you *would* if you could. —If your landlord allowed it, for instance. I bet you'd love having a dog so much, you'd campaign to allow them to ride with officers on duty. Whether they're K9-trained or not. Dogs humanize us."

"I think you mean *animalize*," Meredith objected.

"Normalize?"

As Howie was sitting on the rug of Peter's study at the moment, the sheepdog Ney's besotted head on his leg and one paw thrown over his ankle, while Howie tugged gently and repetitively at each of Ney's fluffy ears, he was in no position to dispute Peter's judgment. He caught the gist of Merry's point, but chose not to pick up on it. She was nitpicking, something she was allowed to do to her husband, but Howie understood that in such a situation there was nothing useful he could add. Side with Peter, and he'd alienate his boss. Side with Merry, and he'd look like he was brownnosing.

He contented himself with stroking the most neutral party in the room, instead.

Merry had suggested that they meet back at her home that night to pool their resources. Share information and connect the

dots between their particular murders, before surfacing at the station the following morning to neaten everything up for the official
record. As a member of the general public, Peter was not supposed to be a party to any of these discussions. Confidentiality
in an investigation was critical. Except in the case of Peter, who
had fed them a *very* late meal of cornbread, chili, and coleslaw,
and was now tending the fire in his comfortable room, where
Merry was sprawled on a lounge chair and Howie's back was
against the sofa.

They had told him almost nothing. The bare outlines of a
double-murder case. The confidentiality was intact.

"I'll leave you to it," he said now with a sigh. "And take myself
off to a book and bed. It's nearly eleven, by the way, so don't burn
too much oil."

Merry had changed into sweats and fleecy slippers. She tucked
her blond hair behind her ears and stared at her laptop distractedly as Peter left the room. Ney instantly dragged himself to his
feet, and exited without a backward glance at Howie.

"Traitor," he said.

"Loyal to the death." Merry stabbed at her keyboard. "Just
not to you. Which, by the way, is worrying me. Ney's getting
old. Peter's his world, and vice versa. We need a puppy, Seitz. If
you come across anything on your travels, lemme know, okay?
It should be good with sheep. And preferably female. I'm so
outnumbered."

"Everything on the island is a Doodle these days."

Merry waved a dismissive hand. "You talked to Brittany?"

"Yeah," he said. "Sonnenfeld asked her to spy on her boss.
And on his own wife. How weird is that?"

Merry glanced up. Her green eyes had deep shadows under
them, and Howie realized the load she carried was catching up
with her. It wasn't enough to be appointed chief after her pre-
decessor resigned under a cloud; she'd had to grapple with the

public safety concerns of the pandemic, and then Ralph Waldo Folger's loss. He had no idea if she'd even found a way to grieve for her grandfather—the isolation of the past year and Howie's own preoccupation with his beloved Dionis, absent and teaching remotely on the mainland, had thrown a distance between them. He realized suddenly that he and Merry used to talk a lot in the car together, traveling around the island on cases, and that he missed their bull sessions over coffee at the Downyflake.

He wondered if they'd ever do that again.

"Tell me," she said.

He shifted from the floor to the cushions of the sofa, aware as he did so that he might just sink into a profound doze if either of them stopped talking long enough.

"I just asked her about her life," he began, "and she unraveled like a spool of thread."

Brittany loved everything about her job with Mike Struna, and her joy radiated through each sentence she uttered. She loved the open-ended budget, the freedom to experiment with any conceivable cuisine, the exposure to interesting people who gravitated to Ingrid's Gift, the sudden flights to Monterey and Manhattan. She loved the easy hours; the authority she found in being Mike's hospitality point person; the unspoken power of managing the subcontractors.

It was possible, Howie told Merry, that Brittany was completely in love with Mike himself—who was twenty years older than she was. And hadn't even tumbled to that, yet.

There had been nothing to mar the succession of happy pandemic days at Ingrid's Gift, in fact, until the Hollywood People landed on Nantucket.

"That Carly," Brittany sniffed, in the passenger seat of Howie's Toyota as they rounded the Milestone Rotary. "There is no way she understands how amazing Mike Struna *is*."

Not to mention Carly's husband.

It turned out that Vic Sonnenfeld had haunted Brittany in her open kitchen from the first hours of Friday morning, when her excellent European coffee machine had turned out his perfect mug of latte, and her homemade cherry-pistachio scones suited his mood. By the dessert hour Friday night at the Barn, Vic was petting her right hand, clasped in both of his, and raving to anyone who would listen about the sophistication of her palate.

"He told her he was close to some major chef in LA"—the name meant nothing to Howie, although Brittany had uttered it with reverence—"and that if she ever felt like getting off the island, he could hook her up with a job," Howie told Merry. "Not just a job. You know, a huge career leap."

"And Brittany considered it." Merry wasn't typing now, just listening. "This guy was a calculating son of a bitch, wasn't he?"

"Brittany went to bed that night with her head spinning, full of plans—wondering if she could find a way to bring her sister Nora along, swing the rent in SoCal between the two of them. She says she barely slept. Kept jumping up to Google this chef and her restaurants—the woman owns four of them—and the type of clientele they cultivated. She was late, she says, to work the next morning."

"Which was Saturday."

"The day Sonnenfeld went AWOL. Yeah." Howie rubbed his wiry hair with the heel of his right hand. He was drop-dead tired. "Brittany dragged herself in at six, which is late by Mike Struna's standards, and really late for the seven-thirty call sheet Carly Simpson had issued the night before. Luckily, she wasn't expected to serve a full breakfast—just coffee, fruit, oatmeal, baked goods. Juice."

"Tea," Merry suggested.

"Probably. Theo Patel is British." Howie paused. "Sonnenfeld asked if she was going to visit the set that day, and she told him she was due to bring lunch at one P.M. He kissed her hand and told her he was looking forward to it."

"Let me guess. Brittany pulled out all stops to serve a lunch Vic Sonnenfeld would never forget."

"Basically. She said she ran out to Bartlett's Farm for all kinds of fancy stuff she thought would impress a guy used to California cuisine. Sort of Nantucket locavore, but with an *elevated* twist, is how she put it."

"Not your basic chowdah." Merry grimaced. "Christ, what a clusterfuck."

"Anyway, she gets to the Field Station at twelve-thirty and there's Vic, wandering around in his shearling coat and hand-made shoes, slapping the Talent on the back and dropping a word in everyone's ear. She starts setting out lunch, she's got a team of people serving, because there's fifty or so clients on the set who have to eat in a short amount of time, and Vic pulls her aside . . ."

"And what, asks her for a hand job?"

Merry had, by this time, heard enough about Sonnenfeld's habits.

". . . asks her for a ride back to Ingrid's Gift."

"He's not staying for lunch."

"Not even. Brittany's really bummed, of course, that she's busted her ass trying to impress this guy who's not going to be eating a bite of her swordfish poke with umami vapor, or what-ever it is. But she's not going to pass up the opportunity to have a conversation alone. So she jumps in her catering van and offers him the passenger seat."

Merry sat back and stared at Howie. "*He left the Marsh* with the chef?"

"You know it."

"Brittany knows exactly what time Sonnenfeld disappeared!"

"*And* where he went."

Merry smiled. "Hit me with it, Seitz."

"Vic was following a mapping app on his phone."

"He had his phone?"

"He did when Brittany last saw him."

"Good to know. And?"

"He told her to turn up the Wauwinet road."

"To the Squam Swamp parking lot."

Howie nodded. "She dropped him there, Mer, at twelve-fifty-one P.M. He told her he was meeting someone, who'd get him back to the house."

"Did he say who?"

"Winter Candler." Howie's expression sobered. "Brittany said he was smug about it, like he had a hot date."

"Oh, shit, no. *Not* Winter."

There was silence for an instant, as each of them considered this. Merry had only seen Winter Candler once, that afternoon at Stella Maris, but Howie knew the idea of the waif with the drowning eyes killing Vic Sonnenfeld was a hard sell.

"That's physically impossible," Merry said, frowning, "if we believe either Ansel MacKay or Winter's account of yesterday. Both of them say she was in town, at Stroll, at that time."

"So does her father, who was worried sick about her bodyguard losing her in the crowd," Howie added. "He showed me the texts he exchanged with this woman named Laura at twelve-forty-two, which he says is right around when Sonnenfeld said goodbye and disappeared from the Marsh."

"So Winter *wasn't* verifiably in town," Merry mused, "if her bodyguard lost her! We have only Ansel's word they were together on the shuttle. He could be covering for her."

"And she for him."

"So they're working together?" Merry queried, her nose wrinkling.

"How? And why? They both said they met for the first time here, on Friday."

"Do we believe that story, though?"

"There's another thing, Mer. Candler tells me he got a Runner—that's somebody who drives cars from a film set when powerful people tell them to—to drive him into town when they broke for lunch. Which, according to the call sheet, was at one-thirty. He says he went looking for Winter. Only he didn't find her."

"So either Chris Candler or his daughter could have met Vic Sonnenfeld in Squam Swamp with a shotgun."

"Only if we're writing a TV serial, here." Howie sighed heavily. He was extremely tired. "I don't know. What *do* we believe? What *is* evidence, anyway? Does truth or fact even exist, or is it all *interpretation?*"

"Here's a fact," Merry said practically. "The NRTA shuttle driver will remember two people in their early twenties riding out Polpis Road yesterday, and getting off at an unscheduled stop for Stella Maris. They'd have to have been on the twelve-forty shuttle. Not many people were headed out that way while Santa was parading up Main."

"Okay," Howie said. "Say the driver confirms Winter was on the shuttle and not at Squam. How's this for an alternative? Sonnenfeld *thought* he was meeting Winter. He was somehow egotistical enough to believe this twenty-year-old girl he assaulted the previous night would be attracted to a guy old enough to be her grandfather. The killer—Chris Candler?—knew this, and *lured* him to Squam Swamp."

"That makes Ansel and Winter's version of events completely truthful, makes the timeline fit, and makes me happy," Merry concluded. "But it's tentative, Seitz."

"It is," he admitted.

"Is Brittany being truthful? Is it possible she drove Sonnenfeld to the Swamp, told him to walk to Marker Thirteen, then stalked him with a shotgun she'd hidden in the back of her van?"

"It's not *impossible*."

"Except then she'd never get her dream job in LA."

"Yeah. Well . . . there's a story about that."

Merry went very still, her gaze fixed on Howie. "The offer was rescinded?"

"It came with strings." Howie sat upright, the better to ward off sleep. "On the ride to Squam Swamp, Vic told Brittany he'd love nothing more than to get her a job at L'Enclos—that's the famous chef's restaurant in Brentwood—and that he'd even find a slot for her sister Nora. Provided Brittany could do him a favor."

"Ah. The noose closes."

"He wanted her to download some financials—proprietary info—from Struna's computer in the main house. The one that sits in his office, where I took statements tonight. He thought Brittany would have access to it in her role as housekeeper. He gave her a list of entities and portfolios he was targeting."

"In *writing?*" Merry asked, aghast.

"One of the drawbacks of being seventy-three," Howie observed. "The man was old school."

"Does she have this list?"

Howie shook his head. "Gave it straight to Struna, next time she saw him. And put all thoughts of LA out of her head."

ANSEL MACKAY WAS restless tonight, a sensation that in past years he would not have known how to manage. As a child he'd struggled with an excess of energy common to boys with active brains and bodies, and a succession of teachers, flummoxed by his demands, had advised his father to medicate him for attention-deficit disorder. This had begun in kindergarten and continued through eleventh grade, with the amphetamine dosages increasing every six months as Ance's body grew. By the age of seventeen, at six foot three and one hundred ninety pounds, he was so accustomed to prescription speed that he needed something stronger to accelerate his mind. He found it one day in the lunchroom at school, when a friend offered him a line of cocaine.

Expensive recreational drugs were a dime a dozen among the wealthy elites of DC's private schools, and simple networks existed for their purchase and consumption. Rarely did the clandestine activity in controlled substances surge above the radar, resulting in notoriety or painful consequences; the time a girl from a neighboring school went into toxic shock from a drug dropped anonymously in her drink; or the clutch of five kids that hit a tree at 3 A.M. and were tossed through a windshield in a crystal splatter of blood and bone. Ansel curated his habit like a connoisseur, shepherded it to college at Colgate, where he played rugby. A collarbone injury there introduced him to opioid pain management, and the euphoria attendant upon Oxycodone. A combined cocaine/opioid dependency only caught up with him when he was forcibly ejected from school in the spring of his third year.

Now, on a Sunday evening in December three years later, he was no longer an adolescent. The frontal lobe of his male brain was steadying. He felt, most days, like a reasoned observer of his own impulses, not the plaything of them. He had learned, with the help of methadone and patient professionals, to exercise restraint.

So when the restlessness hit like a curling wave, and he propelled himself out of his chair and paced his bedroom, he knew enough to understand that his emotions could not be subdued by chemicals.

He walked downstairs to the library, where his father was staring at his phone.

There was no sign of Janet.

"We're cleared to leave tomorrow morning," Ron said.

"The police are letting us go?"

"About time." Ron glanced up at him. "None of this would have happened if you'd left that woman alone."

"She'd still be dead. And she'd still be my mother."

Ron held his gaze a moment, contemplating various answers, then to Ansel's surprise, he sighed wearily. "I'm sorry, kiddo. I should have told you far more about Mary Alice while she was still alive. You might have avoided so much pain, and so much unnecessary and destructive learning. I know my apology is completely inadequate. I haven't handled much about your mother, or this weekend, very well."

"That's because you're afraid," Ansel said.

"Afraid?" His father was taken aback, about to bristle with denial.

Ansel sat down next to him and reached his hand tentatively to Ron's knee. "Afraid of losing me, like you lost her. That's why you clamped down so tight, the whole time I was growing up, and still can't let go of your surveillance. It drives me crazy, but I understand it."

"It's not *surveillance*, Ance. It's—" He hesitated, searching for a neutral word.

"Hypervigilance," Ansel said quietly, "brought on by past trauma. I've got all the language for these therapeutic situations. But I'm not fucking up, Dad, and I'm not going anywhere. At least—not for good."

"You could go back to college," Ron said hopefully.

"That's a conversation for another day." Ansel rose and held out his hand. "Tonight, can I just borrow the car?"

"So it's possible, I suppose," Meredith said as Howie cleared his dishes and followed her to the kitchen, "that Struna was so pissed at Victor Sonnenfeld for trying to steal his proprietary business information, that he went after him with a shotgun."

"But he'd be targeting the man *after* he was dropped at Squam Swamp," Howie pointed out, "not luring him there *first*. Brittany gave Struna the list a couple of hours after Sonnenfeld got out of her van. She went right back to the Field Station to finish serving lunch, and didn't return to Ingrid's Gift Saturday until a few minutes past three o'clock."

"And our working theory is that somebody else lured Sonnenfeld to Marker Thirteen around twelve-forty-five, in the belief he was meeting Winter Candler." Merry ran some water into the dirty dishes and left them piled in the sink. "But that doesn't square in the slightest with the tracking information Struna found from targeting Vic's phone."

Which had him in Town a few minutes after 2 P.M. "No. And given that we haven't found that phone . . ."

Merry rested her hands on the edge of the farmhouse sink, a sponge gripped in her fingers. "I'm thinking the phone's a decoy. You know? Candy's folks will definitely find it, somewhere at Four Howard Court. Because the killer deliberately dropped it far from Squam Swamp."

This was probably prophetic, Howie, thought, and brought coherence to what was otherwise inexplicable. Tracking Vic's phone was not the same as tracking Vic, once phone and man were separated. An inherent flaw in Mike Struna's GoldenEye.

"I'd have dropped it in the ocean," he said.

Merry laughed. "Because you're not subtle enough. *This* killer thought it could be a useful distraction. A beacon leading everybody in the wrong direction. Which suggests that he—or she—knows something about Mike Struna and his software's capabilities."

"I suppose." Howie considered this. Marni LeGuin had known

everything about it. "We still need a connection to Mary Alice Fillmore."

"There *is* a minor one."

"Between Sonnenfeld and Fillmore?" Howie looked suddenly alert.

"Between Ingrid's Gift and Stronghold. Sonnenfeld threw a fundraiser for Janet Brimhold MacKay a few years back. Then he asked her chief of staff to help him with his wife's film permitting on Nantucket."

"But Mary Alice was at Stella Maris. That's pretty slight."

"I agree."

"Still, a weird coincidence."

"And we don't believe in those." Merry dried her hands on a towel. "Also, Ron MacKay visited Mary Alice's house yesterday, right before dinner."

"*What?*" Howie said. "He went to Stella Maris? He told me this morning he had no idea Fillmore was on the island!"

"He still says that." Merry leaned against the kitchen island, her slippered feet crossed. "The Dip Security guy gave me his gate access records. They show that Ron MacKay left Stronghold at five-twenty-seven P.M. in the secretary's official SUV. He returned at six-forty-two, in time to escort her to the second seating at Company of the Cauldron, one of her favorite restaurants."

"Good on Ron," Howie said.

"His reaction, when I confronted him with this, was interesting."

In fact, Ron MacKay's shifting moods had taught Meredith something about conscience and guilt. She had asked to see MacKay in the library that night after she'd concluded her conversation with Ansel. When he blustered into the room, it was clear that MacKay's primary concern was for his son—not himself.

"This is starting to feel like harassment, Ms. Folger," he'd said. "And I want you to know that we're leaving tomorrow morning, whether you like it or not. You know where to find us—the whole world does. My wife hasn't seen Mary Alice since they were girls, playing together at Children's Beach, and Ansel has nothing more to tell you. His knowledge of his mother is extremely limited."

"—To the past three days," Merry said quietly, "and the finding of her body. Grant me the courtesy of admitting I have every reason to question him."

MacKay laughed abruptly. "As long as you don't scapegoat him!"

"Is that what this feels like?"

"It's constantly happening to Ance! Talk about always being in the wrong place at the right time—the kid can't catch a break! *I will not allow him to be saddled with Mary Alice's murder.*"

This was a side of Ron MacKay Merry hadn't glimpsed, and with a sudden shaft of understanding she saw the pieces on the investigative board shift slightly before her eyes. Ron would not scapegoat his son; so who did he believe was doing it? Janet? Her staff?

Was one of them strategically throwing the shadow of blame on the most vulnerable person at Stronghold?

Micheline. Who would protect Janet above and beyond anyone else in her life.

"I promise you that I will conduct this investigation as objectively as I know how," Merry told Ron, "and that I will only bring charges that I can prove. I am capable of nothing more, nor less."

"I realize that," he said unexpectedly, and sank down into the chair Ansel had vacated. "I've been researching you."

Merry blinked at him. "And?"

"You have an impressive and unimpeachable record. I can see

why you hold the position you do, regardless of your relatively young age."

Merry waited a beat before saying, "Then you'll understand why I'm showing you these records, Mr. MacKay, and requesting your honest response to them." She handed him the gate access time sheets. "You left the house yesterday evening at 5:27 P.M. Where did you go?"

His lips compressed. "I took a drive out around the island."

"Hmmm." Merry was deliberately noncommittal. "Just like you took a drive around town Friday?"

"You can go stir-crazy, even in a house as gorgeous as this, when your every movement is watched and codified," he said.

"Is that why you haven't pressured Ansel about his spontaneous walks?"

"He didn't sign on for Janet's life. I did."

Merry inclined her head. "I like your son, for what it's worth."

"What can you possibly know about him?"

"He's kind. And empathetic. He's capable of forgiveness."

"None of which I've taught him."

"Sometimes life is the best teacher."

"Some people would say that Ance is incapable of learning anything," Ron observed bitterly.

"They'd be wrong. Everyone grows up. Whether they're forced, or not." Merry made a show of looking at her computer screen. "What if I told you, Mr. MacKay, that there was a witness to your car on the Polpis road yesterday?"

It was a gamble, but Merry had nothing to lose by taking it.

Ron was tired enough, or guilty enough, not to fight her. "Then I'd have to admit I was there," he said succinctly.

Merry waited.

"*Yes*, I drove out to Stella Maris. It was an impulse. I hadn't seen the place for years."

Merry still said nothing. Just kept her eyes trained on MacKay's face.

"I keep paying the property taxes on it, but otherwise the house might as well have been wiped off the face of the earth," he muttered. "I didn't want to see it, didn't want to think about it—"

"Why not sell it?"

"Because it deserved to die."

The bleakness of the words sent a chill through Merry.

"And yet, we had such wonderful times there! *Once*. We were married from that house—did you know that?"

"No. Tell me," Merry suggested.

He let out a shaky breath, and ran his fingers through his hair. The gesture was so like his son's, and yet so uncharacteristic of Ron's tidy self-control, that Merry was slightly jarred. "I couldn't believe how terrible it looked. Like an open wound. Like the marriage we had. Not a shred of paint left, the roof sagging, a front window smashed in . . ."

"I've seen it."

"Then you know. How could she possibly live there??"

The final words were agonized.

"Comfortably enough."

"I cut the utilities long ago!"

"She was burning wood in the kitchen's iron stove. She cooked on it, too—and I suspect she took showers at the local health club. I'll be checking tomorrow whether she paid for a membership there. She kept a low profile at the house because she knew very clearly she was inhabiting it illegally—but she moved around the island at will. It helped that the pandemic encouraged isolation."

Ron put his head in his hands. "I hated her for so many years. For the way she abandoned me, abandoned *him* . . ."

"What happened to your marriage, Mr. MacKay?"

"Drugs happened." His face emerged, still cupped in his hands. "And she would not give them up, no matter how much I tried to force her. You say you didn't find anything in the house when you searched it?"

"I think she was clean," Merry said. "She was successful at what she did. She'd made quite a name for herself as a photographer over the past twenty years."

"Oh, she was always a gifted artist. I think that was the problem," he said. "She felt stifled, living with me. Forced to conform. So she rebelled in the most thorough way she knew how, and went off to wander the earth."

"You punished her by destroying the house."

"And telling Ance she was dead." He laughed again, this time brokenly. "That worked out really well."

"I suspect he rebels when forced to conform, too. Did you confront Mary Alice, yesterday?"

"At the house?" Ron MacKay finally met Merry's eyes, returned from whatever dream he'd been drifting through. "No. I told you, I didn't know she was there. I just walked around the wreck and tried the doors. It's still boarded up, there's trash strewn around . . . Her mother would be devastated, if she could see it. Maeve loved that place."

"Maybe you can come to a different arrangement," Merry said, "going forward. It's a priceless piece of land."

"I know," he said, and she was startled to detect the shine of tears in his eyes. "Would you believe me, if I said everything about the time we had there was priceless?"

28 | Stroll, Sunday Night

WINTER STOOD LISTENING in the main room, her breath
suspended, for the slightest sound from the far side of the Guest
Cottage. Her father's bedroom and that of his assistant, Carlos,
were beyond the kitchen area. Hers was on the opposite end.
There were no lights under her dad's door, but a thin line of yellow still showed beneath Carlos's. She imagined him sitting up
with earbuds, talking to his girlfriend or listening to music. In
either case, he wouldn't be hearing *her*.

She moved noiselessly across the floor and slid through the
front door. It closed behind her without a groan—the advantage
of Mike Struna's impeccable building standards—and she flitted
like a shadow down the drive.

At the Polpis road gate, she waved at the person on duty—
a woman this time, working the night shift—and said blithely,
"Just meeting a friend! Back soon!" as she ducked under the
barrier.

Ansel was waiting there, in a late-model Subaru Forester plas-
tered with Nantucket beach permits. His stepmother's car. Ron
had given him the keys.

"Hey," he said, as Winter pulled open the passenger door.
"Thanks for coming out."

"Are you kidding? I was dying to get away."

They grinned at each other, faces lit only by the dashboard
lights, but her eyes were still brilliant in her pale face, and Ansel

thought she was the most beautiful thing he'd ever seen. She buckled the seatbelt over her lap. Ansel pulled away.

"So you're definitely going back to DC tomorrow?" she said, as he headed toward the Rotary on the Polpis road.

"Apparently. We'll see if the next twelve hours make any difference in the murder investigation."

"Oh my God!" Winter exclaimed. "I totally forgot! You haven't heard! *Vic Sonnenfeld is dead.*"

"I know. The police were at my stepmother's house."

He had kept his text message brief: *Leaving in the a.m. Feel like going for a drive? Be there in fifteen.*

And she'd been similarly terse. *I'll meet you at the end of the road.*

"They talked to you?" Her eyes were enormous. "They talked to me, too. He was killed the same way as your mom."

"Yep. They think there's a connection."

"But not a deer hunter."

He shook his head. "Crazy, right? I mean, we both come to Nantucket for Stroll weekend—"

"And have no idea the other exists—"

"And then murder happens."

Winter giggled. "It's like an HBO show!" Then she clapped her hand over her mouth, horrified. "Ance—I'm so sorry. I mean, this is *your mother*. Vic was a shit, so I don't give a fuck about him dying, but—"

"He was?" Ansel said, glancing sideways. Winter was staring straight up the road toward the Rotary, her thumbnail in her mouth. "Why?"

She shrugged, her frail shoulders pivoting like the ends of a hanger under her oversized sweater.

Ansel reached out with his free hand and took hers. It was the first time he had really touched her. "You've been jumpy all weekend. You've been scared. If you want to talk—"

"I'm all right," she said, on a quavering note. But her fingers gripped his, and she wasn't letting go.

"It occurred to me that you've seen nothing of Stroll except Santa," he said, "and I might be gone from your life in the morning. Tonight, we're hitting my favorite high spots. Nantucket According to Ansel. You game?"

"Game," she said.

And squeezed his fingers tightly.

THEY STARTED BY dumping the car on Water Street, which was virtually empty of life at 11:04 P.M. on a Sunday night.

"This is Old North Wharf," Ansel said, throwing his arm around Winter's shoulders for warmth and steering her toward the water in front of them, "and this is the Boat Basin. Beautiful, am I right?"

"That tree!" she cried. "In that little boat! All lit up! It's magical!"

"You thought Santa flew with reindeer," Ansel said, "but in fact he sails, with a tree in his prow. All the red Christmas bulbs—that's where the Rudolph legend comes from. He drops anchor in your chimney, and then sails on across the clouds to the next dreaming girl or boy."

They gazed out at Killen's Dory, bobbing gently now in the water; waves were whishing right at their feet, but there was little other sound. "High tide's in about an hour," Ansel said.

"It's gorgeous." Winter was leaning into him, completely trusting, and he felt his heart turn over. He couldn't look at her; just focused on the wharf to his right, where there were Christmas trees set out and decorated near the Wharf Rats Club. "Come on," he said. "Let's walk up Old North. It's the most wonderful place in town, and most people don't know it."

They held hands, arms swinging, as they walked between the silent wharf houses lining each side. A few had lights still glowing; there was a sprinkling of cars. "Years ago," Ansel said, "this was scallopers' and fishermen's shacks. They'd bring the boats alongside and unload the catch. Now it's all high-end real estate. Because, the best view on the island. Although there are a lot of contenders for that."

Ghosts, too, he might have added, but he didn't want to sound too weird. He hoped, all the same, that Winter felt the presence of unseen things as he did on Old North. The way the past and present flowed together like the tides between the buildings, so that walking down the quahog shell surface of the wharf, you weren't quite sure exactly what century you'd landed in.

He stopped short, at the narrow passage between two buildings, and pivoted her shoulders ninety degrees. "Look," he commanded.

Perfectly framed in the spare yard between the two walls, flaming like a beacon, was Killen's Dory again. A different viewpoint, from a ninety-degree angle, and pinned like a jewel on the sliver of visible water. Winter drew a quick breath.

"It's like I've never seen a Christmas tree before," she whispered. "Who puts it there?"

"The same family, every year. For like, forever."

"I love this place," she said spontaneously. "When my dad said we were coming, I was like, *yeah, whatever.* But even with how horrible some of it's been, I wouldn't have missed this for the world."

What's horrible, Ance wanted to ask, but he didn't. It was possible she meant the murders, but he suspected it was something much more personal she was unwilling to talk about yet. He remembered the look of fear she'd given him when he'd surprised her in town, Saturday afternoon, and suppressed the impulse to ask questions. He just walked to the end of the wharf, tiptoeing past the houses that capped it, and which looked unoccupied tonight but might hold sleeping residents; and they stood, for a moment, shivering on the platform in the middle of the water.

"Okay," he said. "Next stop on the Ansel MacKay Nantucket Tour." And steered her back to the car.

THEY DROVE UP Cliff Road, so Winter could see the epic captains' houses behind majestic white gates, garlanded with greenery and red velvet and twinkling lights; out to Steps Beach, where they walked through towering, silent hedges to the public beach access, and stood for a moment on the landing above the crazy criss-cross flight of stairs that descended to the sand; out to Prospect Hill, and the old Quaker gravestones tipping along the hillsides; then out to the Rotary again, and a swift drive to Sconset, where Ansel walked Winter across the wooden bridge behind the Market to stand staring out at the Atlantic, an improvised sundial pegged on the darkened home at their backs.

"From here, it's straight out to Europe," he said. "Nothing but the wreck of the *Andrea Doria* in between."

He told her, then, a story from his childhood—about the year 2000, and New Year's, when he'd been two years old.

"My parents were trying to save their marriage," he said. "They came to Nantucket for the turn of the Millennium, and stayed for a week at Stella Maris."

"You remember?" Winter asked, awed.

Ansel shook his head. "My dad told me about it tonight. When we were talking. He said they drove out here, just like we did, because midnight would come to Sconset first, of anywhere on the island. It's the eastern-most point that greets the sunrise. He said he thinks it's the first place midnight hits in the United States, in fact, but he might be wrong about that. Anyway— enough people believed it, that there was a huge crowd here, on the bridge and the road beneath, welcoming in the next thousand years."

It seemed impossibly quaint, twenty-odd years on. They stood there a moment, trying to imagine it. There was absolutely no one else in Sconset on this bridge on this night, and the stars were a vast vault overhead, more stars than Winter had ever seen, with the great shaft of light from Sankaty slicing through the dark every 7.5 seconds. It was inevitable to feel as though important things were happening to them both.

"Your dad told you this? Tonight?"

"He said it gave him hope. Things were so bad . . . but it was a new year. A new millennium. And they were here . . ."

"Hope," Winter said.

"He kissed her, at midnight. And felt it," Ansel said.

She was staring at him, her eyes huge. He reached out his hand and cupped her chin.

"It's midnight somewhere," she whispered. "Kiss me."

29 | The Station, Monday Morning

"THESE ARE PHENOMENAL," Merry said, an ecstatic note in her voice that Howie Seitz had never quite heard before.

They were staring at a screen in the station's conference room, where Merry had set up one of Ralph Waldo's old slide projectors and was clicking through a round carriage-worth of images. Almost all of them were of birds.

Meredith and Howie had agreed to meet over coffee Monday morning at 7:15 A.M., well before Janet Brimhold MacKay was scheduled to depart the island. Their intention: to study Mary Alice Fillmore's precious slides, all twenty months' of them, retrieved from her ancient green touring van.

Howie had brought coffee, from The Bean.

Merry had stopped at Downyflake for Scotch Irish cake, warm from the oven.

They were trying not to spill anything on the pictures.

There was a snowy owl, ghostly and haunting, captured in midflight over the sands of Coatue.

"Hedwig," Howie said, citing the bird from Harry Potter.

There were gulls, of course—but every kind of gull to grace the island: ring-billed and herring, great black-backed and lesser; Bonaparte's gulls, and Icelandic ones, only seen rarely, in winter, out on the farthest reaches.

There were snow buntings, and eastern towhees, and

red-winged blackbirds; yellow-rumped warblers, and common house sparrows. Juncos, coots, and sapsuckers.

And then there were the magnificent herons, the egrets, and the birds of prey: ospreys and harriers. Even cormorants.

"But look at these gannets," Merry said, reverently.

This was a clutch of shots Mary Alice had culled from the most recent slides in the lot. Diving, plummeting, spiraling gannets plunging into the waters off Great Point, the dates on them from Friday.

"She must have taken these right before she died," Merry said, subdued. "And picked them up Saturday. They're so full of life."

Howie understood her point. The personality of a murder victim is muted by the act of death; the investigator teases it out in the course of the investigation. Sometimes, that personality remains opaque. Sometimes, as in the case of Vic Sonnenfeld, the victim's personality is so dominant it threatens to skew the course of inquiry altogether, possibly in the wrong direction.

But in this case, Merry and Howie had been granted a gift: the essential soul of their victim, free of the burdens of her past transgressions, her current preoccupations, or the reasons she had died by violence, was arrayed before them in all its glory. Mary Alice's art was her greatest testament. It screamed at them: *Justify this.*

"She was here producing art," Merry said. "So why did someone kill her?"

"Revenge?"

"You mean, the husband?"

"Or the kid."

"Even if we could tolerate either choice," Merry protested, "which you can't convince me we will, Seitz—that doesn't explain Vic Sonnenfeld."

"So let's look at it the other way around," he said reasonably, as he studied the image of a great cormorant, snapped the previous summer off Children's Beach. "We don't know exactly when Vic was shot. He may have been in town first, or he may have died shortly after Brittany dropped him at Squam Swamp. But let's just say he was killed *before* Mary Alice. On Saturday afternoon. Never mind *why* or *where*. And then, somebody shot her Sunday morning. *Why did she have to die?*"

Merry stood silent in thought, her fingers clicking among the images. "What a way she had with light," she murmured. "And what an eye."

Then she stood still.

"Seitz," she said. "*What an eye.* What if she saw something— photographed it—that she didn't even realize she'd seen?"

They stared at each other, transfixed.

"Imagine it," Merry persisted. "Mary Alice with her camera lifted, eye in the viewfinder, totally focused on a bird . . . while in the background . . ."

"Someone is committing murder."

"In Squam Swamp," Merry finished.

"Mary Alice was a witness," Howie said.

"Of Vic's murder."

Howie's mind raced backwards. "She was in the swamp. *That day.* Winter said she was driven out of the Field Station by all the activity, Saturday—she couldn't stand the noise and the camera cranes, fifty people disturbing the birds—"

"So she moved her show to Squam Swamp."

Merry rifled furiously among the storage boxes scattered on the broad conference table. There were hundreds of slides, but the boxes were carefully dated.

"The most recent we've got are from Friday." She looked up, dread in her heart. "Seitz, the murderer tore all the film out of her cameras—"

"That's why he targeted Mary Alice," Howie said. "Winter went back to Ingrid's Gift Saturday, and showed the whole room

Mary Alice's Instagram account. She *fan-girled*, as she put it—talked up this woman photographer who'd been at the Marsh, then moved on to the Swamp—"

"And shot something she wasn't supposed to see. The killer heard Winter, and was afraid he'd had a witness he never knew about."

"He went over to Stella Maris first thing next morning, and shot Mary Alice. Tore apart her camera equipment."

"Which was right," Merry said, defeated. "It was the right thing to do, Seitz. He got the film and destroyed the evidence."

"Not necessarily," Howie objected. "Where were all of these developed, Mer?"

"Right here in town," she said. "At the place above Mitchell's."

"She dropped off Friday's film and picked it up Saturday," Howie said, pointing to the shots of gannets. "What if she *dropped off* Saturday's film at the same time? After she was done with work and Ansel?"

"I suppose it's just possible," Merry acknowledged, not wanting to hope. "It's worth a try, Seitz."

But he was studying a text while she thought out loud.

"From Candy," he said. "Her intern just pulled Vic Sonnenfeld's phone out of trashcan on Howard Court. The rental agents say the house was locked and empty all weekend."

IT WAS AS Howie was rocketing out of the parking lot in his Toyota that he saw something unexpected: Ansel MacKay, walking toward the station entrance, when he should have been on his way to Ackerman Field, and the secretary of state's government flight home.

Howie pulled up beside him, rolled down the window, and said, "Ance!"

The young man turned. "Detective Seitz. The person I came to see."

Howie was supposed to be driving into town to consult a film developer. He glanced at his car's dashboard clock; the camera store would not be open yet. He looked at Ansel.

"Aren't you supposed to be flying out?" he said.

"I have some things to do first."

Howie nodded. The Scotch Irish cake had been excellent, as always, but he was still hollow inside.

"Can I buy you breakfast?" he asked.

"WINTER CANDLER TALKED to me last night," Ansel began.

They were sitting companionably at a window table in the Downyflake, a stone's throw from the station and, Howie reflected, the quickest route to the airport, if Ansel felt his obligations were satisfied once he'd come clean to the police.

"You saw her last night? After . . . after we'd taken statements from everyone at Ingrid's Gift?"

Ansel wrinkled his brows. "Dude. How old *are* you? The night was young when you left the place."

Howie laughed. He supposed Ansel was right; or right, at least, for his generation. The gulf between twenty-three and thirty had never felt so huge.

"So, you two got together last night."

While I was hanging with Ney.

"Yeah," Ansel said. "It was . . . pretty special." He shifted on his bench seat, and toyed with his poached eggs. "She hadn't seen much of the island. During *Stroll.* Which, you'll admit, is an absolute crime. So we took a drive. And Winter talked to me."

He looked suddenly miserable, and Howie realized he was about to receive a confidence, and that Ansel felt guilty about sharing what might be his *girlfriend's* deepest secrets with the police.

"She shared something really personal?" he said.

Ansel nodded.

"Was it about Vic Sonnenfeld? And sexual abuse?"

Ansel looked suddenly astounded. He glanced around, as though there might be a hidden camera recording his reaction. "Wait. She *told* you? About her *mom?*"

"Her mom? *What?* No," Howie retorted, confused. And feeling as though he'd touched a live wire, or a burning hot stove. "What are you talking about?"

"What are *you* talking about?" Ansel demanded.

"Vic Sonnenfeld groping Winter, at dinner Friday night."

"He *did* that? Shit. She didn't tell me." Ansel slid across his seat. He was planning to flee the restaurant. Howie reached out and grasped his wrist.

"Hey," he said. "Sit back down. I'll tell you what she told me first. Then *you* can tell me what she said last night. We're only going to get through this if we help each other."

"Okay," Ansel said, breathing hard. "But I'm *so* going to find Winter once this is over."

HOWIE TONED DOWN Victor Sonnenfeld's invasive hands, and exactly where they had gone, because he felt Ansel was volatile at the moment. But he conveyed the essence of what had happened, and while Ansel absorbed it all, managed to finish his scrambled eggs.

"Now you," Howie said, draining his coffee.

Ansel nodded. He was breathing somewhat normally, again.

"Winter said that this guy Sonnenfeld was the Evil Genie behind everything that was happening at Ingrid's Gift, and that she wasn't sorry he was dead," Ansel began.

Howie nodded encouragingly, and took a bite of sausage.

"From what Winter said, I guessed he was a Hollywood mogul— sort of a power broker, in the Majority Leader sense, only with movies."

The metaphor didn't speak to Howie, but he recognized that it helped Ansel. He nodded again.

"Winter said he was a creep. A guy who thought women existed to be used. I didn't realize he'd treated her that way —"

Ansel started to scooch across the seat again and Howie said, "Ance."

"Okay." He took a deep breath, ran his fingers through his Technicolor hair. "After dinner Friday night, Winter was alone in the Guest Cottage. Sonnenfeld walked right into the place without knocking, and Winter was kind of trapped. Her father hadn't come back yet from the Barn—that's what she said, I guess they were having dinner there . . ."

"Uh-huh," Howie said.

"It's just so weird," Ansel fumed. "I *knew* when I ran into her Saturday afternoon that she was freaked out."

"In town?" Howie asked.

"Yeah. By the Pacific Club. There was this look of fear on her face when I touched her shoulder . . . I've been worried about it ever since."

Further confirmation that the two had been where they said they were, Howie thought. Ansel was too angry to be checking his statements.

"She was afraid. Really spooked. Like she was running from something, alone in town. It took me until last night to get enough confidence built up, for her to tell me . . ."

Ansel stopped short. He looked at Howie.

"Sonnenfeld stood at the bar in Winter's guest house and opened a bottle of scotch. He poured himself three fingers, while she stood, backed up to the fireplace, hoping she could text her dad or somebody for help before he made his next move. But he wasn't interested in Winter's body that night. It was her *mind*."

"Her mind?" Howie repeated, perplexed.

"Of course. That's how these fuckers work—they victimize

you mentally first. After that, everything else is easy. You're vulnerable."

"Okay," Howie said. "How did he do that?"

"He started talking about her mom. What do you know about Sonya Rostov Candler?"

"Nothing at all," Howie admitted. "I haven't had time to explore every nook and cranny of this case."

"She was a rising star when Winter's father met her," Ansel said. "I've looked it up. She was more famous than he was. He was waiting tables when she was being talked about as an Oscar nominee."

"Huh," Howie said.

"Anyway—she married Chris, and his career started taking off, and they were both represented by CMI. That's . . ."

"Vic Sonnenfeld's agency. I know," Howie said.

"And then a few years after Winter was born, something went wrong. Sonya blew up. She started drinking uncontrollably— I'm not judging, believe me, I know what addiction is like—and then she killed herself. And Winter found her."

Howie hadn't known any of this. He'd had his head focused entirely on who, what, when and how—for the murder at Stella Maris, and then Squam Swamp. There'd been no time to dive down the rabbit holes of Hollywood or Washington.

So he might be forgiven for feeling, suddenly, that everything Ansel was saying was irrelevant. None of this connected Sonnenfeld to Mary Alice. He should have kept going on his errand to the camera store.

"Why are you telling me this?" he asked.

Ansel looked at him, defeated.

"Because I think Winter killed him," he said.

MIKE STRUNA WAS readying his classic cabin cruiser, *Equity*, for a jaunt out into Polpis Harbor, when he noticed his personal chef striding down the path between the hedges, toward the boathouse and the dock running out beside it.

Almost everyone else was off again today to the UMass Field Station, for the third day of filming in Folger's Marsh. Even Winter Candler had gone to the set to watch her father and Marni film. It didn't matter how many bodies fell in the neighboring landscape; the show, it seemed, must go on. Vic's murder had barely broken Carly's stride. To Mike's surprise, she had nodded in the direction of death, called her producers to reassure them, tightened her film schedule and budget, and moved on.

Mike had told Carly he was there for her—that he'd always be there for her—and he had tried to tamp down the flare of hope that had flickered for years in his soul: that someday, she'd see the devotion right in front of her, and reward it. Because of Carly, he'd never been able to sustain a serious relationship with another woman, no matter how hard he'd tried. Because of Carly, he'd moved heaven and earth to prove himself a successful man, worthy of her trust. He'd made a vast fortune because Carly might, eventually, need it. He'd offered her the run of Ingrid's Gift so she'd recognize just how much he'd acquired—and that he was no longer the inconsequential kid from Queens she'd first encountered a quarter of a century ago.

It had not been enough.

Nothing would ever be enough.

Brittany's auburn hair was undone today, flowing long and wild over her shoulders, and she was staring out at the spectacular shoreline at the end of the dock. He was impressed that she'd come to him immediately Saturday with Sonnenfeld's extortion. He never assumed he could trust his employees to have his back—everyone, Mike knew, had a price.

He waved to her, and she smiled back.

"Hey, Boss. Watcha doin'?"

"Getting ready to take this beautiful girl out for a spin."

"Anywhere special?" she asked, coming to lean in the barn door.

He shrugged. "Probably the Wauwinet."

"It's closed." Brittany ran her eyes over *Equity*, looking wistful. Mike couldn't blame her. The boat was hard not to love. He'd never taken Brittany out in her, either, which was something he'd have to address.

"Run across to Coatue instead," she suggested. "There's supposed to be a snowy owl over there—and they're rare. Besides, you were just at the Wauwinet, weren't you?"

His hands stilled on the mooring line. He rose and studied her face. "What do you mean, Brit?"

"Saturday. You were at the Wauwinet. I saw *Equity* moored there."

"Really? When?"

She suddenly looked hesitant. "It was me, you know. Who gave Mr. Sonnenfeld a ride. He asked me to drop him at Squam Swamp—while I was serving lunch at the Field Station. I ran him over there, and came back right away. I didn't take very long."

"But you went up the road to the hotel?"

"Yeah," she said uncertainly. "I had to pee, to be honest, and was hoping somebody was there, so I could use the bathroom. But nobody was. I had to go in the port-a-john near the Great Point guardhouse."

"And God, does that *stink*," Mike said. "Hey. You've persuaded me. I think I'll go to Coatue after all—I've never seen a snowy owl. Would you like to come with, Britt?"

Her face lit up, then fell. "I'm on lunch duty again, today."

Mike pulled out his phone. "I'll call in takeout to the Marsh. You deserve a day off, girlfriend. I owe you, after all you've done for me."

"SONNENFELD APPARENTLY SEDUCED her mother," Ansel was saying. "Or assaulted her. Or something. He made her trade sex for Chris Candler's roles. His meteoric stardom. And threatened to expose her to all of LA as a whore if she ever breathed a word about it."

"He told Winter all this?" Howie asked, amazed.

"Friday night. In her own guest house. Which was totally typical—he brought his threat right where she was *sleeping*, where her *father* was sleeping, to prove that nowhere was safe, and no one could protect her."

"Why?" Howie asked.

Ansel simply stared at him, stunned at Howie's naivete. "He was trying to get Winter under his power," he said. "He shared this horrible secret with her—that her mother was so ashamed of her life and what she'd done, that she'd gone insane and killed herself—and then threatened Winter in the same way."

"Pretty risky," Howie said.

Ansel leaned across the table, hammering his point home between the ketchup and mustard bottles. "Sonnenfeld told Winter that if she didn't do what he asked, he'd tell her father about Sonya. The bogus version, of course—how she'd been unfaithful. How she'd had an affair with Vic, and when he wouldn't betray his great and beloved client *Chris*, she'd killed herself.

"Winter was blown away. Devastated. All she could think about was shielding her father."

"So you think she somehow went and found a shotgun, and killed him the next day."

"He completely triggered her." Ansel sat back. "She had a relapse that night—started binging and purging. The whole thing that had sent her into rehab in the first place. I can completely see how she could have killed the guy."

Howie was older than Ansel, and should have felt more experienced than the younger man across the table. But he was realizing, as he investigated more cases of violence, how little of life he had truly experienced.

He was forced to ask himself what Chris Candler had truly known about his late wife, Sonya, and the man he'd trusted with his career for twenty-five years. Candler was an actor. He was supremely capable of selling his innocence to Howie—even if he was guilty as hell of murder.

You don't mess with Chris Candler's women, Winter had said. Sonya's exploitation and suicide gave Candler a powerful motive. But could he have killed Vic Sonnenfeld in Squam Swamp when he was supposed to be on camera at Folger's Marsh all day?

There was that lunch hour. Nobody could prove Candler had actually gone into town.

Howie sighed. He was going to have to check with everyone in production Saturday for the Runner that Candler claimed had driven him to Stroll. But that still wouldn't explain how Candler might have gotten a weapon.

—Unless there was one sitting right in front of him.

"Props," Howie said out loud. "Shit. There are probably weapons right there on *The Hopeless* set. It's a crime drama."

"What are you talking about?" Ansel demanded.

Howie brought his attention back to the matter at hand.

"Look," he said. "Winter couldn't have killed Vic Sonnenfeld. She was with *you* during the period of time we believe Sonnenfeld died. There was no way you could have known that—we've been deliberately vague about the time frame—but I think she's in the clear."

"You do?" he said, his expression lightening. He sat up straighter in his seat. "You really think she's okay?"

"You found her Saturday downtown. You visited Mary Alice together. Your mother dropped her back at Ingrid's Gift, and she reported in to Laura and her dad. We can double-check those times with Laura. Winter says she talked about Mary Alice and her Instagram account in front of everyone before dinner—and other people in the room have confirmed that. Her movements Saturday are accounted for. Winter didn't kill Vic. I don't see how it could have been done."

Ansel rubbed his eyes, as though banishing an unpleasant vision. "You're sure?"

"There's another thing. No matter how great her motive for offing Vic," Howie added, "Winter had absolutely no reason to kill your mother."

30 | Stroll Monday

THERE WAS CLOUD cover rolling in from the mainland as *Equity* passed through the channel leading from Polpis Harbor into the greater Nantucket Harbor beyond. The channel was narrow, with Quaise Point on the left hand and Pocomo Head on their right. The tide was still coming in, and would not be fully high for another hour. There was a light mist throwing a scrim over the landscape, and an occasional scattering of rain, but it was warmer today than it had been all weekend—in the mid-fifties, ridiculous for December. By evening it would be colder, Mike knew, and the mist would turn into full-blown rain.

Brittany was taking advantage of the warmer day, with a light windbreaker over her work sweater. She had pulled her hair up into a knot secured with elastic, and was sitting beside him in the Chris-Craft's main cockpit. She was grinning from ear to ear. He would, Mike thought, offer to let her steer. But not until they were in the middle of the harbor; there were sandbars, and he did not want *Equity* grounded.

"Whereabouts was the snowy owl sighted?" he called over the sound of the inboard engine and the churn of the waves.

"Coskata," she yelled back. "But I think it could be anywhere. Maybe there's more than one!"

Coskata was on the eastern end of Coatue, closer to Great Point and its over-sand vehicle traffic than Mike wanted to be. He was making for Five-Finger Point, dead ahead. It was roughly in the middle of Coatue's barrier beach and one of its notable cuspate spits.

"Here," he said, rising from his seat. "You take command. I'll ready the anchor."

Brittany scooched over, lifting her feet to clear the chrome gear shift, clearly thrilled to have her hands on the wheel. "What am I steering for?"

"Keep the nun to port," he ordered, with a gesture to the red buoy, "and head straight for that point of sand."

"Okay, Boss!"

Mike smiled at her wind-whipped head. Then he crawled back over the second cockpit and engine hatch to the third cockpit, in the stern. Lying at the bottom, bundled neatly in a tarp, was his shotgun.

"WHAT'VE YOU GOT for me, Seitz?"

"I was right." Howie placed the packet of slides he'd retrieved from the developer on Merry's desk. "Mary Alice *did* take Saturday's film into the shop that evening. They hadn't developed the slides yet. I showed my badge, and they did it while I waited."

"Great." Merry reached for the packet.

Howie followed her into the conference room. She'd left the slide carousel on the table. "Let's hope we've got something other than birds," he said.

Carefully, Merry dropped the slides into the carousel and flipped on the switch. "Hooded mergansers," she said, clicking through the first few; "those, and the pictures of buffleheads would be from right after dawn or so, when she started out at Folger's Marsh. Then the film production people startled the wildlife, so she upped stakes and moved to Squam Swamp."

A few catbirds and some black-capped chickadees filled the next few prints. Mary Alice had focused on them closely, beaks open and toes clenched on swaying branches. "What's really stunning is how she's caught the light shafting through these thickets. Look at the red bittersweet against those pale white trunks!"

"She went up the Wauwinet road for a bit, too. Some of these are from Great Point."

Merry flipped to the last pictures from the roll. These had been taken away from the woodlands of Squam, among deserted sandy dunes. "Harbor seals," she said, "at a haul-out. Probably Coskata. I guess they're part of her story on climate change, too."

The seal population was growing on Nantucket, as it was throughout the Cape and Islands district; and with seals came sharks, hunting them. Howie bent closer to study the images; Mary Alice again had focused directly on their faces, so that each liquid eye and quivering whisker was etched against the backdrop of sand. "I think she was closer to the hotel," he said. "Isn't that their dock in the background?"

Merry glanced again at the shot, then squinted. "The Wauwinet is closed for the season. What's a boat doing tied up there?"

The hotel owned a launch it used as a water taxi—*Wauwinet Lady*—but that boat was white, Merry thought. She walked toward the screen and peered more closely at the projected image.

"Look at this, Seitz," she said.

Howie joined her. Half the image was projected onto his shoulder. "That's a vintage Chris-Craft runabout," he said appreciatively. "Don't see those every day."

Merry stared at him. "Look at you! When did you become a wooden boat aficionado?"

"You kidding? Those things are *money*, Mer."

She turned back to the screen. "Mary Alice was focusing on the seal, and probably never realized she caught this in the background." Mary traced the outline of the Chris-Craft's hull with her finger. "We've been thinking in terms of roads. Roads and parking lots and *cars*. We never thought of someone coming and going to the Squam Swamp area by boat."

"Where's a map?" Seitz said.

"I've got a chart." Merry skittered out of the room and returned with a large roll of paper, three feet wide and five feet long. The nautical graph of Nantucket's waters was more useful than any map, indeed, because it showed the depth of every inlet and channel, from Polpis Harbor straight over to the Wauwinet Hotel's dock.

Squam Swamp was a stone's throw from the mooring. A brisk walk on a sunny Saturday. And with the hotel closed for the season, there would be no one to watch a killer come and go.

"Seitz, does the name *Equity* mean anything to you?"

He shook his head. "I can find out who it's registered to."

"Do," Merry said.

THE RAIN STARTED coming down in earnest on Folger's Marsh at 1:39 that afternoon, as the cast and production crew were dipping into the offerings of a local food truck sent by Mike Struna.

"How lovely of him," Carly said. "But he shouldn't have. I contracted with his chef for lunch catering. She's being paid extra to do it."

Marni LeGuin leaned into Winter Candler and murmured, "Checking every line item in her budget, I see. This would *not* be the time to ask where the vegan options are. Or if *we're* allowed to charge extra for standing out in the rain."

"Next time," Winter said. She was huddled beside her father, who held an umbrella protectively over them both.

"Would you like to go home, sweetie?"

"To the house? Or California?"

"Actually," Carly interjected, looking up from her phone, "I think we should all call it quits for today. We're not going to shoot anything useful in these conditions. And it's supposed to get worse as the day goes on."

Somewhat dispiritedly, the production packed up its equipment and Talent, stowing all of it in various vans, and headed back up Polpis Road to Ingrid's Gift.

"Brittany better not expect to be paid for today," Carly said to Chris Candler as they drove under the arch at the Barn. "And I intend to ask her for an explanation."

But there was no sign of Brittany when they walked into the main house.

The police, however, were waiting.

MEREDITH AND HOWIE walked together down to the boathouse. They left Tori Ambrose in the great room, with orders to keep everyone inside. They had hoped that Mike Struna would be alone when they approached him, his houseguests absent at their work. But the weather had changed everyone's plans.

It was quiet when they reached the dock, but the lights were on in the boathouse's second-floor windows.

Meredith mounted the stairs, her eyes on the apartment door, while Howie slid open the barn door and checked on the Chris-Craft inside. They did not expect to find a weapon after all this time, but thought it was worth a look.

"It's possible someone other than Struna took out the Chris-Craft," Howie pointed out. "I mean, why would *he* shoot Vic Sonnenfeld?"

"*Why* doesn't matter," Merry reminded him, "once you know *how*. It's a quick walk from the Wauwinet to Squam Swamp, and he could easily transport a weapon in his boat and take it back to Ingrid's Gift without anyone being the wiser. Nobody thinks twice about the property owner going out on the water—he's not part of the film production. Nobody's watching him."

And it was a short walk, too, from Ingrid's Gift to Stella Maris the following morning—when Mary Alice Fillmore died. Ansel and Winter had walked over Sunday afternoon.

"Struna was probably spooked when Winter Candler showed everyone her Instagram account Saturday night," Merry said. "He'd have been in the great house before dinner, looking at the pictures. She told them Mary Alice was at Squam Swamp that afternoon—with a camera."

"But unless we find the shotgun," Howie objected, "it'll never stand up in court."

Now, standing in the boathouse, Howie placed his hand on the hatch over the Chris-Craft's motor and frowned. The wood was slightly warm; it had been out recently. Dumping the weapon? He would have to get Candace Moriarity here to search the cockpits and storage lockers for shotgun residue.

He tensed suddenly, horrified. What if Struna had the shotgun with him—upstairs?

Howie sped back out of the boathouse and up the outdoor steps, his hand on his holster.

Meredith was just disappearing through Struna's front door.

But before he could follow, she was back again.

"He's not here," she said. "Trusting soul. Leaves all his doors unlocked. It's almost as if he has nothing to hide."

31 | Ingrid's Gift, Monday Afternoon

IT WAS THEO Patel who changed the course of everyone's day.

The Englishman arrived from a jaunt to town in one of the production's cars, exiting from the back seat with a clutch of shopping bags and an attitude refreshed by a two-hour massage.

"Marni, darling," he announced as he entered the great room, "wait until you *see*. The hats I bought you at Peter Beaton! And the Jessica Hicks pieces! You'll be trending as soon as we throw them up on Twitter. Complete and utter *swoon*."

Marni clapped her hands and made room for him on the sofa. "Here I was resenting your spa day," she exulted, "and all the time you were thinking of *me*."

"*I have loved none but you. For you alone I think and plan*," he proclaimed. "Jane Austen's *Persuasion*, Wentworth's letter. Like you, Poppet, a *classic*."

Theo enjoyed an audience, and today he had one: they were all assembled around the fire, even Winter and Carlos and Laura and Mike Struna, silenced by his effusive entrance.

He lifted the lid of a hat box with a flourish. "Leghorn straw, large brim, wide black grosgrain. Bow down before me, do."

Only once Marni had set the confection on her head and moved to admire herself in a mirror did he notice Howie, standing with Meredith Folger.

"The policeman's back," Theo sighed. "Don't tell me someone else has been murdered."

"Mr. Patel," Howie said, "this is Chief Folger, of the Nantucket Police. You're the last person to return to the house today, so we'll make our questions brief. Have you seen Brittany Novak, Mr. Struna's chef? Mr. Struna has reported her missing."

"She served breakfast," Theo said, glancing around his fellow guests. "Not all of us take our meals like slugs, in bed on trays. I was down here bright and early for the divine café au lait and figgy pudding. Surely someone else saw her."

"Yes," Carly Simpson said. "She brought my tray to the room herself. Sometimes her sister does it, but not today."

"And her car is still here." Mike's expression was worried. "That's what's so odd. She wasn't in the house when I walked up midmorning, and I expected her to be fixing lunch—she was supposed to cater again down at the Field Station. When she hadn't shown up by eleven, I tried to raise her on her cell. Nothing. I texted her—and finally ordered fifty boxed meals from a food truck." He turned to Carly. "I didn't want to let you or *The Hopeless* down."

"You never do," she said caressingly. "You're a lifesaver, Mike."

"And a complete wanker!" Theo delivered the line in his archest manner. "What have you done with her, Mike? Tell us the story! We're all *agog* to know."

Mike frowned. "I don't know what you mean, Theo. I'm as confused as anyone. It's not like Brittany to go AWOL. She's been so dependable the past two years—"

"Silly!" Theo walked toward him, wagging a manicured finger. "I saw you jet out in that gorgeous boat myself, as I was getting into my car this morning. And Brittany was right beside you— that red hair is *unmistakable*."

Mike drew back his fist and struck Theo squarely on the jaw. Then he turned his back on the front hall, where Tori was standing, and pulled open the great room's French doors. Before anyone in the room could react, he took off toward the boat-house at a run.

Howie Seitz leapt across to the doors and went after him.

"Tori," Meredith called, "radio for a police boat. He'll make for the Jetties."

But as Tori turned away, they all heard distinctly and unfor-gettably, through the back door, the report of two quick shots in succession. There was a guttural yell, and then silence.

"Howie," Merry said, and lunged outside.

"WHERE IS SHE?" Seitz said urgently, his hand on Mike Struna's collar. The man had kept running even after Howie's first shot caught his leg, only falling to the ground when the second shot clipped his thigh. Blood was streaming through Struna's fingers, clutching at the wound, and his teeth were clenched.

"I need a doctor."

"Tell me where she is!"

"Five Finger Point," Struna gasped out.

"Coatue," Howie told Merry as she caught up with him, sprawled next to Struna on the grass path leading to the dock. "He took her to Coatue. Is she *alive?*" he demanded.

Struna nodded. "I couldn't do it. Not to Britt. She was . . . a friend."

"So you left her to die of exposure, on an isolated beach in December, with a storm coming in." Merry pulled a pair of hand-cuffs from her jacket pocket and wrested Struna's hands from his leg. "I'd hate to be your enemy. Seitz, call an ambulance. I'll fix a tourniquet."

The rest of the guests from Ingrid's Gift were spilling out onto the rain-swept lawn. Carly reached them first, crying out as she saw Mike's bleeding wounds.

"What have you *done* to him?"

She fell on her knees beside the handcuffed man, her mouth open in anguish.

"He murdered your husband." Merry ran to the boathouse. She glanced around for a length of rope—found it—grabbed a screwdriver she saw lying on a tool bench—and hurried back to Struna.

Carly had pulled off her sweater and was pressing the wadded wool against his thigh. Merry slipped the rope around the leg above the wound, twisted it, and, using the screwdriver as a lever, tightened it to strangulation point.

"Keep your sweater there," she told Carly tersely; but the woman wasn't looking at her. There were tears on her face.

Chris Candler and Winter came up to them, staring mutely at the scene.

"The ambulance is on its way," Chris said. "Is there anything I can do?"

"Tell Detective Seitz to send the police boat to Five Finger Point," Merry said. "Brittany Novak is marooned there."

"*Why*, Mike?" Carly asked.

He stared at her, gasping slightly. "Because I'm not like other people, Carly. Neither are you. We make our own rules."

"What does that even *mean*?"

"I needed you to *see*. With your own eyes. That Vic didn't deserve your loyalty. That he treated you like dirt. That he wasn't worth the pain he caused. So I invited you all here. And set certain events . . . in motion."

"You killed him with a shotgun," Carly said. "In that swamp. Then lied to me about your special tracking program."

"I never lied. His phone was at Howard Court."

"Because you put it there," she said bitterly. "And bought yourself time. While he was out there all night—and I ignored it . . ."

"That doesn't matter." Struna's face was whitening, a reaction to shock and loss of blood. "I was going to *save* you, Carly. Vic was dead. Your funding would disappear. I was going to under-write *The Hopeless*."

"I don't need your blood money." She raised her chin defi-antly. "And I can save myself."

"I did it for both of us." He closed his eyes, gasping again in pain. "If you don't understand that, nothing matters."

"Mary Alice Fillmore mattered," Winter Candler quavered as she stepped toward him, her hands balled into fists. "She was someone's *mom*, you asshole. Did you ever think of that?"

"She was an old woman. Squatting in a dump of a house," he retorted.

"—who took a picture," Merry finished, "that will convict you of murder."

32 | Ackerman Field, Monday Evening

"WE'LL BE IN touch," Ron MacKay said as he offered his son his hand. He was standing with Janet in a small area to one side of the TSA screening line, which was completely empty of both security personnel and passengers; the government jet provided to the secretary of state was the only plane on the tarmac at the island's small field. Micheline had already boarded, along with her staff and one of the DSS agents; Frank and Sasha were positioned between Janet and the rest of the terminal, like two attack dogs holding the world at bay.

"I won't be far behind you." Ansel took his father's proffered hand, but pulled him instead into an embrace. "Thanks for understanding."

The two men stood like that an instant, their arms around each other in a fragile and unaccustomed way, before Janet said quietly, "Ron," and MacKay broke his son's hold with a clap on his shoulder.

"Keep me posted." He turned, while Frank sprang forward and held open the door for Janet. Sasha followed immediately behind. Ron smiled at Ansel quickly, then walked out across the blacktop to the plane.

It was good, Ansel thought, that his dad hadn't asked him one more time if he wanted to come home. It meant he was beginning to accept that home was no longer with him.

They had talked about it for over an hour after Ance returned from breakfast with Howie Seitz. Ron had delayed his departure for Washington, in fact, to hash out the details. Ansel was going to take over Mary Alice's house, Stella Maris. For the next few months, he would line up contractors. He would supervise the drafting of renovation plans. He would carve out a place in the old structure—one with a northern exposure—to set up a studio. He would try to put together the book of photographs Mary Alice had left behind. And when he could, he would start again to paint.

"We'll make most of the house a lock-off rental unit," he told Ron, "so that the place is earning income. With that location— and private beach access . . ."

"It'll sustain itself," Ron agreed.

And me, Ansel thought. *It will sustain me.*

He watched as the jet's stairs were pulled away and the doors closed. Pressed his hand against the window glass so that it was visible as the plane started to taxi.

Even after it lifted in the air, he watched it dwindle in the clouds blanketing the island until it was no more discernible to a human eye than a gull on the wing.

Then Ansel walked toward the entrance with a sigh. He had a shuttle to catch. Some bags to pack. A move to undertake.

But first, there was a girl he needed to see.

"She called the secretary of state?" Peter said, as he handed Merry a towel that Tuesday morning. "Directly? At home?"

She was bent at the waist, her blond hair streaming over her head, fresh from the shower. Drops of water glistened on her shoulders and the backs of her knees and he barely resisted the urge to gather her up and carry her back to bed. She had responsibilities, now. People waiting for her.

She swaddled her head in the towel and rubbed briskly. Her voice, as a result, was muffled.

"From the cell records, Mary Alice definitely called Stronghold Saturday night. But I'm not sure whether Micheline Tran took the call, or Janet Brimhold MacKay. Or maybe the housekeeper answered the phone—Miranda Stephenson, the artist, you know her? Apparently she's worked for the Brimhold family forever."

He knew Miranda's name. She painted extraordinary landscapes, full of fog and storm and birds on the wing. He had caught Meredith standing wordlessly in front of one a few months before, at an Artists Association show. He would have to consider a Stephenson for her next birthday.

Merry stood upright, the towel slipping from her head. "It's one of those unanswerable questions, Peter. What were the last words, the last thoughts, of a woman who died a few hours later? Did she call Stronghold because she wanted to talk to her ex-husband? She wasn't trying to reach her son—she had Ansel's cell number. Or did she think she could plead with Ron's wife? They had been friends, it turns out, as girls. Or did the competent, all-knowing personal aide run interference, and Mary Alice's urgent message never reach the person she wanted?"

"I vote for Micheline Tran," he said. "She sounds like the type who'd follow orders without a thought, and confession would not be in her arsenal. She took the call, drove out immediately to Stella Maris, and told Mary Alice she'd expose her to Ron if she didn't leave Janet alone."

"You could be right," Merry said.

"But she didn't kill the woman." Peter brushed her wet hair from her forehead. "You found out who did. Which is all that matters."

"Mike Struna," Merry said ruminatively. "Not only did he infiltrate Vic Sonnenfeld's phone—he hacked into Winter Candler's, too. He was able to send Vic a text that looked like it came straight from Winter. Setting up that meeting on the hiking trail."

"So he didn't give a damn if she was suspected of murder? That's almost as unforgiveable as killing people," Peter said soberly. "Implicating that poor girl."

"I told her about it. I thought she should know. Rage can be a positive emotion, sometimes."

"It's more empowering than fear." Peter's hand stilled on her cheek. "You did a great job, chief. Ralph would be so proud of you."

She caught her breath. "You *know*, don't you?"

"Know what?"

"How much I've missed talking through this case with him." She said it wistfully. Ralph had always been her favorite sounding board in the throes of investigation—wiser than her father, and less prone to judgment.

"You still can," Peter said gently. "Only when he answers, you'll hear his voice in your head, not your ear."

"You think?"

"He gave you all the answers you need, long ago."

She reached for him then, and he held her.

"Hey, Mer?"

"Yes, Peter?"

"Have yourself a Merry little Christmas."

"Okay," she said, her cheek against his shoulder. "I will."

ACKNOWLEDGMENTS

WRITERS ARE FREQUENTLY advised to "write what you know."
I have always had a different philosophy—I write about what
interests me, and attempt to educate myself to do it compe-
tently. I would be lost, however, without the kindness of those
who patiently provide me with information in areas where I'm
clueless. For example: Marcus DelNegro, Hollywood camera-
man, offered me Cliffs Notes on everything to do with film
sets and production crews. Kenneth Mayo Johnson, avid bird
photographer on both Cape Cod and in the American West,
offered his insights on equipment, bird populations and migra-
tory patterns, and photographic techniques, as did Jo DelNegro,
who was invaluable on the subject of old-school film and slide
photography—particularly in the matter of lenses. Any errors in
translation are mine, and unequivocally not their fault.

Virginia "Ginger" Andrews, longtime birdwatching colum-
nist for Nantucket's newspaper of record, the *Inquirer & Mirror*,
was a serendipitous source. I struck up a conversation with Ms.
Andrews, who is also an accomplished landscape artist, while
she was staffing the Artists Association of Nantucket gallery
during Stroll Weekend. Although in the moment I had no
idea who she was, I had been reading her column for years—
and was astonished when she identified herself. She graciously
shared some birding tips for the winter season on Nantucket,
and discussed the hyper-focus of birders gazing into their camera

viewfinders or binoculars: intent upon sighting an elusive snowy owl or rare whimbrel, to the exclusion of everything else (mur-der) on the edge of the field.

I am grateful to Liz Ferretti for sharing a story at least a decade ago that I could not get out of my mind: that of a friend whose husband allowed a beloved Nantucket home to fall down into dust, as revenge for a marriage gone wrong.

Sam Mathews enlightened me on surveillance software, and remote backdoor-access to cell phones. Kristen Blomstrom gra-ciously answered questions about high jumping, equestrian training, and the Selle Francais. I learned about hand-feeding of wild birds from Jocelyn Anderson Photography's marvelous video postings, on Twitter, Instagram, and her website blog: jocelynandersonphotographyshop.com.

Nantucket Book Partners were, as always, deeply welcoming during my Stroll Weekend signing at Mitchell's Book Corner. So were the lessors of 4 Howard Court, an absolutely lovely short-term rental I happily occupied (without Vic Sonnenfeld) during my time on-island.

Finally, I would like to thank my agent, Rafe Sagalyn, for his insight and advice during the crafting of this novel, as well as his assistant, Emily Sacks. I would be lost without the fine professionals at Soho Crime: Bronwen Hruska, Publisher; Juliet Grames, Editor and Associate Publisher; Erica Loberg, Publi-cist; Sheri Cheatwood, Events; Taz Urnov, Editorial Assistant; Rachel Kowal, Managing Editor; Paul Oliver, Director of Public-ity; Janine Agro, Art and Production Director; Rudy Martinez, Marketing Director; and Steven Tran, Sales Manager.

And lastly, deepest thanks to Mark and Stephen, who sup-ported me so well during both the pandemic and the writing of this book.